THE EXPLOITS OF SOLAR PONS

by Basil Copper

Books in the macabre field by Basil Copper

Non-fiction
The Vampire: In Legend, Fact and Art
The Werewolf: In Legend, Fact and Art

Short Stories
Not After Nightfall
Here Be Daemons
And Afterward, the Dark
From Evil's Pillow
Voices of Doom
When Footsteps Echo
Whispers in the Night

Fantasy Novels
The Great White Space
Into the Silence
The Horror on Planet X

Gothic Novels
The Curse of the Fleers
Necropolis
The House of the Wolf
The Black Death

The Solar Pons Series
The Dossier of Solar Pons
The Further Adventures of Solar Pons
The Secret Files of Solar Pons
Some Uncollected Cases of Solar Pons
The Exploits of Solar Pons
The Recollections of Solar Pons

THE EXPLOITS OF SOLAR PONS

Basil Copper

Illustrations by
Stefanie Kate Hawks

Minneapolis, Minnesota
1993

THE EXPLOITS OF SOLAR PONS

Copyright ©1993, by Basil Copper

Illustrations © copyright 1993, by Stefanie K. Hawks

First Edition

All rights reserved. No part of this book may be reproduced in any form or by any means without written permission of the author, except for brief quotations in critical articles or reviews. Address all queries to: FEDOGAN & BREMER, 700 Washington Ave., S. E., Suite 50, Minneapolis, MN 55414.

ISBN: 1-878252-11-9 (Trade Edition)
ISBN: 1-878252-14-3 (Limited Edition)
Library of Congress Number: 93-073410

Book design by Felix Bremer

Following the Characters Created by August Derleth

The Solar Pons Stories written by Basil Copper are the only ones authorized by Arkham House Publishers Inc., by whom they were first commissioned, and by the Estate of the late August Derleth.

The novellas contained in *The Exploits of Solar Pons* have never before been published.

This One is for Dixon Smith and Madeleine Henry; husband and wife, gifted authors, loyal friends; with gratitude for their help and encouragement.

CONTENTS

The Adventure of the Verger's Thumb 5
The Adventure of the Phantom Face 55
Death at the Metropole 129
The Adventure of the Callous Colonel . . 173

THE EXPLOITS OF SOLAR PONS

THE ADVENTURE OF THE VERGER'S THUMB

THE ADVENTURE OF THE VERGER'S THUMB

1

"**M**ANY A SLIP, Parker, many a slip!"
I looked up from my corner of the first-class railway carriage and smiled at my friend Solar Pons as he sat opposite me, spare and trim in a tweed country suit.

"I do not understand you, Pons."

My companion blew a plume of fragrant blue smoke up to the roof of the compartment.

"It would not be the first time, Parker. I was referring merely to that contraption you were fiddling with."

"I see!"

I held it up so that he could have a closer look.

"What on earth is it?"

I smiled again.

"I thought you were supposed to be the detective, Pons."

My friend looked at me with eyes in which little flecks of irony were dancing.

"*Touché*, Parker. You are developing a very pretty wit of late. I must confess I am in turn developing a taste for it."

"You flatter me, Pons, but you have still not answered my question."

"It was I who questioned you," Pons corrected me. "I am on holiday, remember, and giving my ratiocinative faculties a rest.

It was your idea, Parker. You said, if I recall the extravagant phraseology rightly, that the Norfolk Broads would be a tonic."

He smiled wickedly.

"Which means that we find ourselves on the way to the unquiet metropolis of Norwich."

"Come, Pons," I protested. "Norwich is one of the most beautiful cities in England. It is in the centre of the Broads and if I had taken you to a small village . . ."

Solar Pons held up his hand.

"It was merely my feeble attempt at a joke, Parker. You are perfectly correct. I was there once only, for half a day, but to the best of my recollection all your eulogies are well-deserved. Though we are still faced with the basic problem."

"You are referring to this?"

I still held the object between thumb and forefinger and I passed it over to my companion. It was a beautiful day in early June and we were passing through the flat, lush countryside of Suffolk, typical Constable terrain in which fields of fat sheep, fine old trees and glossy streams competed for attention in the eye.

"Ah," said Pons. "Some sort of apparatus for tying artificial flies for trout fishing, is it not?"

"You are right, Pons," I said. "It is new on the market. I purchased it only yesterday."

Solar Pons passed the miniature vice back with a thin smile. "I did not know you were a fisherman, Parker."

"Neither am I, Pons," I said ruefully. "I used to be fond of fly-fishing when I was a youngster but I have had little time in latter years. I thought I might take it up again."

"You will find small opportunity on the Broads, Parker."

I laughed.

"Of course not, Pons. It was merely that I felt I might spend some spare time so. It is a soothing enough occupation."

My friend nodded and turned back to the pages of the learned journal he had been immersed in when my experimental overtures with my new toy had attracted his attention.

The bright June day continued, the engine joyfully shovelled black smoke over its shoulder as it vibrated its way over the flat countryside and in an astonishingly short time, it seemed, we were descending amid the noise and bustle of Norwich Thorpe Station, bedecked with coloured posters featuring Broadland yachts apparently sailing across the rich fields and shouting the attractions of Yarmouth as a seaside resort.

"Did I not say it was agreeable, Pons?"

"Indeed, Parker," said Solar Pons drily, skilfully dodging aside to avoid a covey of small boys carrying fishing rods.

We had nothing except light hand luggage so after surrendering our tickets, we walked out into the brightness of the station concourse, avoiding the taxi-rank and instead crossing the road to walk by the broad, brown waters of the Yare, where tall-masted sailing boats bobbed alongside the quay at Norwich Yacht Station.

Across the bridge, we let the flow of pedestrians take us into the heart of the city where the great spire of Norwich Cathedral floated like some huge ship at anchor, and reported ourselves at the Royal George Hotel, where we were expected. A shocked attendant took our luggage and whisked it immediately to our comfortable rooms. When we had again descended, Pons consulted the huge grandfather clock in the hall.

"It is still only a quarter-past twelve, Parker. What say you to another short promenade before lunch?"

We slipped out of a side-entrance; it was market-day apparently and a rich display of stalls, selling a fantastic variety of goods stretched as far as the eye could reach across a vast square near the Cathedral, the reds, golds and greens of their canvas roofs making a colourful, mediæval pattern that was eye-aching in the bright summer sun.

Solar Pons looked at the rich life about him, his keen eyes taking in the details of the individual faces, a thin plume of smoke from his pipe rising into the warm air. After a short while wandering about in this manner we turned our steps back in the direction of the Cathedral, pausing in the Close to examine the moving memorial to Nurse Edith Cavell and then crossing the road to traverse the quaint old alley of Tombland with its houses leaning at crazy angles. Neither of us talked much, we were so taken with the charm of the place, and I was delighted by many subtle indications in my friend's attitude and demeanour that he thoroughly approved of his surroundings and my suggestion to take this much-needed holiday.

As possibly the world's greatest private consulting detective Pons had been extremely overworked in the spring of the year; he had been drenched in a mountain stream in Switzerland in one case; set upon by thugs in another; and had found even his iron strength severely taxed in a long and complicated affair which had involved him in covering miles of rough and almost impassable Scottish countryside on foot.

As his medical adviser as well as his friend I had long urged caution and proper rest and the amiable landlady of our quarters at 7B Praed Street, Mrs Johnson, had joined her injunctions to mine so that we were both delighted when at last we had prevailed upon my companion to take a brief fortnight's respite from the clatter and bustle of London.

Indeed, I congratulated myself highly on my strategy as we sat down to an excellent lunch at The Royal George because I could see that already my friend was benefiting from the change of air and the agreeable atmosphere of Norwich in this perfect June weather.

After lunch we strolled along the banks of the river for a while, the moored yachts and motor-boats bobbing gently at anchor, while the hum of the city rose around us like that of a hive of bees. Solar Pons glanced at me ironically, as though he could read my thoughts.

"You were right, Parker," he said genially. "I must congratulate you on your choice. It might take much longer than a fortnight to exhaust the possibilities of such a city."

My cheeks glowed at such unwonted praise from my companion.

"I am glad to hear you say so, Pons."

He said nothing more and we walked on in silence, climbing some steps to gain an iron bridge and eventually finding ourselves, as though by tacit consent, in front of the mellow bulk of the Cathedral. A section of the vast double doors was open, showing a black oblong and the deep basso of an organ's treacly notes percolated to the street.

It was cool and shadowy inside after the brilliance of the exterior and it took some minutes before my eyes had adjusted to the diffused lighting; the sun's rays being broken by the rich reds, greens and ambers of the mediæval stained glass in the rich windows and scattering like powdered gold across the delicate tracery of stonework and timber in that magnificent interior.

Evidently some sort of service had just concluded because people were dispersing down the long aisles and the wooden chairs were thickly occupied by seated worshippers. The unseen organist continued with his recital as the vast building emptied, though visitors were constantly stepping through the great doors from the street behind us.

I paused to examine some carving in a side chapel while Pons wandered on, his keen eyes shooting glances up to the vaulted ceiling high above and then at some detail of the ancient stonework nearer at hand. It was an agreeable occupation and we had spent some half an hour in such gentle perambulations before we were brought up in front of a massive archway, half hidden by the vast stone pillaring. Steps led downward into the gloom.

"This would appear to be the crypt, Pons."

"Would it not, Parker," said my companion, little flecks of amusement dancing in his eyes.

"Shall we go down?"

"By all means, my dear fellow. A great cathedral is nothing without its crypt, which is as necessary as cloisters and Norwich is nothing if not a great cathedral."

I followed my companion as he led the way down the sunken stone steps into the shadowy realms below. Naked electric bulbs illuminated the honey-coloured stonework and our steps echoed loudly on the flagstones beneath the vaulted ceiling. There was evidently some work going on, for scaffolding surrounded some of the tombs and great beams barred off portions of the crypt. I had noticed evidence of the same activity in the church above.

"Interesting, is it not, Pons?"

"Indeed, my dear fellow. No doubt it appeals to your romantic instincts."

"Perhaps, Pons," I replied cautiously. "But at any event it would not take much imagination to picture strange things happening in such a setting."

Pons chuckled quietly, looking about him.

"You are certainly correct in that supposition, Parker."

It was indeed a formidable and strange realm in which we now found ourselves. Great stone pillars going up into the massive vaulted ceiling; flagstones beneath our feet; shadowy corners and turnings inadequately illuminated by the electric light bulbs suspended at intervals; some curious tombs and statuary, with here and there the massive beams and timbers of the renovation work. All overlaid by the echoing footsteps of the few visitors down here and their sibilant whispering which seemed to reverberate curiously about the catacombs.

The hush was abruptly broken by the sound of hurrying footsteps and round a pillar came a curiously assorted couple. A girl of about twenty-eight, her fair hair flying, her expression furious. Behind her a tall, sullen, bearded man in his forties, rage and anger flaring on his face. Oblivious of their surroundings, they hurried on toward the entrance steps, the girl shaking off the man's restraining arm.

"Pray control yourself, Elise," said the man in low, urgent tones, glancing about him.

"It was promised!" she said in furious tones. "You said it would be today!"

The muttering continued as the odd pair half-ran from the crypt and we could hear their agitated progress up the worn stone steps until the sound died away in the distance. Pons looked at me thoughtfully.

"Curious, Parker," he murmured.

I smiled.

"A lover's quarrel, Pons?"

"Perhaps," he said shortly, an expression on his lean, feral features I had come to know well.

I led him forward to where a Norman noble's effigy rested on the cover of an ancient tomb. In the far corner an imperious statue raised its arm aloft.

"I hope you are not seeking mysteries here, Pons. We are on holiday."

"I have not forgotten, Parker," said Solar Pons placatingly, though I noticed his keen eyes were darting about the crypt, resting first on one detail and then another.

"Hullo! Someone has dropped something."

He darted forward round the edge of the tomb and picked up a small object resting on the flagstones.

"What do you make of this, Parker?"

I glanced at the thing in the palm of his hand curiously.

"It looks like a cotton-reel, Pons."

"Does it not? However, I think there is a little more to it than that."

He held up the little wooden cylinder, holding it toward the illumination provided by the nearest bulb. There was no-one else near us in this secluded corner, where we were screened by the massive groyning of the crypt. He twisted it gently, giving a grunt of satisfaction as it came apart.

Within the hollow interior was a slip of paper. Pons unfolded it and smoothed it out with his fingers. I looked over his shoulder. Printed on it in ink was a meaningless jumble of symbols, composed of random groups of letters.

"It is of no value, Pons, that is evident."

"We shall see, Parker, we shall see," my companion returned mysteriously, thrusting the slip and its container into his pocket.

"I think we have seen enough for one afternoon. Let us adjourn to the open air."

We were ascending the steps to the Cathedral now.

"Should we not report the finding of this article to the church authorities, Pons?"

"All in good time, Parker."

Solar Pons' face was tense and abstracted and I looked at him curiously. A moment later I saw what had attracted his attention. The bearded man we had seen in the crypt was coming back down the nave, a worried expression on his features. He passed without noticing us and darted into the entrance which led to the crypt.

To my astonishment Pons led me into the shadow of a great pillar and seating himself on one of the wooden chairs which faced the altar motioned me down beside him. He put his fingers to his lips to enjoin caution.

We waited perhaps ten minutes and then footsteps were heard ascending. A moment later the man with the beard, looking more worried than ever, appeared. Pons was already on his feet and strolled casually after him. I followed, considerably perplexed and not a little irritated.

We gained the Cathedral entrance and watched the tall figure of the bearded man striding away into the heart of the city. Pons followed and I had difficulty in keeping up with him. After a short while, however, my companion slackened his pace. He was smiling.

"Ah, Parker, we are in luck. The gentleman is evidently staying at The Royal George or taking tea there."

"Indeed, Pons."

I followed his gaze and saw that the bearded man was ascending the entrance steps of our own hostelry. As we crossed the road, pausing to allow a bus to pass in front of us, I caught Pons' arm.

"Is it not possible that the thing you have just picked up belonged to that gentleman, and that he has been back to the crypt to find it?"

"It is entirely possible, Parker. Come, I have a notion to see what our friend will do next."

And he led the way into the lobby of the hotel.

2

I sat down in a corner of the tea-lounge, the three-piece orchestra playing a dreamy melody from Strauss. The girl who had been in the cathedral was sitting three tables away, looking tense and irritated. Pons had asked me to keep an eye on her while he went on some mysterious errand of his own. I must confess I was put out at the turn things had taken; after all, we had come here for a much-needed holiday and such little mysteries as the one we had just witnessed were an unwarrantable intrusion.

I ordered afternoon tea for Pons and myself and waited, glancing idly about the room. The place was full and the agreeable hum of muted conversation drifted up to the beamed ceiling. I should have been extremely content if it had not been for the strange incident in the crypt and my pique continued as the minutes passed and my companion had still not appeared. The waitress had already brought the tea, the buttered scones and the selection of cakes before Pons hurried through the door to join me.

As he did so he almost collided with the bearded man; the latter drew back with an apology for he had thrust his way through the door with unceremonious haste. Pons stood back and beckoned him forward with a gracious gesture, a smile on his lips. The bearded man continued over to the girl's table and as he sat down I could see from his hunched shoulders and strained tense attitude that the row we had witnessed in the crypt was continuing in this more salubrious atmosphere.

Pons sat down opposite me and rubbed his thin hands, looking at the delicacies on the table before us with keen anticipation.

"Excellent, Parker. I can see that this holiday will suit me. Even Mrs Johnson could not have done better."

"You may well say so, Pons," I rejoined, my spirits rising considerably. "But where on earth have you been? I was afraid the tea would become cold."

"No fear of that, Parker," said Pons, holding out his cup for the sparkling measure I poured for him. "I was just engaged in a pleasant conversation with the young lady at the reception desk."

I looked at him in surprise.

"For what purpose, Pons?"

Solar Pons chuckled.

"Surely it is self-evident. I was merely trying to establish the identity of our fellow guest. I told the young lady I thought he was a friend I had met in America. She obligingly looked him up in the register. He is Herr Karl Koch of Stuttgart. He has been staying here for three days."

The resentment and surprise in my eyes must have shown for my companion had mischievous little glints dancing in his own.

"Come, Parker. I have no wish to let such poor ratiocinative gifts as I possess rust in this mellow holiday atmosphere. I must confess I am curious and decided to find out a little more about this oddly assorted couple."

"So long as it is only that, Pons. I have no wish to see the holiday spoiled."

"And neither have I, my dear fellow. Though some little problem in our present genteel surroundings would constitute the perfect holiday for me."

I thought it wiser to say nothing further on those grounds and sought to divert Pons but it was obvious by the way his deep-set eyes were glancing over the far table that he was deeply interested in Koch and his companion.

"You did not find out anything about the young lady, Pons?" I put in mischievously.

He shook his head.

"Miss Elise is not staying here, Parker."

"I am surprised that you do not simply ask Mr Koch if the thing we found in the crypt belongs to him, Pons?"

My companion shook his head, a faint smile flickering at the corners of his mouth.

"That would spoil the game entirely, Parker. I have a mind to hold on to it for a little while. It can do no harm, surely, and I understand our strange friend is staying here for several days longer."

I glanced at the animated couple again.

"As you wish, Pons. Pray try these excellent scones; they are still hot."

But it was evident that though Pons ate heartily and enjoyed the tea his mind was elsewhere. Three times I saw him shoot penetrating glances in the direction of the other table and long after the couple had disappeared he had an abstracted air about him.

We had finished the meal and were about to withdraw from the lounge when there came an interruption. A short, rather shabby-looking little old man in dark clothes had been hovering about at the entrance to the great room. I had noticed him at the cash-desk talking to the manageress and now I found him at my elbow, his eyes deferential and apologetic.

"Mr Pons? Mr Solar Pons?"

"This is he," I said, indicating my companion.

"I am sorry to disturb you, gentlemen, but we are in some trouble. The Dean sent me specially."

Solar Pons smiled, sitting upright in his chair in an alert and wide-awake manner.

"Will you not introduce yourself? I must confess your sentence makes little sense at the moment."

The little man looked confused and shot an apologetic glance at the manageress over Pons' shoulder and then at my friend himself.

"My apologies, sir. My name is Miggs. I am the Head Verger at the Cathedral yonder. Strange things have been happening."

"Indeed?"

Solar Pons' eyebrows were drawn across his brows in a hard, straight line.

"Will you not sit down and tell us about it?"

Our strange visitor shook his head.

"My thumb is still sore, gentlemen, and the Dean himself bade me make haste."

"You seem determined to present us with an enigma, Mr Miggs," said Solar Pons with a dry laugh.

"I take it you want us to come with you?"

"If you would be so good, sir. The thing is so mysterious, you see."

"May I ask how you knew I was at this hotel?"

"The Manager of the hotel, sir, worships at the Cathedral. Of course he's well-known in Norwich and when the Dean was speaking about our troubles yesterday Mr Kellaway immediately said you were coming to stay here today. I do hope it has not caused any offence . . ."

"By no means," said Solar Pons, rising from his seat.

"Mr Kellaway would have spoken of it himself, sir," continued Mr Miggs apologetically, "but he's been called away today. He telephoned the Dean who asked me to come straight here."

Solar Pons smiled thinly as I got up and indicated my willingness to accompany him.

"Am I to understand that the Dean of Norwich himself wishes to consult me on some matter?"

The little man flushed.

"Begging your pardon, sir, explaining things is not my strong suit. You have hit it exactly, Mr Pons. Canon Stacey is a charming gentleman and is quite at his wit's end. We all are, I can tell you. Such goings-on!"

He wiped his forehead with a handkerchief he took from the side pocket of his old black coat.

"I know it's your holiday, sir, but if you could spare some time we'd all be grateful. The Canon's house is in the Close, quite nearby. Just a step, sir."

He delivered his monologue with such a rueful, apologetic air that I had a job to keep a straight face, however irritated I might feel at this potential interruption to our holiday.

"Very well. Let us go there straight away," said Solar Pons crisply. "You can tell us about your thumb on the way. You must find your work at the Cathedral a great deal different from shoe repairs."

"Eigh?"

Mr Miggs looked at Pons in great astonishment, his mouth all drawn up on one side. His eyes had a strange expression in them.

"How on earth could you possibly know that, Mr Pons?"

"Ah, I am correct then?"

"I was in the trade for more than thirty years, sir."

"That accounts for the callouses on your thumb where you hold the leather as you shape it on your last. They are quite distinctive. When I see in addition that your left shoulder is slightly lower than your right I conclude that you are right-handed and that you have been in the habit of bending over your work in the manner peculiar to cobblers. Thirty years of that would certainly have its effect on your physique and it is typical of the trade."

Mr Miggs continued to stare at my companion in astonishment.

"Wonderful, Mr Pons! Wonderful!" he breathed. "Canon Stacey will be pleased. Mr Kellaway said you had miraculous powers of reasoning, sir, but I did not realise you would demonstrate them so soon."

Solar Pons chuckled.

"Let us hope that neither you nor Mr Stacey will be disappointed when I get to grips with your little problem."

Mr Miggs shook his head.

"I am sure that will not be the case, sir."

3

Despite his age he led the way at a furious pace through the streets of the old city, until at last we came to the hush of the Cathedral Close, with its handsome old houses flanking the green lawns and gravel driveways. He ushered us up white steps to a gracious Georgian portico, its discreet pale-blue painted door glittering with brass ornaments. The white paintwork gleamed on the fanlight above the door and on the small-paned windows set in the façade of the house and a profusion of flowers made bright splashes of colour in the black window-boxes and perfumed the air for yards around.

"This is Canon Stacey's residence, gentlemen," said Mr Miggs, his voice involuntarily lowering. Pons gave me a faint smile above the old man's bowed head.

"You have not yet told us about your thumb, Mr Miggs."

"Ah, sir. All in good time. The Canon said I wasn't to mention that until you had heard what he has to say."

"Very well, then," observed Solar Pons. "We shall just have to curb our impatience, eh, Parker?"

"Certainly, Pons."

A trim parlour-maid had now opened the great front door and ushered the three of us into an elegant and soberly furnished hall, whose beauty was enhanced by the bowls of cut flowers in vases set about the interior and by the exquisite Indian rug at the far end, that glowed like a great ruby on the black and white tiled floor.

A regal, grey-haired woman whose features bore the dark tint that skin acquires after long years of exposure to tropical sun, came out of a room adjoining the hall and advanced toward us with a smile of welcome.

"Mr Solar Pons? And Dr Lyndon Parker? It is indeed good of you to interrupt your holiday in this fashion."

"Not at all, Mrs Stacey," said Pons, shaking hands. "Dr Parker and I will be only too pleased to help in this little matter."

Mrs Stacey's hand flew to her throat with a nervous gesture.

"Oh, you will not find it a little matter, Mr Pons. Mr Miggs here has been half-frightened out of his wits. And my husband is gravely perturbed. Gravely perturbed."

There was more than worry in her eyes and Solar Pons glanced at her solemnly.

"Indeed, Mrs Stacey," he said soothingly. "Nevertheless, we shall do our best to set things to rights."

He smiled reassuringly at the grey-haired woman, who led us without more ado to the door of her husband's study, where she rapped at the panels and then ushered us in.

"Will you not come in, Mr Miggs?" she asked the verger kindly.

"If you'll excuse me, m'am, I'll wait in the hall until the Canon should require me."

"As you wish. This is my husband, Mr Pons. Dr Lyndon Parker."

The tall, distinguished-looking man in the neat grey suit rose from his desk in the cluttered study as we advanced toward him. A vase of roses made a blaze of colour in the handsome stone fireplace and the sunlight glinted on the spines of the thousands of leather-bound volumes that filled the glass bookcases which stretched from floor to ceiling. Beyond the tall, elegant windows with their gauze curtaining could be glimpsed the tranquil Close with its passing visitors.

Canon Stacey was a man of about sixty-five, with a pleasant, open face and an unlined complexion though, like his wife, he still bore a deep tan. His silver hair rose in thick waves on his head so that it almost resembled an eighteenth century powdered wig. His white, even teeth gleamed in a welcoming smile but I could see anxiety and doubt in the steady brown eyes.

"It is extremely good of you, Mr Pons. We are at our wit's end. Will you not sit here, gentlemen. Winifred, perhaps you could see about some tea for our guests."

"Pray do not put yourself out," said Solar Pons to the Canon's wife. "We have just had tea."

"In that case you will not mind if we indulge," said the Canon with a faint flicker of a smile. "We usually have ours at this time of the afternoon."

"By all means," said my companion. "Your Mr Miggs tells me you have a problem which is worrying you."

Mrs Stacey, with a quick glance at her husband, went out to give the orders for tea and Pons and I sank into comfortable leather chairs at our host's invitation. Glancing anxiously from one to the other of us, Canon Stacey without further preamble at once plunged into his story.

"There are strange things going on in the Cathedral, Mr Pons. I am worried, gentlemen. Extremely worried. Your coming to Norwich was like the answer to my prayer. And I have no wish to involve the police in this matter or there might be a public scandal."

Solar Pons said nothing, merely sat back in his chair, his long, slim hands in his lap, his lean, ascetic face gilded with golden stripes by the sunlight. He looked reassuringly at the Canon who licked his lips once or twice and continued with his apparently random musings.

"It started about two weeks ago. I was walking through the Cathedral at dusk when I became conscious of a low whispering. It was fairly late, there were no services taking place and the spot was dimly-lit and lonely. I am not a fanciful person in the ordinary sense of the word, Mr Pons, yet there was something unpleasant and inexpressibly furtive in that mumbled colloquy taking place in that sacred place. I caught only one or two words, savagely and more loudly spoken than the others. They made my heart beat faster and I moved behind a pillar in case the hidden talkers should see me."

"Why was that, Canon Stacey?"

The distinguished-looking churchman hesitated.

"A good question, Mr Pons. Really, I believe, because there was such menace in their tones. I am a gentle, peace-loving man as befits my cloth and I instinctively shrank from such voices in a holy place."

"I see. Male or female voices?"

"Male, Mr Pons. Extremely rough. Working class and not at all the sort of people I should imagine would have found much time for organised religion."

The Canon looked apologetically from one to the other of us.

"I must confess that does not sound very Christian, Mr Pons. After all, the church is open to everyone. But I would be less than honest if I did not frankly indicate my feelings."

"Your attitude does you credit, Canon Stacey. Just what were these words which so startled you?"

"'Robbery' and 'killing', Mr Pons."

There was a long silence between the three of us.

"Hmm."

Solar Pons pulled reflectively with thin fingers at the lobe of his right ear.

"You did not see the men?"

Canon Stacey shook his head.

"Not at that point, Mr Pons. They were behind the chancel screen, you see, and I should have been seen had I quitted my position at the pillar. Something compelled me to stay there, as though harm might befall me if I were to make my presence known."

The Canon lowered his voice and looked around him as though the room were dark and gloomy and the time winter, instead of light and bright with the brilliant summer sunshine streaming in. He hesitated again and then went on.

"You will think me even more fanciful, Mr Pons, but I had the strangest impression as I stood behind that pillar and listened to those evil voices."

"And what was that, Canon Stacey?"

"That the two men were lying out full-length on the pews in order to avoid being seen as they plotted something horrific and criminal."

4

We were interrupted at that moment by a rap at the far door and Mrs Stacey re-appeared, followed by the same maid who had let us in, wheeling a tea-trolley. Pons and I remained silent until the tea-preparations were completed and the girl had withdrawn. Mrs Stacey shot a glance at us.

"I will just take Miggs a cup," she said. "I will see that you are not disturbed again, Howard."

The Canon smiled graciously.

"Thank you, my dear."

He waited until his wife had quitted the room, drumming nervously with slim fingers upon his desk.

"Your experience was certainly a strange one, Canon," observed Solar Pons, tenting his thin fingers before him. "And something one would not expect to find within the precincts of a great Cathedral."

"There is more to come, Mr Pons," observed the Canon sombrely.

"I had hoped to hear something further but unfortunately there was a loud noise in the distance, probably caused by one of the volunteer cleaners, which startled the couple. I heard the scraping of heavy boots and moments later saw the dark shadows of two large men, making off down the aisle."

"You did not observe them clearly?"

"Well, Mr Pons, I waited until they had got to a more brightly lit portion of the interior, slipping from pillar to pillar so that they should not see me. All I could make out was that they were dark, tall and wore rough clothing."

"I see. Pray continue."

"About an hour later I was called by Mr Miggs, who was rather agitated and upset. He has a great sense of propriety and is one of the most zealous guardians of the Cathedral and its fabric."

"He struck me as being exceedingly conscientious, Canon," I put in.

Canon Stacey nodded and then went on, as though a flood of thoughts were waiting to be liberated.

"Miggs took me to the spot near the pillar where the two men had been lying. We found the lid of a tobacco tin which had been used as an ash-tray. The floor was littered with cigarette ends and packages of food had been opened and sandwiches eaten. The mess was disgusting! Smoking and eating in the Lord's house, Mr Pons! It was my firm opinion that the men were waiting until after dark, when the Cathedral would be locked, and intended to commit some mischief."

"But were apparently disturbed and fearing detection made off?"

"Something like that, Mr Pons."

My companion nodded slowly.

"It is one possibility," he said. "There is more to come, I take it?"

"A good deal more," said the Canon grimly. "There are priceless treasures within the Cathedral. The plate alone . . ."

"We will take that for granted, Canon," Solar Pons interjected. "Facts, if you please."

"I am sorry, Mr Pons. My nerves have been ruffled, I must confess."

Canon Stacey cracked his knuckles several times in succession in an irritating manner as though to prove the point and I noticed that his action seemed to be having the same effect

The Adventure of the Verger's Thumb 21

upon Pons. Then Stacey took up the threads of his story once again.

"A few days later, Miggs again came to me in great agitation to say that one of the side-chapels was in considerable disorder. I went there immediately and I must say I was extremely shocked. Chairs had been thrown down, some of the carvings disfigured, all the altar ornaments had been removed and ornamental candlesticks unscrewed. I had never seen such a mess!"

The Canon's anger and distress was patent but it appeared to me that Pons was having some difficulty in keeping a straight face as our host's tale proceeded. But he sat upright in his chair, his face alert and intent, his eyes shining.

"What you have just told me is extremely interesting," he said.

"Such hooliganism, Mr Pons!"

Solar Pons shook his head.

"I think not, Canon. These are the marks of something deeper than that."

"What do you mean, Mr Pons?"

"I would prefer not to speculate at this stage, Canon. You say you did not call the police?"

Our host hesitated, drumming his fingers again.

"No, Mr Pons. There was a very good reason. Any publicity might have frightened these men off. I wanted, if possible, to catch them red-handed and we could not do that if newspaper reports of this sacrilege were to appear in the local press."

"I see."

"The next thing that happened, Mr Pons, was shocking and inexplicable. There has been a great deal of re-building and maintenance work going on at the Cathedral over the past three or four years. This has obviously necessitated parts of the building being closed and some inconvenience occasioned to both the staff of the Cathedral and the worshippers. Not to mention the general public who merely regard the building as a tourist attraction."

The Canon poured himself another cup of tea and stared at Pons as though expecting him to agree that tourists were an unmitigated nuisance. Pons waited politely until the churchman had taken two or three sips, though it was obvious to me that he was intensely interested in the Canon's story.

"I had gone down into the crypt. I think to verify an inscription on one of the tombs for a learned paper I am at present writing concerning the history of this noble edifice. It was late afternoon and there was no-one but myself there. I was up in a far corner, translating the Latin inscription, and could not have been visible to anyone coming into the crypt. I had been engaged so for some five or ten minutes when my attention was arrested by a slight noise. Work on the foundations in the crypt has necessitated the re-positioning of some of the tombs."

"Naturally, being scholars and historians as well as churchmen, we have tried to do as little violence to the original scheme of things as possible, but the Cathedral architect had insisted that the tomb of Bishop Lascelles would have to be moved to one side to allow underpinning and draining of the foundations. The tomb itself is of no great historical value; the good Bishop died in 1812 and so far as I know there are no members of his family extant so we did not have to apply for permission."

"The Bishop's tomb is where in the crypt, Canon?"

"I can take you there, Mr Pons."

"We have already been, Canon Stacey, though I should like you to refresh my memory."

"It is the third memorial down, on the right-hand side as you get to the bottom of the crypt stairs, Pons," I said. "I noticed it particularly, as it has somewhat hideous cherubs on the sarcophagus and wooden beams and scaffolding around it."

"Correct, Dr Parker," said Canon Stacey, beaming.

"Excellent, Parker," said Pons drily. "You are constantly improving."

"Well, gentlemen," continued the Canon. "That is the place, right enough. You can imagine my horror when I heard a low groan and the creak of wood. As I started from my corner I was appalled to see that the temporary wooden cover on the tomb—we have removed the inner shell containing the remains of the Bishop pending his re-interment—was beginning to move upward. I could see that there was a lean, dirty arm and hand inside, pushing the lid up toward the ceiling. I am afraid that I gave a terrified cry, the lid collapsed with a loud crash and in the shock of the moment I beat an undignified retreat up the stairs."

"I am not surprised, Canon," said Solar Pons, conscious of the apologetic expression in the churchman's eyes. "You did wisely."

"Ah, then, you believe in the supernatural, Mr Pons?"

Solar Pons shook his head slowly, producing his pipe from his pocket. He lit it at Canon Stacey's extended permission and puffed thoughtfully, sending fragrant blue plumes of smoke up toward the gracious plaster-work of the ceiling.

"On the contrary, Canon, I am inclined to believe the problem is more tangible than that."

Puzzled, Canon Stacey turned to me as though for an explanation. After a moment he continued, albeit more hesitantly than before.

"I lost no time in summoning help, gentlemen. With Mr Miggs and several stalwart workmen I again descended to the crypt. We got that heavy temporary wooden lid off the tomb. Mr Pons, it was absolutely empty!"

5

Solar Pons had a thin smile on his lips.

"I should have been extremely surprised had you found anyone there."

"Good heavens, Pons!" I exclaimed. "How could you possibly know that?"

Solar Pons' smile widened a little.

"Intuition, Parker. Combined with certain theories which I have already formed."

Canon Stacey smiled also.

"Ah, Mr Pons. I was correct in my supposition that you would soon get to the heart of this awful mystery."

My companion held up his hand.

"Not so fast, Canon Stacey. I am far from doing that. And I have no wish to raise your hopes unduly. But what you have told me so far leads my thoughts in certain directions. Apart from that I would prefer to say no more at the moment."

"Very well, Mr Pons," said Canon Stacey, but there was evident disappointment on his face.

"I come now to the last of these mysteries. Yesterday evening, again near dusk, Miggs himself had a terrifying experience. Otherwise, I might have felt my own to be the result of some strange delusion or fancy. Perhaps you would like Mr Miggs in now?"

"By all means. It was by his own wish that he was excluded from this conversation."

"Miggs has odd little ways," said the Canon, with a wry smile.

He got up and went over to the study door, reappearing a few seconds later with the diminutive figure of the verger, who was looking apprehensive and carrying his cup and saucer in his right hand. He seated himself on the very edge of the chair the Canon produced for him and sat looking round him as though prepared for some inquisitorial ordeal. As he showed no inclination to speak Pons himself opened the conversation.

"Canon Stacey has told us something of the strange events in the Cathedral, Mr Miggs. I should now like to hear from your own lips of the experience you yourself had last evening."

Miggs moistened his lips with his tea and shot an uneasy glance at the Canon.

"We are all friends here, Mr Miggs," said the churchman with a kindly smile.

"Well, gentlemen," Miggs began. "It was just about dusk last night. I was going around locking up and seeing that everything was secure. There were still visitors in the main body of the Cathedral but they were few and far between and it wanted but half-an-hour to the closing and locking of the main doors. There was a little job I wanted to do in the Montresor Chapel, which is half-way down the body of the church."

Miggs cleared his throat apologetically and took another sip of the tea as though to sustain himself during his ordeal.

"I had my cleaning materials with me and it was my intention to burnish the brasses a little. There's the most magnificent . . ."

"Yes, yes, Mr Miggs," the Canon interrupted. "I'm sure Mr Pons doesn't want to hear all that."

"Just tell us what you did," said Solar Pons quietly, his lean, feral face expressing the keenest interest.

"Well, sir," said Miggs, turning toward him. "I had been working away for a few minutes, when I had a strange feeling that I wasn't alone. There's a quaint old altar piece up in one corner, with an ancient confessional box. It has a font with a carved gargoyle's head posed above it, as though it used to be a fountain at one time. I saw something in the bowl of the font, which arrested my attention, Mr Pons."

"And what was that?"

The Adventure of the Verger's Thumb 25

"Something that looked like a cotton-reel, Mr Pons. I bent forward to pick it up and as I did so I became aware of red eyes like an animal's glaring at me from the gloom of the confessional box. At the same time the gargoyle bit me!"

Solar Pons leaned forward, his face grave as a carven statute.

"Bit you, Mr Miggs?"

"Yes, sir. Something sharp like a tooth in the mouth of the thing! It drew blood and I dropped the wooden reel and fled!"

"I can't say I blame him, Pons," I exclaimed. "That would be enough to frighten anybody."

"Indeed, Parker."

"Just let me have a look at your thumb, Mr Miggs."

The indignant verger drew a grubby piece of plaster aside on his right thumb and allowed me to examine the wound. He winced as I fingered the skin around the puncture.

"It is deep, Pons. Something has either stabbed or bit him. Something with a very narrow entry point."

"Thank you, Parker. This is exceedingly interesting. You have nothing further to tell us, Mr Miggs?"

The verger shook his head.

"Only that when I came back with Canon Stacey and some of the workmen there was no sign of anyone in the confessional box. And the wooden thing in the font had gone!"

Solar Pons rubbed his thin hands together. He rose to his feet.

"I think we have heard everything that is likely to be of use, Canon. I would now like to go over the ground."

"By all means, Mr Pons. I will myself accompany you. Perhaps you would lead the way, Mr Miggs."

Pons was silent as we walked across the Close to the great façade of the Cathedral with its massive carved stonework at the entrance doors. Once inside the dim interior with the glutinous notes of the organ sounding we were again in another world.

"This is the place, Mr Pons. The Montresor Chapel."

Solar Pons' clear-minted features expressed the greatest interest. He hurried forward through the wrought-iron entrance gate and stood for a moment, looking intently about him. The Canon, Miggs and myself remained outside for a moment while he made his preliminary examination. There were few people about here and the light coming in through the stained glass in the early evening of this beautiful June day cast segments of blue, red and gold across Pons' alert face.

"This is the bowl of which I spoke, Mr Pons," said the verger pointing out the altar piece in question. I followed behind him and the Canon and I watched while Pons produced his magnifying glass and went carefully over the stonework.

"Why, there, Mr Pons!" said Miggs pointing with a quivering forefinger. "There is a drop of my blood!"

"Indeed," said Solar Pons abstractedly. "I had already observed it. But I am more interested in this gargoyle. Ah, that is singular, is it not, Parker?"

I followed Pons' glance and saw that the mouth of the thing was hollow. Pons was within the darkness of the confessional box now and I could see his eyes gleaming in the shadow as he surveyed us.

"Significant also, Parker," he said, his voice muffled from within the huge wooden structure. I squeezed in beside him and found that I could survey the chapel and a good deal of the Cathedral interior on this side without being seen myself. Pons was crouching down and I saw a beam of light illuminate his features.

"Just look at this, Parker."

I put my eye down and found that there was a large hole, apparently at the back of the gargoyle's head. The light from the cathedral interior was shining through the mouth.

"Good heavens, Pons, this is curious!" I exclaimed. "This must have been part of a fountain once."

"I am inclined to believe you, my dear fellow. Undoubtedly the water supply passed through this channel. It is highly significant."

We were interrupted at that moment by Canon Stacey, who was obviously keen to show us the spot connected with his own little adventure. In the shadow of the great pillar to which he led us Pons carried out a minute examination, and then glanced at the pews on which the two men were carrying out their mysterious conversation when observed by Stacey.

"There is little to be learned here, Parker," he said briefly. "But then I did not expect there to be. I should like to see the crypt now, if you please, Mr Miggs."

"Certainly, sir."

The verger led the way at a fast trot, fussy and full of self-importance and I could see a wry smile creasing Pons' features as I followed my friend down the steps. There was no-one else in the crypt so we were free to carry out our examination unhindered.

"Now exactly where were you standing when you saw this apparition?" Pons asked.

Canon Stacey gave a nervous glance over toward the scaffolding and sarcophagus in the corner.

"By this tomb here, Mr Pons."

He led the way and Pons took up the position indicated by him.

"I see. That squares perfectly with what you have already told us."

Pons stood for a moment, the fingers of his left hand pulling reflectively at the lobe of his left ear. Then he walked back down to the tomb of Bishop Lascelles. As the Canon had told us a heavy wooden lid temporarily covered the top, where the massive stone original had previous rested. This itself was on the paving at some distance, with a rope barrier around it.

"What was the exact purpose of this lid, Canon?" Pons asked.

"Why, Mr Pons, it was a question of time, you see. It was quite an undertaking getting the original off and then we had to remove the body. It could not be done in a day or anything like it, as our masons had to have scaffolding to lift the inner shell with the Bishop's remains. So we had the wooden cover made to conceal the inner coffin while the work went on. There was so much to be done here, you understand, that we should have had to have closed off the crypt to the public for months otherwise."

"I see."

Pons bent down and picked up a long thin strip of material. I glanced at it and saw that it was a wood shaving. I saw Pons' gaze resting on the various tools scattered about in this corner.

"And the lid was lifting by itself, you say? Or rather under the pressure of a hand and arm within the sarcophagus?"

Canon Stacey swallowed and turned a little pale. Looking round the dim crypt I had an idea of the shock the experience must have given him; even with the four of us here it was an atmospheric, evocative place.

"That is correct, Mr Pons. I shall never forget it."

"I am not surprised. Let us just see what weight we have to deal with."

Pons lifted one end of the lid.

"Oh, yes, it is not all that heavy."

He casually levered it to one side so that we could all look within at the dry, ancient stonework of the interior.

"There was nothing there, as you see, Mr Pons."

"Exactly, Canon."

Solar Pons stood looking reflectively down into the tomb. I saw that holes had been drilled through for the heavy bolts of the lid and helped Pons to replace it in its original position. Solar Pons dusted his hands, his eyes bright as he glanced at me.

"I think I have seen enough, Canon. Thank you, Mr Miggs. It has been extremely enlightening."

Canon Stacey had an eager expression on his face.

"You have learned something, Mr Pons?"

"I have learned a good deal. Whether I shall be able to draw any valid conclusions from my data remains to be seen. Come, Parker."

And he led the way from the crypt.

6

"Now, my dear fellow, let us just have your invaluable thoughts on this matter."

We were sitting at ease in the hotel dining room, having just concluded dinner, in that agreeable interval between the dessert and the entrance of the coffee and liqueurs. I fiddled with the fly-tying vice in my pocket, conscious that the original purpose of our holiday was fast becoming as the substance of a dream.

"You think this Herr Koch might have something to do with the extraordinary events in the Cathedral, Pons?"

"It is not beyond the bounds of possibility, Parker. You will have observed that Mr Miggs' account of the article in the basin of that fountain was extraordinarily similar to the thing we ourselves picked up in the crypt this morning."

"You think it was another message, Pons? In code?"

"It is extremely likely, Parker. Though the code itself is childishly simple."

"I did not find it so, Pons."

"That is because you are not bringing your mind to bear upon the subject, Parker."

"Enlighten me, Pons."

We were sitting in a secluded corner with no-one else near us and Pons waited until the waiter had brought the coffee and glasses of cognac before he produced a slip of paper from his pocket.

"I have the original safely upon me, Parker, but I do not wish to display it in a public place, for obvious reasons."

He thrust a folded sheet of paper toward me.

"I made an exact copy. You have it there. Let us just see what you make of it."

I smoothed out the paper and looked at the roughly inked characters upon it. Some of the symbols were hard to make out.

"Done in a hurry, Pons. There are many mistakes."

My companion shook his head.

"I think not, Parker. Slowly and laboriously indited by one of inferior education and extremely dull mind."

I stared at Pons in astonishment, replacing my coffee cup in my saucer.

"How can you possibly say that, Pons?"

"For the simple reason, my dear fellow, that a number of the letters are crossed out. The man had only the elementary rudiments of his own alphabet."

I stared at the groups of letters.

"I see the crossings out, but why slowly and laboriously? Just as easily hurriedly and carelessly, surely?"

Again Solar Pons shook his head.

"You will notice, Parker, that the worst-formed symbols, apart from those scratched out, are all upon the right-hand side. Surely that suggests an obvious explanation."

I shrugged helplessly.

"Not to me, Pons, I am afraid."

"That is only because you are not giving the matter sufficient attention. The message was obviously written within the Cathedral near dusk."

"But why, Pons?"

"Because of the light, Parker. Whoever wrote this message, sat in the western aisle of the cathedral to catch the last of the light. The right-hand edge of the paper was in semi-darkness, which was why he had such difficulty. It was obvious the light had almost gone altogether."

"But why would he wait until darkness, Pons? And why was he in the Cathedral at all at that time?"

Solar Pons chuckled.

"Ah, if we knew that, Parker, we would know a good deal. It is my guess that one of the men surprised by Canon Stacey wrote this."

"I see, Pons! I must confess I am completely baffled. Why on earth would they be hanging about here? And I am still no nearer to deciphering the message."

I looked at it again. All I read was: SNN CZMFDQNTR VD LTRS VZHS. Three letters were crossed out and made again and Pons' careful copy emulated all the blurred and wavering lines of the letters I had already noted in the original. I put it down at last.

"I am afraid it is no use, Pons."

My companion gave a thin smile and lifted his cognac glass to his lips. He replaced it on the table with an expression of satisfaction.

"Excellent, Parker. They have a first-rate cellar. You will find the answer on the unfolded portion of the paper beneath your hand there. The writer simply transposed the letters of the alphabet. One merely shifts the entire message to the right, as it were."

I turned the paper over.

In Pons' strong black capitals I now read: TOO DANGEROUS. WE MUST WAIT.

I looked at my companion in stupefaction.

"Brilliant, Pons. But what does it mean?"

"Elementary to the first, my dear Parker. And I do not know, to the second. But we progress."

He rubbed his thin fingers together with satisfaction as I traced out the simple message from the apparently chaotic jumble of letters.

"You will notice, Parker, that as is common with such simple cyphers when he reaches *A* he merely goes back to the end of the alphabet and substitutes *Z*."

"I see, Pons," I said. "This is extremely important. Ought we not to tell Canon Stacey?"

Solar Pons shook his head.

"Not unless we wish to frighten our men off altogether, Parker. We must tread very carefully indeed."

"If you say so, Pons. But I must say all this is a far cry from our peaceful holiday."

My companion's eyes were alert and shining.

"On the contrary, Parker, I am in fine form. I have all the benefits of a holiday together with the mental concentration on a criminal problem which so appeals to my peculiar nature."

"You think Koch and the girl are involved?"

"I should be extremely surprised if they were not."

"But what is all this business about two rough men, Pons, and coffin lids in the crypt rising?"

Solar Pons smiled enigmatically.

"The whole thing is linked, Parker," he said in that maddeningly omniscient way of his. "They are merely using the Cathedral as a dead letter-box."

"As a letter-box, Pons?"

I gazed at my friend in bewilderment. He leaned toward me across the table.

"So far as I know that is the means by which they communicate. As to the link which binds these disparate elements together, so far I have not been able to discover it. There is one simple, obvious fact staring me in the face but I cannot see it."

"Ah, well, Pons," said I, leaning back in my seat, "if you will forgive me I will leave these difficult problems of yours and immerse myself in the evening paper. I feel a little out of touch once I am away from town."

"By all means, Parker," said Solar Pons affably. "I will just put this ridiculous cipher away and enjoy an after-dinner pipe. Are you game for a stroll about the town before we turn in?"

"Certainly, Pons," I said. "Providing you give me half an hour in which to digest my dinner."

Solar Pons smiled, glancing round the half-empty dining room and tamping the bowl of his pipe. He was soon contentedly wreathed in aromatic blue smoke while I occupied myself with the day's news.

"Hullo," I said at last. "Here is an item concerning your old friend Superintendent Stanley Heathfield. And he is in the Norwich area!"

"Indeed?" said Solar Pons coolly, wrinkling up his brows at me through the pipe-smoke.

"It seems to be a desperate business, Pons. Two hardened criminals have escaped from prison in the Midlands and are believed to be hiding in Norfolk. Superintendent Heathfield was responsible for sending them to prison and has been sent up from the Yard to assist in the hunt, as he knows them both personally."

"When was this escape, Parker?"

There was an urgency in Pons' voice which had not been there before.

"About three weeks ago, Pons," I said, checking the article.

"I think you had better let me have that, my dear fellow," said my companion, stretching out his hand for the newspaper.

"Apparently they robbed a bank in Norwich itself of £20,000 two years ago, Pons. The money was never recovered. We seem to be the centre of excitement wherever we go."

"Do we not, Parker," said Solar Pons, his brows knotted over the newspaper account. "This is extremely interesting."

He put the journal down and sat frowning into the far distance. I knew better than to interrupt him. Presently he rose from the table.

"If you have finished, my dear fellow, we will take our walk. According to this account Heathfield is making The Bull his headquarters. I think we will pay him a little call."

7

"Mr Pons!"

Superintendent Stanley Heathfield's keen, military-looking face with its iron-grey moustache, was suffused in smiles as I followed Pons into the bar.

"I am as surprised as you, Superintendent," said Pons drily.

"You know Dr Parker, of course. I only read of your presence in the city in the newspaper this evening."

"Ah, that."

A shadow passed across the Superintendent's face. He moved farther down the polished bar of The Bull to give us room.

"Will you not join me in a drink?"

"Delighted," I said.

When Heathfield had given the order to the attractive girl behind the bar he looked at us quizzically.

"I am not quite clear what you are both doing in Norwich."

"We are nominally on holiday," I said somewhat bitterly, "but Pons has already found a problem with which to occupy himself."

Superintendent Heathfield smiled a thin smile.

"Trouble seems to follow us both, Mr Pons. Health to you."

He raised his glass in salute, looking critically at the milling people in the bar around us.

"Let us find somewhere more quiet, Mr Pons. I would be glad of your advice."

Solar Pons had an ironic look in his eyes.

"Our co-operation may be mutually beneficial, Superintendent. I suggest we adjourn to the hotel lounge. It appeared to be almost empty as we passed through the entrance hall."

"As you wish."

The Superintendent's tall figure led the way to the oak-beamed lounge. There were only a few elderly people dotted about in arm-chairs and the pleasant summer breeze came in through the open windows, bringing with it the scent of cut grass and roses.

"It takes a good deal to beat England at this time of year, Superintendent."

"You are right, Mr Pons. But you did not come here to discuss gardening."

My companion chuckled, easing his lean form into a deep leather chair in the secluded corner the Scotland Yard man had chosen.

"As always, your reasoning is accurate. You are looking for two escaped convicts. I am involved in a problem which concerns four people. I think our pooling of ideas may be mutually beneficial."

Superintendent Heathfield twisted his grey moustache with sensitive fingers.

"You think the two things are connected?"

Pons nodded.

"Before I begin I would like to extract a promise from you."

Heathfield shifted in his chair and looked at my companion with serious eyes.

"That depends upon the promise."

"I do not think it is one you will find hard to keep. It is just this. I do not wish to have the full panoply of the law involved in my own problem. My suggestion is that you alone should be concerned."

The Superintendent raised his glass to his lips.

"The three of us in other words?"

"At this stage, yes. You know the persons, after all. I have only half the threads in my hand."

Heathfield nodded, looking from my companion to me.

"What have I got to lose, Mr Pons? Naturally, I shall have to hear the whole story from your own lips. But I think I can give that promise in advance."

Solar Pons smiled.

"Very well, Superintendent."

He looked at me with an almost dreamy expression. He fumbled in his jacket pocket, producing the small wooden container we had picked up in the Cathedral crypt.

"Before we let our friend in on the little secret, Parker, I think we should just compose a suitable message in order to bring our quarry to the bait."

"How do you mean, Pons?"

Solar Pons shook his head.

"I know that we are nominally on holiday, my dear fellow, but you have not been following my line of reasoning."

I frowned.

"You mean the message in that little spool was intended to be picked up by somebody and went astray?"

"Of course, Parker!"

Solar Pons slapped his thigh with his right hand, making a cracking sound like a miniature pistol-shot.

"It is palpably plain. Unless I miss my guess the drama we have seen in part played out in the Cathedral and the Dean's story are interconnected. It should not take too long to unravel the loose ends providing we take things in sequence and tread carefully."

"What do you suggest, Pons?"

"After I have taken Superintendent Heathfield into our full confidence we must invent something that will bring events to a climax. We shall need the Dean's co-operation as I shall require darkness for what I have in mind. We can only do this at night or they will be on to us, which means a door must be conveniently left open."

Superintendent Heathfield had a frown on his face now.

"I hesitate to appear over-inquisitive, gentlemen, but I would be grateful for a little light myself in this matter."

Solar Pons smiled disarmingly.

"By all means, Superintendent. If you would just order another round of drinks, Parker, I will put our friend in possession of the facts."

8

"But why are we going to the Cathedral, Pons?" I said.

My companion frowned.

"I have a little errand to take care of, Parker."

We were threading the crowded streets of Norwich in the late afternoon sunshine of the following day. Pons had been moody and taciturn following our conversation with Heathfield the previous night and had spent a good deal of time keeping Koch and his female companion under discreet observation. He had been busy in the writing room of the hotel earlier in the afternoon and when he joined me for tea had been a little more communicative.

We had walked by the riverside for a little while and now, as we made our way toward the towering pile of the Cathedral, he became almost expansive.

"Let us just put our thoughts in order, Parker. Give me the benefit of your observations on this little problem."

I fingered the fly-tying device in my pocket thoughtfully.

"I am beginning to see some light, Pons. But the whole thing seems bizarre. The Canon's fright in the crypt and the hand coming out of the tomb; the Head Verger's thumb dripping blood; the two rough men; the couple we saw; the coded messages. Some of it makes sense viewed separately but frankly I find the whole thing a fantastic jumble."

"That is because you are not looking at the complete pattern, Parker."

Solar Pons blew out a lazy trail of blue smoke over his shoulder.

"But why the Cathedral, Pons. So public . . ."

My companion smiled.

"Exactly, my dear fellow. A great public building is the perfect place of concealment. Hidden amongst the crowd, as it were."

He frowned up at the magnificent façade of the church as we advanced across the forecourt in the mellow light of early evening.

"A dead letter drop. It could not be more convenient."

"But what do you propose to do now, Pons?"

"Why, deliver my own message, of course, Parker."

I looked at him in astonishment.

"For what purpose?"

"Why, to arrange a rendezvous for tonight. Only we will keep the appointment as well."

I felt my irritation rising but bottled it back.

"As well as whom?"

"In addition to those expected, Parker. I think midnight would be ideal. It is traditionally the witching hour, is it not?"

"I give up, Pons," I said, as we walked down the shadowy aisle, through bars of dusty sunlight that fell as if sub-aqueous through the stained glass windows.

"I trust that all will be made clear soon," said my companion as he led the way cautiously forward, turning toward the dark recess that was the Montresor Chapel. The pompous form of Mr Miggs was hurrying toward us and at Pons' suggestion he waited until the last visitor had left the chapel and then himself closed the wrought iron gates behind us and stood on guard until we had concluded our business.

Pons looked round carefully and then went casually forward into the area of the confessional box. He placed something into the ancient stone bowl and then rejoined me. A few seconds later Mr Miggs had noiselessly re-opened the gates and followed us down the aisle. Pons turned to the little man and put his hand to his lips.

"Absolute discretion, Mr Miggs. Do not go near the Montresor Chapel again this evening."

Miggs looked puzzled and disappointed.

"I do not understand, Mr Pons."

"No matter. It is for your own good. Now, if you would be so kind as to let him know, I should like a word with Canon Stacey."

"I believe he is in his garden, Mr Pons. He keeps bees."

"That will do well enough. Kindly tell him that we shall attend him there within a few minutes."

Mr Miggs bustled off and Solar Pons looked thoughtfully after him. I glanced around the massive stone columns.

"You are sure we have not been seen going into the chapel, Pons?"

"As sure as one can be of anything in this life, Parker.

"I asked Miggs to make certain we were not disturbed but he immediately drew attention to our visiting the chapel by closing the gates. An over-officious little man but one whose heart is in the right place. However, the men we seek are undoubtedly well off the tourist track and Koch and the girl are out on the river this afternoon. They have hired a motor-boat from Norwich Yacht Station."

I looked at my companion in surprise.

"How do you know that, Pons?"

My companion pulled thoughtfully at the lobe of his right ear.

"Because I have made it my business to know, Parker. I followed Koch when he left the hotel after lunch. He went straight over the bridge near the railway station and booked a powerful launch at the Yacht Station office there."

"Indeed, Pons. For what purpose?"

"That remains to be seen, Parker. But it would be an unobtrusive way of getting those two men away from here. There are two hundred miles of Broads in which they could lose themselves."

"I see you have given this a lot of thought, Pons."

"Have you ever known a time when I have not, Parker?"

"How do you know they have not left already?"

Solar Pons shook his head.

"Simple observation, Parker. Those two are still quarrelling and on edge. If they had achieved their objective they would have quietly left before now."

"But why are they out on the Broads this afternoon, Pons?"

Solar Pons clicked his teeth in a deprecatory manner.

"Simply in order to learn the controls of the boat, Parker. Like most people who come for a Broadland holiday they have little knowledge of sailing or motor-boats. When I left this afternoon the man from the Yacht Station had detailed his assistant to teach them the controls. The last I saw of them they were heading down river toward Brundall. It is my guess they may make for Breydon Water before turning back so that has given us a few hours."

He consulted his watch and said nothing further until we had gained Canon Stacey's garden, where Mr Miggs was again waiting by a side-gate in the Close to conduct us to his superior.

As Miggs had indicated, the Canon was indeed among his bees and as Pons appeared to be as impervious to those insects as to those of a criminous nature I stood some way off among the apple trees and admired the beauties of the garden until my friend had finished. The two men had an amiable conversation for about two minutes, the churchman in his bonnet and veil while Pons stood, a lean and imperturbable figure, among a cloud of buzzing insects. Mr Miggs, a slightly comic sight, stood halfway between myself and the two men by the beehives.

When Pons re-joined me he was smiling and rubbed his thin fingers together in jaunty fashion.

"The Canon has given me the key of a small door leading on to the cloisters. I think that should be sufficient for our purposes."

"What are our purposes, Pons?"

"To apprehend criminals, Parker. It is a pity that you did not bring your revolver, for these are desperate men."

I frowned.

"I thought we were on holiday, Pons. I do not usually bring deadly weapons on such trips."

"No, of course not," said my companion soothingly. "Are you game for the midnight jaunt tonight?"

"Of course, Pons."

Mr Miggs was deep in conversation with the Canon now so Pons and I came away, walking back slowly through the Close. I was about to make some commonplace remark when, to my surprise, Pons caught my arm in a powerful grip, almost making me cry out.

"They are back earlier than I thought, Parker."

I followed his glance toward the broad concourse in front of the Cathedral and saw that the girl called Elise was walking purposefully across toward the great main door. We followed unobtrusively. The vast church was still half-full of people wandering about and we had no difficulty in keeping the girl in sight. From where we stood by a massive pillar we could easily see her slip through the wrought-iron gates into the Montresor Chapel.

She was absent for but a minute and when she came out it was obvious from her expression that she was excited and tense. She sat in a chair some distance in front of us, across the aisle, her head bowed as though in prayer. Pons' voice was calm, his manner distant as he whispered.

"She has deciphered it, Parker. Unless I miss my guess she has taken the bait."

We waited while the fair girl rummaged around in her handbag. Once again her head was bowed.

"She is composing her reply, Parker."

Less than a minute later she was on her feet, making her way with confident strides up the aisle toward us. Pons and I slipped round the pillar, as though examining architectural features, but she obviously had no eyes for us. As we watched she descended the stairs to the crypt. I made as though to follow but once again Pons' hand was on my arm.

"There is no point in following, Parker. Apart from the fact that there may be someone watching inside the church and we do not want to tip our hand. She is undoubtedly agreeing to the rendezvous proposed and will leave her message in a pre-arranged place below."

He moved out from behind the pillar.

"I think we may as well get back to the hotel."

"But are we not going to wait, Pons?"

My companion shook his head, a slight expression of irritation passing across his features.

"There is no point, Parker," he repeated.

He was proven right a few minutes later when the girl passed us in the street as we walked slowly toward our hotel. Solar Pons looked at me enigmatically.

"Now all we have to do is to prime Heathfield and settle down to wait," he said gently.

9

I shifted my cramped position behind the pew and once again mentally criticised the hardness of the floor. Pons was still and alert at my side. On the summer breeze the silvery notes of church bells—dozens of them from the myriad churches of Norwich—had just pealed for half-past eleven. I leaned toward my companion to whisper.

"It is a pity I did not bring my revolver, after all, Pons."

Faint light glinted on my companion's eyeballs in the dusky interior of the great cathedral.

"This heavy walking stick will have to do, Parker. Though Heathfield and his men will not be far."

"You think these desperadoes will come?"

"Undoubtedly."

"Koch and the girl also?"

"Koch, certainly. I am positive that she will remain with the boat."

I glanced at my companion's almost invisible form.

"But how would Koch get into the church?"

"He would not need to, normally. The exchanges take place in daylight. My guess tonight is that his two companions in crime will unbolt or break open a small, little-used side-door. Ah, what did I say!"

A faint creaking noise, seemingly far off, echoed and reverberated in an eerie manner through the vastness of the empty cathedral. There was a long silence and then the furtive sound of shuffling footsteps. Pons put his mouth up against my ear.

"One is coming up from the crypt. The other has already gone to open a door. We shall not have long to wait."

No sooner had he spoken than there came the faintest pin-point of light, close to the floor and bobbing along the far aisle of the church. It passed away and as we turned to keep it in view, it was blocked from time to time by the vastness of the pillars which supported the roof of the cathedral.

Presently there came the noise of metal on wood and a loud creaking sounded throughout the building. There were low voices now and the distant sound of footsteps and then two more shadowy figures came hurrying along the aisle and passed in the direction of the first.

"Excellent, Parker," Solar Pons breathed. "My theory was correct."

"I do not understand you, Pons."

"There has been some muddle over the place of concealment, Parker. It is just as I thought and accounts for the disorder discovered by Mr Miggs."

I gave up at this point and concentrated on the faint reflections of light and the sounds coming from a side chapel farther along the aisle. We waited perhaps half an hour, until the noises had died away. Then three shadowy figures crept back. A distant door closed.

"Quickly, Parker!" said Solar Pons, all caution abandoned.

I hurried forward in the thick, glutinous darkness, hard put to it to keep up. He went straight to the area just vacated by the three men. Inside the railed-off chapel interior everything was in confusion. In the light coming through the stained glass window from the city outside I made out a gaping blackness in the oak altar-piece.

"It is as I suspected, Parker," said Solar Pons. "We have not a moment to lose."

In a few moments we had let ourselves out into the cloisters and a short while afterwards were hurrying at an undignified pace through the streets of Norwich. Presently Pons slackened his pace.

"There is no hurry now, Parker," he said calmly. "Our men are just ahead, emerging from that side-street."

The three shadows were visible ahead and I turned into a shop doorway with Pons. To my astonishment I saw, from the light of the street-lamps, that two of the men wore clerical surplices.

"Are you sure this is right, Pons?" I asked. "These men look like clergymen."

Solar Pons chuckled softly.

"Do they not, Parker. The best disguise in their circumstances. They would find everything they want in the Cathedral."

We followed at a discreet distance as the trio moved down Bishopsgate and into Riverside Road. I noticed that the third man seemed to be moving more slowly, weighed down with a suitcase. Now and again the cadences of their voices came to us on the summer breeze. They seemed to be arguing about something. As though he could read my thoughts Pons commented succinctly, "They have not yet realised that a third party was responsible for this midnight meeting. Let us hope they are aboard before the truth sinks in."

We were nearing our destination now; there were only a few passers-by at this late hour but it was such a beautiful night that a number of people were abroad, strolling in the scented air; some walking dogs while others, obvious lovers, were making for the waterside where the River Yare passed by Norwich Thorpe Station.

Our trio made for that area too but without even pausing at the Yacht Station or glancing at the lighted windows of the small hotels and guest houses on the other side of the road, continued along the tow-path in the Yarmouth direction. The faint beat of a motor-launch came to us down wind.

"Should they be moving at this time of night, Pons?" I asked.

My companion shook his head.

"My guess is, no. All Broadland craft are obliged to tie up at dusk. It is forbidden to move at night without proper navigation lights and hired holiday craft do not have them."

He frowned.

"As their launch is the only craft moving it should not be too difficult to pick them up again. I think we will take to the road, Parker. According to the maps I have studied there should be another bridge a little farther down."

I hurried after him up the steps at the side of the tow-path and we walked along a well-lit, metalled road.

"Lack of navigation lights will make it difficult for us to pick them up, Pons," I said.

"True, Parker," my companion agreed. "But you forget that no part of the Broads is more than an hour away by car. There is ample time to cut them off when we give Heathfield the word to move. We want all four, on board, and with the money."

I glanced at my companion's tense, aquiline face.

"You think they are making for Great Yarmouth, then?"

"Undoubtedly that direction, Parker. The police are watching the roads about Norwich and the launch is their only way out. I have no doubt they intend to transfer to a motor vehicle when they reach some pre-arranged lonely spot. Now we must be sparing of talk as we have some stiff walking ahead of us."

He said nothing more as we walked briskly along the road, following the course of the broad, sluggish river; we could hear the launch clearly but as we had left the tow-path which the three men had taken, they were no longer in view. The noise of the launch was clearer now, the slow beat of its motor echoing back from the banks.

Then it increased and as the throttle opened it settled into the familiar rhythm of a motor vessel under way. Pons glanced at his watch as we passed under a street-lamp. His face expressed satisfaction.

"All four safely aboard, Parker," he said. "I think we might make our move now, before they get too far down-river."

"You are showing remarkable knowledge of the locality, Pons," I commented.

My companion chuckled.

"I have not wasted my time and this afternoon I studied a large-scale map of the area. Unless I am much mistaken, there is a bridge about a mile ahead which will do very nicely."

I tucked my arms into my sides for the lean, athletic figure had increased its pace and I am afraid I was a little blown before we had reached our destination. The river twisted here, for the sound of the launch was fainter, though we had evidently gained upon it, for I could see the faint cabin lights between the trees down below. The road, of course, ran straight, taking no account of the river, which veered away at this point and in remarkably quick time we had come to a broad road-bridge across, guarded by a low parapet topped by iron railings.

Pons had reached it first and stood awaiting me impatiently, his eyes dancing with excitement. He still carried the heavy stick and his keen eyes were fixed on the bend of the river behind us.

"I think this will do nicely, Parker. The bridge is low and sloping so that they will have to keep in the centre of the stream. The cabin top should not be more than four feet below the arch at this point."

"Good heavens, Pons," I mumbled. "You surely do not intend to drop on to the vessel?"

"That is exactly my intention, Parker. But if you do not feel up to it, I shall quite understand. In which case I should be grateful if you would remain as an observer and sound this police whistle once I am aboard."

He slipped the chain of the whistle about my neck as he spoke but I shook my head.

"I would not dream of remaining, Pons. Where you go I shall follow."

Solar Pons smiled thinly.

"Excellent, Parker. I knew I could rely on you. We must drop quite accurately and make sure we do not get in each other's way. Timing is all important and you must drop three seconds after me. I shall land in the bow and you on the cabin-top that way."

"You seem to have worked it out in a good deal of detail, Pons," I said, looking back at the small circular blobs of light from the launch portholes which were now coming broadside on to us at the far bend.

"It is hastily improvised, Parker, but I fancy it will do," he said casually.

We were quite alone on the bridge and the nearest street light was at the far end, so that we were in shadow here. Pons went over to the other side of the bridge and stepped on to the low wall. He seized the iron railing and eased over. He disappeared and a few moments later I heard his voice echoing upwards above the beat of the launch engine.

"It will not be difficult, Parker. There is a brick groyne here which gives excellent footing and one can hold on to the iron bolts of the railings."

I looked down over the coping and saw that he had spoken the truth; he held the stick under his left arm and balanced himself easily on the brickwork holding on to a long, protruding iron bolt with his right hand.

"It is just a question of timing. Pray go to the far parapet and run back to me as soon as the bow of the craft reaches the bridge. Then we have only to wait until the Moorhen appears beneath us. I estimate she is travelling at only some five knots."

I did as Pons ordered, running swiftly to the far parapet. The dim shape of the launch was already a hundred yards away, the chug of its engine sounding exceptionally loud in the still summer air. As Pons had said she carried no navigation lights but someone had made an attempt to duplicate the green port and red starboard markings by affixing electric torches to the cabin top on either side and fastening coloured mica strips across them.

There was no-one visible aboard but there was a dim light from the steering well and I crouched down, carefully calculating the vessel's progress as she cleaved the dark brown water, briefly turned to silver in the moonlight.

"She is beneath the arch now, Pons!"

I ran swiftly back, my heart thumping and scrambled down next to Pons. He smiled at me encouragingly.

"Three seconds, Parker. No more or you will overshoot."

"I understand, Pons."

The words were no sooner out of my mouth than the bow of the vessel appeared from beneath the bridge, directly underneath us. Pons was already gone, dropping cat-like on to the bow. I finished my counting and was in the air; the cabin-top looked as small as a postage stamp but I landed safely, slithering sideways for one sickening moment, before I managed to steady myself by catching hold of a wire cable which helped to support the short mast of the launch.

The bang I made on the cabin top roused cries of alarm from the interior and I was reassured to see Pons appear beside me; he looked alert and formidable as he brandished the heavy walking-stick.

"I hope this is the right launch, Pons," I said, "or we shall have a suit for assault on our hands."

Pons laughed, his keen feral face clear-minted in the moonlight.

"You never cease to entertain me, my dear fellow. Ah, here they come."

He lashed out as a burly figure flailed its way from the cabin. There was a howl of pain as the heavy cane descended and the big man in the tarpaulin coat backed away. Two men appeared to have collided in the cabin doorway and I leaned over and got in a smart blow at the neck of one of them. A search-light suddenly stabbed out across the water in front of us and the chugging of another launch was heard.

"Ah, that will be Heathfield," said Pons calmly, jumping down into the well of the vessel. "Just sound that whistle, if you please."

I had no sooner given three sharp blasts of the police whistle than the three swearing men were on us. I saw Pons close with one and heard a hoarse shout; a heavy body fell with a resounding splash and was soon left astern. A villainous-looking fellow with a shaven head had his hands at my windpipe but I managed to break his hold and he fell back into the cabin interior where a fair-haired girl was steering the launch and looking anxiously back over her shoulder.

The third man, who could only be Koch had closed with Pons, and was reaching for his pocket. I heard him grunt as my companion caught him a well-timed blow on the face and then he was asprawl on the deck, the revolver falling from his pocket. Pons was on it in a flash and steadied the barrel on the big man who came in a rush through the door.

"The game is up," he said sternly. "Just place your hands on the cabin top."

The big man sullenly obeyed and I went to help Koch up. The other launch was approaching rapidly now, the yellow beam of the searchlight playing on our vessel. Heathfield's voice, clipped and confident, came across the water to us.

"Is all well, Mr Pons?"

"All well, Superintendent. We have our men. You will find one in the river yonder. Fortunately, it is a nice night for a swim."

He chuckled as he glanced at the bearded features of Koch.

"You may tell the lady to switch off the engine now. You have no further cards to play."

The sound of the motor died away and the Moorhen began to drift as the bows of the other launch bumped against the rubbing strake of ours. Heathfield jumped aboard, followed by two uniformed constables. The searchlight beam had picked out the agitation in the water where the third man was trying to swim ashore. He was still some yards from the bank when a constable on a bicycle stopped on the tow-path and waited for him to scramble out. Heathfield rubbed his hands together.

"Excellent, Mr Pons! I am again in your debt. You have handled this in a masterly fashion."

Solar Pons smiled thinly.

"You are too kind, Superintendent. It was a fairly simple matter once I read about your two convicts."

Heathfield looked sharply at the bearded man who stood opening and closing his fists impotently at the cabin-door and then turned to the big man.

"Well, Blakeney, I am sorry it has come to this. Greed has been your undoing throughout life. You have lost your remission and the money to boot."

The big man with the close-cropped head spat angrily into the water and mumbled something unintelligible. There was the flash of handcuffs as two constables closed in on him. The man we had known as Karl Koch stood straight and pale in front of us; there was something noble, almost tragic about him, as he glanced at the slim woman called Elise, who had joined him from the wheelhouse. She carried a heavy black suitcase and Heathfield moved immediately to take it from her.

The girl's face was white and strained.

"Fool!" she told her companion. "This has been bungled from the beginning."

Pons had lit his pipe and now he blew a stream of aromatic blue smoke thoughtfully into the warm summer night.

"Do not blame your husband too much, Mrs Kramer. The scheme was a good one but you relied upon poor tools."

The slim woman turned like a snake. Her eyes were burning savagely as she stared at Pons.

"You know us, then?"

Pons inclined his head.

"Who does not know Karl and Elise Kramer of Zurich in international criminal circles?"

Heathfield turned to my companion, consternation on his face.

"I do not understand, Mr Pons."

"It came to me rather late, Superintendent," said Pons. "I thought the man's face was somehow familiar but I could not at first place it. However, I put through a call to the Sureté yesterday from my hotel and soon had the identification. Mr and Mrs Kramer, alias Koch, are now based in Switzerland.

They are wanted in Dusseldorf as well as in this country so it is rather a question of where the trial will take place as I fancy the Germans will ask for their extradition."

"But what is all this about, Pons?" I burst in.

My companion looked dreamily along the searchlight beam to where the third man was being handcuffed by the constable on the bank.

"I think we have had enough excitement for one night, Parker, and it is now almost two A.M. More detailed explanations must wait until the morning."

"I agree, Mr Pons," said Heathfield. "In any event, so far as I am concerned, it will take most of the night to charge this precious band and to take their statements."

He raised his hand in a signal to the constable who had taken over the controls of the Moorhen. The two launches slowly began to get under way, turning to head up river and back toward Norwich Yacht Station.

10

"It was a remarkable performance, Mr Pons!"

Solar Pons smilingly disclaimed Superintendent Heathfield's statement, the smoke from his pipe ascending in fragrant spirals toward the ceiling of our hotel. We were a small group gathered in a quiet corner of the coffee lounge the following evening and the fragrant perfume of roses came in through the open windows.

"The only thing remarkable about it was the coincidence. There was little of the ratiocinative process involved and, of course, as soon as I knew of the escaped convicts' presence in the city the motivation of the strange events in the Cathedral became clear to me."

"That is all very well, Mr Pons," said Canon Stacey, "but I am inclined to agree with Mr Heathfield. I must confess that I am still in the dark over most of these matters."

"You are not the only one," I said somewhat caustically and Pons turned to me a mocking visage in which one eyebrow was visibly raised.

"Come now, my dear fellow."

He glanced round the small company composed of myself, the Superintendent, the Canon and Mr Miggs who perched somewhat uneasily on a bar-stool in the far corner as though he were excluded both socially and physically from the gathering.

"As soon as I heard Canon Stacey's story it became obvious that the bizarre events he mentioned were interconnected. Let us just recall them, my dear Parker."

"Well, Pons," I said. "As I remember, Canon Stacey first heard evil whispering from two rough men who were lying on the seats of one of the pews in the dusk, eating a meal. The Canon heard them speak of 'robbery' and 'killing'."

"Excellent, Parker," said Solar Pons, his eyes fixed unwinkingly on me. "My training has not been entirely wasted."

I confess I felt a flush rise to my cheek at the compliment as I went on.

"Then, some time later, one of the side-chapels had been desecrated; altar ornaments removed and ornamental candlesticks unscrewed."

Pons nodded, his eyes half-closed now.

"That was extremely significant and you may remember I commended it to you, Parker."

"So you did, Pons. That brought us to the horrifying experience of the Canon, when he saw the lid on the tomb rising in the crypt. Not to mention Mr Miggs' own experience when he went to pick up that cylinder out of the font and was bitten by the gargoyle!"

My companion smiled thinly.

"A fairly accurate and concise, if colourful resumé. I gave a good deal of thought to the matter and had no difficulty in assigning a fairly logical explanation, particularly in view of our own first-hand knowledge of Karl and Elise Kramer whom we saw behaving strangely in the crypt on the first day of our arrival in Norwich. They had apparently dropped or mislaid a coded message in the little wooden cylinder identical to the one Mr Miggs attempted to pick up from the bowl of the font. The code was an elementary one and yielded the message: TOO DANGEROUS. WE MUST WAIT. The longer I thought about the matter the more I became convinced that the two men seen by the Canon and our couple were connected."

I stared at Pons reflectively.

"That the two men and our couple were connected, Pons?"

"Of course. It was, on the surface of things, unlikely, but there are many unlikely things in life which nevertheless come to pass. Without knowledge of the robbery, of course, I did not immediately see the cause, neither did I know the two were escaped convicts but some points of interest immediately suggested themselves. Let us just take them one at a time. I pointed out to you, Parker, that a great cathedral was just the place for people to submerge themselves."

Solar Pons puffed out a cloud of smoke and watched its slow ascent toward the ceiling of the lounge.

"The fact that the men were seen at dusk; that they were eating food; and that they were apparently discussing a robbery immediately suggested that they were hiding—or even living—in the Cathedral."

Canon Stacey gave a muffled exclamation.

"You don't mean to say so, Mr Pons?"

Solar Pons nodded slowly.

"I was never more serious, Canon Stacey. There are dozens of places in such an edifice in which desperate and determined men might hide. During the day they had only to sit in the pews or wander about the building and no-one would give them a second glance. It immediately occurred to me that they might be somehow linked with Kramer and the girl. The couple staying at the hotel could easily leave them parcels of food at pre-arranged places within the Cathedral and they had only to pick up surplices from pegs in order to vary their appearance from time to time."

Superintendent Heathfield nodded.

"It was quite a brilliant scheme, Mr Pons. If I may start at the beginning, Blakeney and Hobbs, to give these two escaped convicts their proper names, were recruited by the Kramers to commit the robbery at the Norwich bank three years ago. They hid the money in the Cathedral, as had been pre-arranged, but were arrested and rather than let the Kramers benefit by the proceeds refused to tell their accomplices its whereabouts. They preferred to serve out their sentences or escape. They eventually chose the latter course and we knew they would make for Norwich for the proceeds of the robbery had never been found."

Solar Pons nodded.

"As you have already learned from the Sureté, Superintendent, the Kramers crossed over from Zurich when they read of the escape in the newspapers and booked into the same hotel to which Parker and I came. I have no doubt the scheme was an alternative one which had been decided a long time ago and the coded messages and their method of passing them was a part of it."

Heathfield drew up the corners of his mouth.

"Hobbs has already confessed as much, Mr Pons. Blakeney will be a tougher nut to crack, though the thing is academic now that we have recovered the money and have all four under lock and key."

Solar Pons resumed, his keen hawk-like face glancing at each of us in turn as he continued.

"I decided then that the two men were staying in the Cathedral for some purposes of their own and the combined stories told by Mr Miggs and Canon Stacey strengthened my premise at every step."

"But the desecration of the side chapel, Pons?"

My companion's eyes gleamed.

"Elementary, my dear Parker. These men, as we have ourselves observed, though hard and determined, are of limited intellect. They were no doubt recruited by the Kramers for just these qualities. They performed the hard, dangerous work of the actual robbery. When it was over they hid in the Cathedral, waited until it was closed for the night and concealed the stolen money beneath the altar in one of the side-chapels. We have already heard from the Canon here that renovation work has been going on in the Cathedral for some years. It is my theory that they used tools lying about to remove panelling to conceal their loot. During the course of their operations they unscrewed some of the ornamental candlesticks on the altar, initially, I venture to suggest, with the idea of rolling up some of the notes and concealing them within the shafts. But even their limited intellects realised this was impracticable, given the sums of money involved, and they abandoned this procedure."

I had been staring at Pons as he proceeded and now I broke in.

"During the time they had been in prison, they forgot in which chapel they had concealed the money!"

"Exactly, Parker. The disorder in which Mr Miggs found the place proved it was so. Moreover, he had disturbed them at their work. They had unscrewed the candlesticks, hoping to identify the chapel, but I have already ascertained that nearly all of such fixtures in the Cathedral come apart in like manner."

"For cleaning purposes, Mr Pons," Mr Miggs put in.

My companion nodded.

"Perhaps you could add to that, Canon Stacey?"

The churchman stirred in his chair, admiration on his features.

"It is amazing, Mr Pons. Unless these men had looked at the brass plates over the chapel entrances, they would have had difficulty in identification for work was going on there three years ago and now the scaffolding and beams have been moved farther down."

"Exactly," said Solar Pons. "Now we come to the incident of Mr Miggs' thumb. It is self-evident that the two groups had a pre-arranged code and that when the time came to recover the money they would have pre-selected places to exchange their messages."

The Superintendent smiled thinly.

"That is so, Mr Pons. Hobbs has confirmed this."

Solar Pons took the stem of the pipe from his mouth.

"I submit that one picking-up point was in the crypt. I noted a stone statue at the far end. The right hand was raised and the carving of the hand, palm upwards, was sufficiently high up to conceal anything placed in the palm. I further submit that Kramer and his wife were in the crypt to pick up a message but that it had either somehow fallen from the hand of the statue or had been removed by a visitor who had let it drop to the floor. They had obviously overlooked it and it was not until I recovered it, that we were brought into the matter. The couple hiding in the church picked up Kramer's messages from the font in the Montresor Chapel. But again, Mr Miggs application to his work threw them off. He came along to clean the brasses and noted the little cylinder in the font. Hobbs or Blakeney had hidden in the darkness of the confessional box. When Miggs bent over to pick up the message from the font the man in the box stabbed his finger with a thin-bladed knife, striking down through the open mouth of the stone gargoyle. This obvious explanation immediately suggested itself and I had only to look at the chapel and its physical properties to see what had occurred."

"Good heavens, Mr Pons!" said Mr Miggs, his mouth half-open. "This is miraculous . . ."

Solar Pons smiled.

"Despite the highly religious atmosphere, Mr Miggs there is nothing heavenly or of the miraculous about it. It is extremely down to earth."

"That is all very well, Pons," I said, "and you have explained it most convincingly. But what about the apparition in the vault?"

Solar Pons shook his head.

"There was no apparition, Parker. Hobbs and Blakeney were merely making use of the existing conditions. One or both of them slept within the tomb at night, where they would be undisturbed. I had only to look at that wooden cover to see that they had used the tools lying about the crypt to drill air holes in the lid. I noticed also, that the clamps securing the cover had been removed so that they could not be inadvertently locked in by workmen arriving unexpectedly."

"Remarkable, Mr Pons," Canon Stacey murmured. "But I still cannot understand what they meant by talking about a killing."

Superintendent Heathfield shook his head.

"I have gone into that, Canon. Hobbs tells me they were discussing the robbery in the cathedral that night. Blakeney, his companion, a desperate and hardened criminal, was merely stating that he would kill Kramer if he betrayed them."

"But what did you put in your coded note, Pons, to bring things to a climax last night?"

Solar Pons turned to me, a faint smile on his face.

"The message purported to come from Kramer. It merely said that they would have to move at midnight if they were to get them away. Fortunately, the two convicts were able to discover the whereabouts of the money by that time and they were too busy arguing among themselves over the division of the spoils to realise that a third party had intervened in their affairs."

He looked around the little circle, his eyes dancing with strange lights.

"A case not without its interesting points, Parker."

He chuckled.

"Perhaps you will still be able to find time for that fly-tying device which has lain so long unused in your pocket."

He turned back to the assembled company.

"And now, gentlemen, if you will give me your glasses, it is my round I think."

The Adventure of

THE·PHANTOM· ·FACE·

THE ADVENTURE OF
THE PHANTOM FACE

1

It was a day of heavy hoar frost in early January, the sky bleak and louring and I had just come in to our cosy chambers at 7B Praed Street as dusk fell, having finished a hard afternoon's rounds. Our admirable landlady Mrs Johnson had a roaring fire going in the hearth and I slumped down in front of it without removing my coat, conscious only of the circulation slowly being restored to my frozen hands.

It was near the hour of tea and I lay back in pleasant anticipation of the hot crumpets and other delicacies which would shortly be ascending to our quarters, borne by our gracious hostess. I was lost in these admirable day-dreams when I became aware of a strange thumping sound which had started up from one side of the room. It seemed to emanate from my friend Solar Pons' bedroom and as it continued the floor began to creak and the volume of noise reached alarming proportions.

I walked over and tapped on the door but on receiving no reply, threw it open. I was astonished to see my friend leaning over a recumbent figure on the bed, belabouring it savagely with a walking cane. He turned a smiling countenance to my astonished features.

"Good afternoon, my dear Parker! It must be rather cold and inclement without."

"But warm enough in here, Pons," I said, glancing at his shirt-sleeved form. "Particularly with such violent exercise."

He chuckled and I followed his gaze down to the bed. I now saw that what he had been maltreating so violently was nothing more than a bolster from his bed, round which his old smoking jacket had been wrapped. He detached the jacket from the pillow and threw the cane down with a grunt.

"It was a foregone conclusion," he said, examining the marks on the material carefully. "Undoubtedly the jacket had been replaced after the man was beaten to death. This final verification will put the last nail in the coffin of Mr Ebeneezer Grunwin, I fancy."

"I wish I knew what you were talking about, Pons," I said, unable to keep the irritation from rising in my voice. Solar Pons looked at me quickly, resuming his maltreated jacket, his lean, feral features alive with suppressed energy.

"Pray do not disturb yourself about it, Parker. Merely a little problem in which our old friend Inspector Jamison has sought my advice. The East End is well rid of another scoundrel."

He led me back into the sitting room, rubbing his thin hands together before crossing to his favourite chair by the fire.

"I see you have had a busy afternoon, Parker."

"Indeed, Pons."

"A long walk too."

"That is correct."

"As far as Aldgate I notice."

I stared at Pons in astonishment.

"How could you possibly know that, Pons?"

"Because the road is up there, Parker, and the whole area in a devilish mess. They are using tar and a peculiar mixture of a distinctive reddish sand in their preparation of the road surface. When I see such an amalgam on your own toe-caps it is fairly safe to assume you had been Aldgate way for I know of no other public works currently taking place in the capital using this somewhat original mixture."

"You are right, as always, Pons," I said grudgingly, taking off my overcoat and sitting down opposite him. Before he could reply there was the sedate and welcome tread of Mrs Johnson on the stairs. She popped her bright, well-scrubbed face round the door-panel with a cheerful smile.

"I thought I heard you come in, Dr Parker, and felt you would not be averse to high-tea on such a cold day."

The Adventure of the Phantom Face

"You are certainly correct, Mrs Johnson," I observed, pulling up to the table.

"We have both taken a good deal of exercise this afternoon."

Solar Pons chuckled throatily.

"You are developing a pretty wit, Parker. But you are not so far wide of the truth. I have been down river and deucedly cold it was. I only came in myself an hour ago."

He looked sharply at our landlady as she bustled about the table.

"Is there any sign of the visitor I expected, Mrs Johnson?"

A shadow passed across our landlady's face.

"I am sorry, Mr Pons. I quite forgot to tell you. He called in the early afternoon and was disappointed to find you from home. I suggested he might come again at seven o'clock and he said that would be quite convenient."

"Excellent, Mrs Johnson. I shall be in all evening and would be grateful if you would show him up as soon as he arrives."

"If you wish I can withdraw after tea, Pons," I offered.

My companion shook his head.

"It will not be necessary, Parker. Mr Michael Balfour has an interesting problem, it appears, and I should be glad of your advice and support."

"You are surely joking, Pons," I said, my mouth half full of hot, buttered toast, as Mrs Johnson left the room.

Solar Pons shook his head, pouring tea from the old stoneware pot.

"You under-estimate your gifts, my dear fellow. I derive a good deal of benefit from your homely summings-up of the little problems that come my way from time to time."

"I know my limitations, Pons," I added, reaching out for my cup. "Who is this Mr Balfour?"

"He wrote me yesterday from Bredewell House which, assuming my gazetteer is accurate, is in a somewhat remote spot in Essex. He is bothered by a phantom face, it appears."

He chuckled drily at my expression.

"Those were the exact words he used in his letter, Parker."

"Good heavens, Pons," I spluttered. "I did not know you had taken up investigating psychic phenomena."

"And neither have I, Parker," Solar Pons said crisply. "I fancy there is something a little more down to earth behind it."

"What makes you say that, Pons?"

"Because phantom faces do not kill, Parker, and this thing has killed, apparently."

"You do not mean to say so, Pons!"

"I was never more serious, Parker."

My companion put down his cup and looked at me closely, his deep-set eyes glinting with strange lights.

"An apparition so horrific, Parker, that a country gentleman collapsed and died upon seeing it. At least, if we are to believe the stories in the current newspapers."

"I have not seen them, Pons."

"That is because your mind is not attuned to the bizarre as is mine, my dear fellow. Kindly pass me that Times from the table yonder."

I reached out my hand to a pile of newspapers on the far corner of the table not occupied by the cloth.

"There, at the head of page five. You might perhaps refresh my memory in the matter."

Solar Pons sat with his thin fingers tented before him as I read out the brief and strange account he had just drawn to my notice.

It was headed: STORY OF PHANTOM IN ESSEX VILLAGE and the sub-heading, in the conservative type favoured by *The Times,* ran: Death of Mr Charles Boldigrew Follows Ghostly Appearance.

The article ran: The Essex village of Tidewater has been terrorised by what local police describe as "a phantom face", a series of appearances of this apparition culminating in the death of a respected local landowner Mr Charles Boldigrew of nearby Bredewell House.

Mr Boldigrew was discovered by his nephew, Mr Michael Balfour, lying near the library window on the ground floor of the mansion on Tuesday evening. Mr Boldigrew was semi-conscious and appeared to be terrified. He told his nephew that he had seen "the face" and died a few minutes later.

According to locals, the weird and sinister apparition has appeared over the past two months in the village and has been seen by at least three people. Inspector Horace Cunliffe of the Essex Police told our correspondent today that robbery did not appear to be the motive, though he discounted the "phantom" theory as the gossip of credulous villagers.

I turned the page, somewhat disappointed, but there was nothing else.

The Adventure of the Phantom Face

"It is a somewhat bald statement, Pons," I said, turning to my companion and resuming by interrupted tea.

"Is it not, Parker. Yet it suggests some possibilities."

"In what way, Pons?"

Solar Pons reached out for the appetising cuts of ham Mrs Johnson had left for us, and deftly transferred two slices to his plate.

"Inspector Cunliffe is either an astute officer who does not wish to display his hand untimely or remarkably obtuse."

"I do not follow you, Pons."

"Tut, Parker, it is elementary. *The Times* does not go in for innuendo and distortion. When their local correspondent avers that this apparition has been seen, not only by one person but by three, then we may take it that he has found his three witnesses in Tidewater."

"I see, Pons."

"Furthermore, my dear fellow, Boldigrew himself, according to his nephew, had seen this horrifying face just before he died. Indeed, the nephew says in his letter that he is convinced that his uncle had see something horrible and had died of the resulting shock."

"Perhaps the Inspector does not wish for too much publicity, Pons."

"Perhaps, Parker," said my companion, biting into the ham with evident relish. "This is really excellent; pray try some."

"I have not yet finished the crumpets, Pons."

Solar Pons smiled thinly, his mind still evidently on the terrorised village.

"I must confess this case has a number of aspects which appeal to me strongly. Not merely this strange death but the bizarre atmosphere surrounding it. And if Cunliffe hopes to avoid publicity he is hopelessly off the mark for the cheaper tabloids have made a good deal of it."

"They did not say of what Mr Boldigrew died, Pons," I grumbled.

Solar Pons' eyes were gleaming.

"Ah, you are constantly improving, my dear fellow. I was wondering when you would come to that. *The Times* would have got the police surgeon's findings had they been available. There is nothing in any of the other papers either."

I frowned across at my companion.

"That presents two possibilities, Pons. Either the police surgeon has not been able to come to any decision, which would be extremely odd. Or he has come to a conclusion but the Inspector is withholding his findings from the press."

My companion had strange lights dancing in his eyes now.

"Ah, there you have hit upon it. Either supposition leads to only one conclusion."

He leaned forward to look me full in the face.

"You surely do not suspect . . ."

"Murder, my dear fellow," Solar Pons interrupted calmly.

And he picked up his tea-cup with great satisfaction on his features.

2

"Mr Michael Balfour, Mr Pons!"

Mrs Johnson smilingly ushered in our visitor and withdrew. Balfour was a frank-looking, open-faced young fellow of about twenty-eight, smartly but sensibly dressed in a checked overcoat which he took off at my companion's invitation to reveal a belted Norfolk jacket, worn over thick tweed trousers. His fresh features were reddened and roughened with the wind and his thick black curly hair much blown about and tousled, for he was hatless.

He sat down appreciatively at our invitation and held out strong, well-kept hands toward the fire. It was just turned seven and Balfour's face brightened when Pons suggested some refreshment.

"Some coffee would not come amiss, Mr Pons, if it is not too much trouble. It is an exceedingly cold night and I must say I have neglected my meals today with the worry over this business."

Our visitor declined any food and when I had again ascended to our quarters after making our wants known to our amiable landlady, Pons had removed a bottle of fine old cognac from the sideboard and had placed three crystal liqueur glasses on the crystal tray he had already put in position.

"I find coffee and cognac give an agreeable lining to the stomach on such cold evenings, do they not, Parker?"

"Certainly, Pons," I agreed, seating myself in my armchair across from our visitor, who occupied a chair by the table.

"Mr Balfour has already asked me to return to Tidewater this evening and I have agreed. He has a car at the door. I do not know how you are placed, Parker, but I would be glad of your presence."

"I had better telephone my locum, then," I said, glancing over at the clock. "Fortunately, there is nothing urgent in the practice and I daresay he will be able to manage for a day or two."

"Excellent!"

Solar Pons rubbed his thin hands together and smiled at our visitor.

"I told you we could rely on Dr Parker, Mr Balfour. I am sure we shall soon see light in these dark matters which have been burdening you."

"It is most good of you both," stammered young Balfour, "especially as I have not yet gone into the details of the business which brings me here. It is certainly dark enough and horrible enough."

"My curiosity had been aroused by the newspaper stories," said Solar Pons swiftly. "I had already made up my mind on receipt of your letter."

"Then I am fortunate indeed," said Michael Balfour, turning candid blue eyes on us both.

At that moment we were interrupted by the entrance of Mrs Johnson with a tray containing earthenware cups and a steaming coffee pot, and the conversation was not resumed until after she had withdrawn.

Michael Balfour sat cupping his glass of cognac, his blue eyes dark and troubled, as he stared into the heart of the comfortable fire that was burning on our hearth.

"I take it you are familiar with most of the salient points from the newspaper accounts, Mr Pons?"

"Pray forget them, Mr Balfour. I prefer to hear your own story, direct from your lips."

Young Balfour smiled briefly. He sipped appreciatively at his glass and then turned again to the large cup of coffee before him.

"I have been much abroad, Mr Pons."

"So I observe, Mr Balfour," said Solar Pons, giving our visitor a sharp look from his deep-set eyes. "You have been back less than a year, I should say."

Balfour's astonishment was evident on his face.

"How can you possibly know that, Mr Pons?"

"Simple observation. Since you have been here I have had occasion to observe you closely. You have twice run your finger along your stiff collar, as though it were chafing you, and as if it were unfamiliar to you. When I further see the traces of a tan on your cheeks and neck, followed by a line of white skin some distance below your collar—for you pulled it well down the last time—I deduce that you have been in the tropics. Only the equatorial sun gives that deep a tan and in my experience a pigmentation of some years, such as that given by a sojourn in Africa, takes from six months to a year to fade completely away on return to this country, depending on the type of skin."

Our visitor's eyes were wide and round with surprise.

"You are correct in every respect, Mr Pons. I have been back from the Gold Coast some eight months. But you make the matter sound so simple."

"That is the tragedy of my life," said Solar Pons, pulling down the corners of his mouth in mock severity as he stared at me. "Friend Parker here has denigrated my theories on more than one occasion in his accounts of my little adventures."

"Come, Pons," I protested. "You are being too hard altogether."

I gave him a penetrating glance.

"And it would take a much more profound mind than mine to demolish your theories, Pons. Take no notice of him, Mr Balfour."

Solar Pons chuckled drily and lit his pipe, sending slow spirals of fragrant blue smoke up toward the ceiling of our comfortable quarters.

"Let us just hear your story, Mr Balfour, and I will draw my own conclusions."

"Well, Mr Pons, as you have already gathered, I have spent some years in the Colonial Service, firstly in Gibraltar and latterly on the Gold Coast. I was called home last summer by my uncle, who appeared to be in failing health. As his only surviving relative I am his heir and I naturally obeyed Uncle Charles' wishes."

"Entirely laudable, Mr Balfour. What age was Mr Boldigrew?"

"A man in the prime of life, Mr Pons. That was the strange thing about it. Uncle Charles could only have been fifty or fifty-five at the most."

Solar Pons shot our visitor a sharp look.

"Come, Mr Balfour, you must have known his age. The newspapers aggregate it at fifty-four and this was confirmed in the police statement."

Michael Balfour turned worried eyes to my companion.

"Forgive me, Mr Pons. Of course you are right. This business has been so upsetting that I hardly know what I am saying at times. He was fifty-four."

Pons tapped the bowl of his pipe against the fender, his lean, feral features concentrated on the young man before us.

"Hmm. You have resigned from the Colonial Service?"

Balfour nodded.

"I got extended leave at first but the situation I found when I arrived at Tidewater soon made me realise that my permanent presence was desired in England. I resigned formally three months ago."

"I see. Before you continue, Mr Balfour, what sort of place is Tidewater and its surroundings?"

Balfour shook his head.

"The village itself is well enough, Mr Pons, but Bredewell House is in a bleak and lonely spot, in sight of the sea and salt-marshes. There is nothing there but pasture and sea-birds and in the winter it is desolate indeed. It was almost as though my uncle wished to bury himself in as remote a place as possible, far from the haunts of men."

Solar Pons paused in bending forward to re-light his pipe, his intent gaze fixed on the young man.

"Why do you say that, Mr Balfour?"

Our visitor shrugged.

"Through various indications, Mr Pons. It dated from the day of my arrival. I had expected to be met but I had to engage a hire-car from the station and had a job to make myself heard at the front door of the house. When the housekeeper eventually opened to me it was not until she had released several bolts and locks. I had never seen such security in an ordinary house."

"That is extremely odd, Parker," said Pons, looking across at me as he blew fresh smoke toward the ceiling.

"Just what I was going to say, Pons. What then, Mr Balfour?"

"Well, doctor, it did not take me long to realise that my uncle was extremely nervous and jumpy. As I have said, he had these extraordinary precautions about securing the house. At night it was quite a ritual, with him supervising Mrs Bracegirdle as she went the rounds of doors and windows. And he asked me, every time I went out, to keep a watch for strangers in the village."

"I see."

Solar Pons lowered his gaze to the fender and gazed at the flames of the hearth as though they held the secret of Bredewell House and its occupant's death.

"There is much property connected with the house?"

Balfour nodded.

"Curious you should ask that, Mr Pons. There is quite an estate. As you can imagine, my uncle's reclusive mode of life had made it difficult to run and things had been slipping badly for some years. I established a small estate office in one of the outbuildings and as I was accessible to all and sundry there, soon began to get things on a sounder footing. My Colonial experiences came in useful, you see."

"Naturally," said Solar Pons blandly. "Just how long had this state of affairs been going on?"

"My uncle had been a fairly jovial sort of man in earlier years, so far as I could gather, Mr Pons. But his change of habit dated from a year or so ago."

"Perhaps the housekeeper could help there, Pons?" I suggested.

Balfour shook his head, a thin smile on his lips.

"You will not have much success in that quarter, Mr Pons. Mrs Bracegirdle is as tight-lipped and reclusive as my late uncle on such matters. I could get nothing out of her but I gathered, from the hints my uncle dropped from time to time, that she was an old family retainer, sworn to secrecy in his service."

Solar Pons pulled reflectively at the lobe of his left ear and leaned forward in his chair.

"We come now to the incidents leading up to your uncle's mysterious death, Mr Balfour. Pray be precise and specific as to detail."

"Certainly, Mr Pons. Though in so strange and horrible a business I hardly know which detail might be significant."

"Just give me all the facts you can recall," said Solar Pons gently.

Our visitor drew up his shoulders in an expressive gesture.

"As you have no doubt made out from the newspapers, Mr Pons, there has been something like a reign of terror in the village of Tidewater, which is the place nearest to Bredewell House. So far as I can make out this terrifying apparition has appeared a number of times to the local villagers. Even our gardener, Stevens, saw it one evening only a week before my uncle died."

"What was it like, Mr Balfour?"

"Extremely hideous, Mr Pons, according to Stevens' description. It was all glowing and luminous, like green fire. The eyes were red and the head was something like a nightmare. At least that was my gardener's description and he is not a man given overly to fancies."

Solar Pons made a dry, clearing sound at the back of his throat which could have indicated derision or sympathy. I shot him a quick glance but could read nothing useful in the concentrated pin-points of his eyes.

"How did it appear?"

"In Stevens' case at the window of his potting-shed, where he sat smoking in the dark. He gave a great cry and ran out; with commendable courage, I thought. But it was pitch-black and there was nothing and no-one to be seen."

"Interesting, Parker."

"Frightening, Pons."

Solar Pons nodded, little lights glinting at the back of his eyes.

"What about the other villagers, Mr Balfour?"

"The circumstances were similar, Mr Pons. The face was seen always at dusk. An old widow woman; two men drinking in the four-ale bar of a local hostelry; an elderly villager in a cottage near a bridge at the far end of the village. Investigations were made in all cases but no-one was seen or apprehended."

Solar Pons smiled slowly and put up his hand to the lobe of his ear, pulling at it thoughtfully.

"And this had been going on for some weeks before your uncle died?"

"Six weeks to two months, Mr Pons."

My companion turned to me.

"This is highly significant, Parker."

"I cannot see it, Pons."

"That is because you are not applying your mind correctly, my dear fellow."

Solar Pons stared again into the fire, as though he could see visions among the leaping flames that were denied to us. I was astonished at his next question.

"How old were the men, Mr Balfour?"

Our visitor looked disconcerted also.

"I do not follow you, Mr Pons."

"Those in the four-ale bar?"

"I cannot remember, exactly. In their sixties, I think."

Solar Pons smiled faintly again.

"These factors are vitally important, Parker. Mark them well. The face appeared only at dusk?"

Balfour nodded.

"And always through windows?"

"That is correct, Mr Pons."

"And every single person who saw the apparition was elderly?"

Again the surprise in Balfour's eyes.

"Well, yes, now that you come to mention it."

Solar Pons rubbed his thin fingers together with satisfaction. Balfour opened his mouth to speak again.

"That is, until I myself saw the phantom two nights ago!"

If I had been surprised before, I was astonished at Pons' reaction.

He leapt to his feet, his penetrating eyes fixed upon young Balfour's face.

"That puts an entirely different complexion upon the matter, Mr Balfour. We have not a moment to lose! If you would be kind enough to telephone your locum, Parker, and pack a valise we will set out for Tidewater at once. I will hear the remainder of Mr Balfour's story *en route*."

3

I adjusted my muffler more tightly round my throat and sank bank into the cushions of Balfour's big touring car as we threaded our way cautiously through the streets of the East End. It was even more bitterly cold than before and frost glittered on the back windows of the vehicle, brushed briefly into diamonds by the headlights of following cars. I occupied the back seat with our two valises piled beside me.

Pons sat in the front passenger seat with our client and continued the brisk questioning which had begun in our sitting room at 7B.

"The circumstances of your uncle's death, Mr Balfour."

"I had been out earlier in the day, Mr Pons. Uncle Charles had been restless and agitated for several days. The stories circulating in the neighbourhood about the phantom face had had a startling effect upon him."

"In what way, pray?"

"He went ashen grey when I first mentioned the matter some weeks before. And then when one of the local newspapers got hold of the story he was so agitated and upset that he burned the newspaper."

"Indeed."

Solar Pons gave me a grim smile as he leaned back toward me, ejecting a thin stream of blue smoke from his pipe.

"Are you comfortable there, Parker?"

"Well enough, Pons," I said. "I am listening carefully."

"Pray do so, my dear fellow. I shall find your thoughts on the matter invaluable later."

He turned back to Balfour, who was handling the car with considerable skill, for we were already clearing the outskirts of the city and beginning the long run through the shabby suburbs in that quarter of London.

"Why should your uncle have troubled himself over this matter, bizarre and unusual though it might be for a small Essex village?"

"I do not know, Mr Pons. It was all part and parcel of his reclusive life-style. He was, as I have already told you, in fear of something and this apparition seemed to crystallise all his terrors."

"What do you think this thing is, Mr Balfour?" I put in.

Our driver shot me a quick glance over his shoulder, as though in surprise.

"I have given it some thought, Dr Parker, as you can imagine. Tidewater is a small place and even a remote dwelling like Bredewell House is not immune from gossip. I can assure you I am as puzzled as the most unsophisticated rustic."

"And just a little frightened, Mr Balfour," said Solar Pons evenly, replacing the stem of his pipe between his strong teeth.

"As you say," said our client frankly. "My uncle has died under mysterious circumstances and now I have seen the same thing myself."

"Oh, I was not criticising in the least," said Solar Pons swiftly, laying his hand on the other's arm in a friendly gesture. "I might well have been shaken myself, under the circumstances."

"That seems difficult to imagine, Mr Pons."

"I am only human, Mr Balfour," muttered Pons deprecatingly. "Were there any other things about Mr Boldigrew's behaviour that commended themselves to your attention?"

Balfour shook his head.

"Nothing stands out in particular, Mr Pons. Except that he was more emphatic than ever when commending Mrs Bracegirdle on the importance of locking and barring the doors of the house at night."

"Which brings us to the evening of his death, I take it?"

"Exactly, Mr Pons."

Balfour spun the wheel smoothly as we turned round a block of gaunt warehouses, the flaring lights of the commercial quarter dying in the dusk. A single thread of road lay before us now and trees and foliage were beginning to obtrude into the landscape, as the ugliness of the suburbs gave way to substantial villas and rows of private houses.

"We are talking now of a fortnight ago?"

"Yes, Mr Pons. Last Tuesday week. The inquest was on the Friday."

"Indeed. I have read the report but I would like your own views in due course."

"Certainly, Mr Pons. To come to the Tuesday in question my uncle had been particularly worried that day. I caught him whispering with the housekeeper on two separate occasions and he had a distinctly furtive, not to say hunted look upon his face."

Solar Pons tented his thin fingers before him in the dimness of the car, his keen eyes staring at the wisps of mist which were gathering before the windscreen and causing our client to slacken the speed of the vehicle a little. The road had become lonely now and the outlines of gaunt, wintry trees, occasional cattle in the bleak fields and now and then a passing vehicle were the only things that broke the monotonous waste of whiteness which was insidiously gathering in the darkness outside.

"Did you speak to him about this?"

Our driver nodded.

"In a tactful manner, Mr Pons. I said he looked worried but he assured me it was the same business. This phantom face had upset him and he hoped it would not be long before the thing, or person perpetrating such a nasty joke, was caught."

"Ah. He, at least did not appear to think it was supernatural?"

"Possibly, Mr Pons. I had not given it much thought but now that you mention it, it might be so."

"Is that important, Pons?" I put in.

My friend turned his lean, feral profile toward me.

"It could be, Parker. At this stage I am merely trying to establish an accurate chain of events."

"I spent a good deal of the evening in the drawing-room reading, Mr Pons. I had been up early and round the estate in the morning. I passed the remainder of the forenoon seeing people in my office at the farm and as the weather was dreadfully cold and inclement, I felt I had had enough for one day."

Pons nodded, sending out a thick plume of blue smoke from his pipe.

"We had high tea together at about five o'clock in the evening. Mrs Bracegirdle served it. That was the last occasion I really had time for an exchange of views with my uncle. The next occasion on which I saw him, he was dying."

Solar Pons nodded again, his eyes hooded and thoughtful.

"It would have been long dark by five o'clock. Had the usual bolting and barring of the house taken place?"

"Oh, yes indeed, Mr Pons. Soon after four o'clock. My uncle and Mrs Bracegirdle went the rounds."

"Did you not find it tiresome, Mr Balfour?" I asked. "I mean, supposing you wished to go in and out of an evening or to the village?"

"Of course, Dr Parker. That is why I have had very little social life since arriving back in this country. I had to make my arrangements to visit people and return in daylight, otherwise it meant a great deal of trouble to my uncle. He hated having to unbolt and unbar the doors to anyone at night, even to his own nephew."

Our client smiled wanly, peering forward through the windscreen as the mist insidiously gathered over the unprepossessing countryside through which we were now travelling. Flat, inhospitable and interspersed with only occasional clumps of trees, it seemed obvious that we were now approaching the area of the Essex marshes in which our client lived. He turned back to Pons for a moment, as he halted cautiously at a deserted cross-roads.

"Of course, it was different in the summer, Mr Pons, with the lighter evenings. I had spoken of living elsewhere or merely moving into one of the outbuildings, which I could have had converted to a dwelling-house, but he would not hear of it."

"He rather looked on you as a sort of bodyguard whenever dusk fell?"

"I had not thought of it so, Mr Pons, but you are no doubt right."

Balfour engaged the first gear again and the car crept forward cautiously through the gloom.

"You said you had high tea, together. What matters did you discuss on that occasion?"

"Nothing of importance, Mr Pons. My uncle was still uneasy but he seemed a little more settled than of late. He had had one or two bills through the post which seemed to cause him some concern."

I saw Pons stiffen on the front seat of the car and throw a swift glance at our driver.

"Bills, Mr Balfour? It hardly seems likely that anything so mundane would bother such a well-propertied man as your uncle."

Balfour's puzzled face was reflected in the windscreen against the white wall of vapour as he changed gear again and we crept forward, more slowly than ever.

"Now that you mention it, Mr Pons, it does seem peculiar. Uncle Charles had several times seemed worried in past months at things that arrived in the post. Once he changed colour at breakfast and dropped the piece of paper the envelope contained, and it seemed as though he would fall. When I questioned him about the matter he said he had received a bill for which there was no justification. Later I saw a heap of ashes on the hearth and gathered, though I did not ask him, that he had burned the offending document."

"Hmm."

Solar Pons pulled thoughtfully at the lobe of his right ear as his keen eyes seemed to pierce the veil of vapour ahead. If anything it seemed colder than when we had started and I pulled the thick car rug even more tightly about me, folding it across my legs.

"That could be highly significant, Parker."

"Of course, Pons," I returned.

"What then?" my companion rejoined.

"As I said, we had tea and then my uncle wanted to write some letters. He went to his study on the ground floor and I myself took a book to the drawing room where I passed a pleasant hour or two by a great fire of logs. I was about to go to my room just before eight o'clock when, as I was passing near the study, I heard a heavy sound as though of someone falling."

"You had heard nothing before that?"

"No, Mr Pons. Just the one sound, as though a heavy sack of earth had hit the floor. I got no reply to my knock and went straight in, as I sensed something was wrong. I found my uncle near the window. The curtains had been drawn back. He was semi-conscious and as I tried to help him up he mumbled something about, 'That dreadful face'."

Solar Pons was silent for a few moments, the car seemingly suspended in white vapour as it continued its monotonous progress through the wastes of Essex.

"You presumed he meant he had seen something at the uncurtained window?"

"Indeed, Mr Pons. I summoned Mrs Bracegirdle and then ran outside but could see nothing. It was a bitterly cold night and there was a thin mist. When I got back inside the housekeeper had already telephoned for medical assistance. Dr Sherlock was round within a very few minutes but there was little he could do and Uncle Charles died about ten minutes after he arrived."

"It was heart, I believe?"

"That is so, Mr Pons."

"Who is this Dr Sherlock?"

"The family physician, Mr Pons, and Uncle Charles' oldest friend. He had moved to Tidewater some years ago in order to be near to him."

"I see. What was the doctor's reaction to all this phantom face business?"

"He inclines to the theory that the local people are superstitious and fanciful, Mr Pons, but he was considerably startled when I told him what my uncle had said just before dying."

"Mr Boldigrew said nothing else?"

"Not so far as I know, Mr Pons."

"Is there any reason why your uncle should have gone to the window?"

"Perhaps someone tapped to attract his attention, Mr Pons."

"Perhaps. Though why would your uncle have gone if he was so mortally afraid?"

"Habit, possibly."

"I do not follow."

"I am sorry, Mr Pons. My uncle had a rather strange inclination. We often sat in his study, which overlooked the front drive. In summer people who called got in the habit of tapping on his window, instead of walking all the way round to the front door. My uncle would come to the window and converse before admitting them. Even people working for him on the estate got into the habit."

"I see. It is curious. But then life has many curiosities, eh, Parker?"

"We have certainly had our share of them, Pons."

Solar Pons chuckled grimly, hunching his chin into the collar of his thick raglan overcoat.

"The window was locked, of course, on this evening?"

"Undoubtedly, Mr Pons. It is of thick glass, secured by a heavy clasp at the top. It slides upward easily, as it was used so frequently that Uncle Charles had the runners greased."

"I see. And it was the only window in the study?"

"By no means, sir. But it was in a sort of small turret which jutted out and was the most convenient window on to which the visitor would come. The view is partly concealed by shrubbery but a portion of the drive can be seen from there."

"Very well, Mr Balfour. You have given me much food for thought. What do you think killed your uncle?"

Balfour shook his head.

"I do not know, Mr Pons. But I fear that it was something so horrible that his heart could simply not stand it."

"You may be right, Mr Balfour," said Solar Pons sombrely.

"You said you had yourself seen this horrible face."

Our client shivered slightly at the wheel.

"Yes, sir. Just two nights ago. Which is what prompted me to come to you."

"You have done wisely," said Solar Pons. "We are moving in dark and muddied waters. Just relate the circumstances."

"I was sitting in the study just after supper, Mr Pons, going through my uncle's papers. It was about nine-thirty P.M. Since my uncle's death I no longer followed his routine. I had given up bolting and barring doors and left the windows uncurtained at night if the mood so took me. On this particular evening I had closed the study curtains but had left the main window in the little turret with the coverings pulled back. Something attracted my attention as I was sitting at the desk writing. I was half-facing the window so at first I did not notice anything."

"It was a foggy night, Mr Balfour?"

"There was a thin mist, yes. I glanced up and was considerably startled to see something that looked like a yellow blob in the middle of the pane. I got up from the desk and walked to the window. I felt no fear, only curiosity."

Balfour changed gear and turned into a side-road, his features expressionless in the reflected light from the instrument-panel.

"Imagine my horror, Mr Pons, when I saw this soulless, inhuman face, seemingly made of wrinkled yellow skin with two black sockets where the eyes should have been!"

"How dreadful!" I exclaimed.

"You may say so, Dr Parker. I am afraid that I let out a cry and dropped my pen. The thing made off like lightning at that. It just withdrew from the window at a tremendous speed and disappeared in the fog. I ran out, roused Mrs Bracegirdle, got a powerful flash-light and searched the grounds."

Solar Pons shook his head.

"Brave but singularly unwise, Mr Balfour."

"Maybe, Mr Pons, but that is what happened. It is my nature to be impulsive."

"Quite so. You found nothing?"

"Not a trace of anything, Mr Pons. And the path beneath the window is hard and would not retain the impression of a footprint. What do you think? I must confess that I have bolted and curtained the windows since that night."

"You are extremely prudent, Mr Balfour," said Solar Pons slowly. "This is a dark and sinister business."

And he puffed silently at his pipe until we had arrived at our destination.

4

This proved to be a large, Edwardian mansion set back in its own grounds. The fog was so thick by this time that we could see little of our surroundings and conditions were so bad that our host almost ran the car past the carriage drive entrance. The tyres crunched frostily over the hardened ground as we eased up through shadowy clumps of rhododendron.

"A melancholy place, Pons," I observed.

"As always, you are correct, Parker. And a suitable setting for such a tragedy as Mr Balfour has unfolded."

We had drawn up in front of the entrance steps and the house was, as I had already observed, even more melancholy and sombre than I had imagined with the thick mist swirling about it. Before our host could descend from the driving seat, Pons had sprung down and with typical energy was already striding toward the façade of the building. I followed and saw, in a gap in the shrubbery, the small jutting turret of which our client had spoken.

There was a tarmacadam path in front of it and Pons already had his pocket lens out and was going up and down the surface, almost on his hands and knees. He rose to his feet, a disappointed look on his face, as Balfour joined us.

"Too hard, as I had expected. There is nothing there. This is your uncle's study window, Mr Balfour?"

"Yes, Mr Pons. As you can see, it is most conveniently situated if visitors wished to attract my uncle's attention."

"Indeed," said Solar Pons drily, casting his keen eyes over the broad expanse of glass, through which could be dimly glimpsed the interior of the room.

"And it is equally conveniently situated for the purposes of someone who intended your uncle harm."

We followed Pons back along the path which ran behind the screen of shrubbery separating it from the main drive, until it debouched near the front entrance steps and the vehicle in which we had just arrived. I assisted Balfour in removing our luggage and then our host led the way up the steps to where the light of an electric lantern over the porch pricked the darkness.

"I will show you the estate tomorrow, Mr Pons," said the young man, ushering us into a spacious hall on one side of which a warming fire blazed in a stone fireplace.

"It has only just turned ten o'clock and I am sure Mrs Bracegirdle will have something prepared for us."

"A light meal only for my part," said Solar Pons. "Though I must admit the journey and the coldness of the evening has put an unsuspected edge on my appetite."

A door opening farther down the hall interrupted the conversation and a tall, distinguished-looking woman with greying hair advanced beneath the light of the electric chandelier which illuminated the hall.

"This is Mrs Bracegirdle," said our host. "Mr Solar Pons and Dr Lyndon Parker, who will be staying with us for a few days."

The housekeeper, who was dressed in a dark tweed suit with a touch of white at the throat bowed courteously.

"Welcome, gentlemen," she said in a low, well-modulated voice.

She was about to pass out of the hall when Pons stopped her with a courteous movement.

"Before you go, Mrs Bracegirdle, there are one or two questions I should like to ask you. I believe you were devoted to the late Mr Charles Boldigrew?"

The woman looked at Pons with eyes which held an enigmatic expression.

"That is perfectly correct, Mr Pons."

"Have you no theory about his death?"

Mrs Bracegirdle drew herself up.

"I do not follow you, Mr Pons."

Solar Pons took off his hat, overcoat and scarf and laid them on top of a massive iron-bound chest that stood at one side of the hall.

"I think you follow me well enough, Mrs Bracegirdle."

The housekeeper did not seem to take offence at my companion's words but she visibly drew herself up as though to brace herself against an impending blow.

"I must repeat, sir, I do not understand your meaning."

She glanced at her employer as though imploring his assistance but receiving no help from that quarter, sighed deeply. Solar Pons walked over toward the massive fireplace and held out his hands to the blaze.

"Oh, come now, Mrs Bracegirdle, it is not so very difficult. Mr Boldigrew had received a number of threats against him . . ."

"Mr Pons!"

Balfour was plainly shocked and staggered and I saw the housekeeper's figure crumple, but she recovered herself admirably, though her face was white.

"How could you possibly know that, Mr Pons?" said the young man.

"It was elementary, Mr Balfour. Gentlemen of Mr Boldigrew's wealth and standing do not change colour and almost collapse on receiving tradesmen's bills. There was only one possible explanation when you told me of these occasions. Boldigrew had received some sort of threat through the post. What was it, Mrs Bracegirdle? Blackmail?"

The housekeeper moistened her lips and glanced imploringly at Balfour.

"Begging your pardon, Mr Balfour. I didn't like deceiving you, but it looks as though this gentleman can read one's very thoughts."

"You are not so very far wide of the mark, Mrs Bracegirdle," said I, with a triumphant glance at Pons.

We were all over by the fireplace now and Balfour gestured us into large leather chairs, set in a half-circle round the blaze. I sat and massaged the warmth back into my half-frozen fingers. The housekeeper, after nervously twisting and untwisting her hands for a few moments, broke the silence which had fallen upon us.

"It is true, Mr Pons. There was something. I had been Mr Boldigrew's housekeeper for over thirty years. There were not many things about the family I did not know."

Solar Pons' face expressed keen interest in the firelight as he glanced at the housekeeper.

"For example?"

"Well, Mr Pons . . ."

The housekeeper's voice was hurried and breathless and again I caught our host's eyes on her with a worried expression.

"There was an Anglo-Indian Company Mr Boldigrew was interested in many years ago. He was a partner and gave his Indian co-director bad advice. The company crashed and ever afterwards Mr Boldigrew blamed himself. His partner committed suicide and the thing had been on his conscience for years."

"Why did you not tell me this before?" asked young Balfour hotly.

The housekeeper looked at him with an expression of mingled pity and resentment.

"Because Mr Boldigrew swore me to secrecy, Mr Balfour. It was a sacred trust. I am only betraying it now because Mr Boldigrew is dead and this gentleman would be sure to find it out, sooner or later."

"You are certainly right there, Mrs Bracegirdle," said Solar Pons mildly, getting out his pipe and lighting it up at our host's express permission.

"Do you know what was in those notes, Mrs Bracegirdle?"

"Not exactly, sir. But Mr Boldigrew intimated to me that they contained threats. I gathered it was something to do with this Indian firm and the suicide of his former partner."

"But if the man had committed suicide where would the threats arise?" I said.

"Mrs Bracegirdle has her own ideas about that, Parker," said my companion with a thin smile.

"It is true, sir. My first thought was that the dead man's son had come to England and was intent on revenge."

Pons sat with his brows knitted, staring into the fire.

"It is a possibility, Mrs Bracegirdle," he said softly. "Did you notice the postmarks of the letters?"

"They all came from London, sir. Mr Boldigrew burnt them afterward."

"And what was your theory about them?"

Mrs Bracegirdle turned to Pons and gave him an almost fierce look from her faded grey eyes.

"Well, sir, and begging Mr Balfour's pardon, I suspected Ram Dass and his followers."

Balfour looked incredulous.

"Oh, come, Mrs Bracegirdle! It is ridiculous. They are a somewhat strange household, I know, but just because my uncle had a quarrel over boundaries with him, that is no reason . . ."

"I do not understand," said Solar Pons, looking from one to the other.

The housekeeper was the first to break the silence.

"They are Indians in the neighbourhood, sir. Mr Boldigrew's partner was named Dass. They are a strange people, and their ways are not our ways."

"Hmm."

Solar Pons' eyes were bright as he turned to Balfour.

"This is extremely interesting. And you say these people had a quarrel with your uncle?"

"That is so, Mr Pons, but it was nothing, really. An outburst of temper on both sides. Certainly not enough to occasion murder."

"However, we must not overlook the possibility," said Solar Pons, rising from his seat. "You have been most helpful, Mrs Bracegirdle. Your sense of duty to the late Mr Boldigrew does you credit. There is nothing else you wish to tell me?"

The tall woman shook her head and rose from her seat also.

"Nothing that comes to mind, Mr Pons. And now, gentlemen, if you'll excuse me I'll see about getting the supper."

5

"I am sure Mrs Bracegirdle is wrong, Mr Pons. The Dass family are peculiar, it is true, but I am not convinced. So far as I know, my uncle never evinced the slightest uneasiness about their presence in the neighbourhood. And the quarrel was purely through my uncle's then bailiff. He had no personal contact with them at all."

We were sitting in the handsomely panelled dining room after supper and the air was blue with tobacco smoke. It was only a quarter past eleven now and it seemed strange to reflect that we had been in Praed Street only some three hours ago, so bizarre was the atmosphere of this lonely old house.

We had seen no other servants and had gathered from our host that Mrs Bracegirdle was the only other person who occupied the house. The rest of the staff came in from the village daily. Pons ejected a plume of blue smoke thoughtfully toward the ceiling.

"Nevertheless, with your permission, I think Parker and I will call upon this Mr Dass some time tomorrow. It is as well to be clear in one's mind about these matters."

"By all means, Mr Pons. Ram Dass and his entourage live in a large house called The Grange, which is about a mile from here, at the edge of the village. It has extensive grounds and Dass' land adjoins my uncle's, which is where the boundary dispute arose."

"I see. And now, if you are not too tired, Mr Balfour, I should very much like to see the study in which your unfortunate uncle met his end."

"By all means, Mr Pons."

Our host led the way back through the hall and into a corridor which was lined with stags' heads and other trophies of the chase. A series of polished teak doors led off it and on the right an oak staircase ascended into the gloom above. Balfour threw open a door on the left, almost opposite the staircase.

"This is the study, gentlemen."

Solar Pons looked sharply at our companion and then glanced swiftly at the stairs.

"You were about here, then, Mr Balfour, when you heard your uncle fall?"

Balfour paused, his hand on the study light-switch.

"That is correct, Mr Pons."

Pons nodded approvingly.

"Show me exactly where you found your uncle."

"I ran straight in, Mr Pons. Uncle Charles was lying here."

Balfour led the way swiftly across the handsome room to the turret window we had already observed from outside. With its serried ranks of leather-bound books; the bright fire burning in the marble fireplace; the polished desk; and all the other evidence of a neat and orderly life, the study should have been a quiet and placid refuge, redolent of peace.

And yet with the mist swirling at the dark window panes, the deathly cold outside and the knowledge of the tragedy that had been enacted here I felt a thrill of horror as the young man indicated the area of carpet on which his relative had fallen to his death. I glanced up at the mist at the window and could easily imagine the appalling shock the old man must have had as the phantom face appeared there.

Yet Pons seemed oblivious of all this atmospheric implication. His lean, feral face was alive with interest. He already had his lens out and was going minutely over the carpet in the small embrasure, to the evident puzzlement of our host. Pons finished his examination and straightened up.

"There is only the one large window which looks directly on to the shrubbery. We must assume that your uncle saw the face there, if indeed he saw anything."

"There were his dying words, Mr Pons."

"That is true."

Solar Pons was silent as he looked narrowly at the window and the tall green wall of shrubbery, sparkling with hoar-frost, dimly visible through the fog which was now descending rapidly.

"Why must Mr Boldigrew have seen the face through the central pane, Pons?"

"Because, my dear Parker, it would have been difficult at the two side windows, which are placed at angles. As you see, the reflected light would have cancelled out any image. Whereas the dark wall of shrubbery there would have enhanced such an apparition."

"You are right, Mr Pons," said young Balfour admiringly. "You think that of significance?"

"It may be so," said Solar Pons carelessly. "Let us just have a look at the window itself."

Once again he went over it minutely, while we both waited and watched in that silent place. For myself I was only too conscious of our exposed position in the little turret and I wondered if the thing which had apparently taken Boldigrew's life in such a shocking manner could still be lurking out there beyond the wall of fog which pressed in slow, oily undulations upon the window glass.

"This is the only catch to the bottom central window?"

"Yes, Mr Pons. It is supposedly burglar-proof. As I intimated, Uncle Charles did not have too complicated a system here, as he liked to open the window to speak to visitors."

"So I believe. You have shutters inside, I see."

"That was another of my uncle's eccentricities, Mr Pons. They are of teak, reinforced with steel, as you will observe. They were always closed and secured with the patent steel bars fitted, before the household retired."

"Would you open the window for me, please."

Balfour stepped forward and made two complex movements with his right hand on the shining steel catch at the top of the window.

"It is a two-stage lock on top, Mr Pons. These were fitted during the past year."

"Hmm. Presumably, after your uncle received the threats?"

"It could be so, Mr Pons."

Again the troubled look on the nephew's face.

"Let me just try this."

Pons leaned forward and slid the window up. It went easily and I noticed there were steel runners at the sides, which appeared to be liberally greased.

"They make no noise, either."

"That is correct, Mr Pons. Now just see what happens when you close the window."

Pons pulled at the lower sash. The cold air and thin streamers of fog which had been wreathing into the room was cut off immediately as the window slid smoothly home, with a barely audible hiss.

"Now try and open the window, Mr Pons."

The Adventure of the Phantom Face

Balfour smiled as Pons struggled to raise the casement. Even by manipulating the catch and exerting all his strength he was unable to make the window budge.

"It is simple once you know the knack, Mr Pons. It is nothing more than these two small buttons, operated first in clockwise and then anti-clockwise directions, which release the internal bolts."

Pons did as our host directed and after a moment or so the window slid open. Pons closed it again, dusted his hands and drew the deep red curtains.

"Excellent," he said drily. "It has just proved one of my tentative theories."

"That Mr Boldigrew could not have been touched by anyone outside the window, Pons?"

"Perhaps, Parker."

My companion was silent for a moment. Then he seemed to recollect himself, going soft-footed about the elegant room, now and again taking down a book. He sat at the desk for a while and measured the distance between it and the window. He turned to me.

"Pray be good enough to go to the window, Parker. Just stand behind the curtain for a moment and tap on the glass."

"Behind the curtain, Pons?"

Solar Pons smiled at my expression.

"If you please, my dear fellow."

I did as he suggested, feeling a slight crawling of the scalp as soon as I got behind the curtain and saw the blanket of oily fog curling against the glass. I drew the curtain to behind me and rapped three times sharply on the glass.

"Excellent, Parker. Your signal is clearly audible from the desk, even with the curtains closed."

I regained the room and crossed to my companions. Balfour had stood, a silent and worried figure, all the while, saying nothing, though his eyes anxiously searched my companion's face. Solar Pons sat on at the desk, his thin fingers tented on the red leather surface before him.

"The sequence seems quite clear. Mr Boldigrew was seated at the desk or was at least somewhere between the desk and the shelves by the window. If he had been any farther into the room he would have been unlikely to have heard the sort of taps friend Parker just made. He crossed to the window, drew the curtains back . . ."

"Saw this horrible face and collapsed," I said. "Mr Balfour heard the fall from the staircase outside and rushed in."

"Thank you for your expert reconstruction of events, Parker," said Solar Pons blandly, searching in his pocket for his pipe.

"You think the thing tapped to attract his attention, Pons?"

"It is entirely likely, Parker. We have heard that the gentleman was in mortal fear and it seems fairly obvious that he would keep the study window curtained after dark. If the shutters had been drawn over the windows, he would not have heard any tapping or, indeed, have been able to hear the sound. Mr Balfour, who did not have the window curtained did not hear any tapping when the face appeared to him."

"That is so, Mr Pons," put in young Balfour. "Though my uncle kept strong precautions so far as locking and bolting the door were concerned, he would not secure the shutters until late at night, just before retiring. He felt too enclosed, otherwise."

"I am surprised," I said. "He had turned the house into a fortress."

"Indeed, Parker," said Solar Pons quietly. "I believe you said, Mr Balfour, that the entire estate devolves upon you now that Mr Boldigrew is dead?"

Balfour pursed his lips.

"On me entirely, Mr Pons. As I have said, the sum involved is considerable. We have not yet gone into it because it is too soon after my uncle's death. Indeed, he was only buried last week."

"Just so," said Solar Pons softly.

Our client again appeared troubled in his expression.

"His lawyer, Mr Sainsbury, would no doubt be pleased to elucidate further, Mr Pons."

"All in good time, Mr Balfour," said Solar Pons quietly, drawing on the stem of his pipe.

We were sitting so when there was a deferential tapping at the study door which made our client jump. A moment later Mrs Bracegirdle had appeared in the opening.

"Dr Sherlock has called, Mr Balfour. He knew you were due back tonight and wanted to know if there was anything he could do to help."

"He has already done quite enough for the household," said her employer. "But we should be pleased to see him just the same."

"He is waiting in the drawing room, sir."

"Just tell him we shall be along directly."

The housekeeper withdrew and Pons turned to our companion inquiringly.

"Dr Sherlock, as my uncle's oldest friend has handled all the arrangements, Mr Pons. I do not know what I should have done without him. The inquest was quite an ordeal but thanks to the doctor things went smoothly and as painlessly as these things can be."

"I am glad the doctor has called," said Solar Pons, getting up from the desk. "I should be glad of the opportunity to ask him a few questions."

"You will find him more than helpful, Mr Pons."

Back in the drawing room we found our host's visitor warming his hands before the fire. He was an amiable, sandy-haired man in his early sixties with gold pince-nez perched on the end of his nose and a rather fussy manner. He came forward from the fire as soon as we were announced.

"I hope my visit is not inopportune, gentlemen?"

Balfour shook his head and introduced us.

"Mr Solar Pons! And Dr Lyndon Parker. This is indeed an honour. I have followed your adventures with the keenest interest, Mr Pons."

Solar Pons took the doctor's hand with an amused smile.

"You must blame your medical colleague for any little exaggerations in the narratives, doctor."

Dr Sherlock's faded blue eyes stared at me ingenuously.

"I am sure that a scientific man like Dr Parker would not be prone to such a failing, Mr Pons."

He turned back to Balfour.

"I trust that all is well with you, Mr Balfour. If there is anything at all I can do . . ."

"You are more than kind, doctor," our host added. "When I told Mr Pons of the trouble that has fallen upon Bredewell House he and Dr Parker insisted on returning to stay with me a few days."

"Most laudable," murmured Dr Sherlock, sitting by the fireside and waving away our host's invitation to sherry.

"I only stopped by to pay my respects as I had to make a call on a patient out this way. I am glad to have had the opportunity to meet you, Mr Pons."

Solar Pons seated himself in a great leather chair across from the doctor and blew out a plume of fragrant smoke from his pipe.

"I may say the same, doctor. I would like your opinion on the phantom face which seems to be haunting this corner of Essex."

The doctor smiled, looking into the glowing heart of the fire.

"The people hereabouts are a superstitious lot, Mr Pons. And there are certainly some strange ones among them. Mr Ram Dass, for example . . . I do not know what you will find here to exercise your talents. The Police Inspector has some fanciful theories but they run counter to informed scientific opinion."

"And what would they be, Dr Sherlock?"

"Mostly old wives' tales and perhaps children playing pranks, Mr Pons. Poor Charles had a long-standing heart ailment. I had warned him to take things more easily, but he spent long hours in the study working on various documents and accounts. He could have had a fatal seizure at any time during the past two or three years."

Solar Pons nodded, his own gaze now fixed on the molten centre of the fire.

"So he died of heart disease, then?"

The doctor nodded.

"Undoubtedly, Mr Pons. I have a copy of my post-mortem findings here, if Dr Parker would care to peruse it."

He rummaged in his medical bag which I now noticed at the side of his chair and came up with the official form, covered with his small, meticulous writing. I studied it with interest.

"An extremely advanced form of heart disease, Pons," I said, passing the document to him.

He scanned it swiftly, his lean, eager face tinted bronze by the fire-light. Young Balfour stood midway between the groups of hearthside chairs, looking now at one of us, now at another, a worried frown upon his brow.

"There seems no doubt of it," said Solar Pons, passing it back. "But that still does not explain his dying words."

Sherlock shook his head.

"Dying men often say strange things, Mr Pons. I am sure Dr Parker will bear me out."

"Undoubtedly," I said.

Solar Pons pulled thoughtfully at the lobe of his ear with fingers as delicate as the antennae of an insect.

"He said nothing while you were with him?"

Dr Sherlock shook his head.

"Poor Charles was on the point of death, Mr Pons. I doubt if I could have helped had I been there when he had the seizure."

"What exactly happened that evening?"

"I was summoned by Mr Balfour and arrived within half an hour of the attack. There were only Mrs Bracegirdle and Mr Balfour with him. I soon saw that it was hopeless and cleared the room in order to spare them further distress. In spite of an injection I gave Mr Boldigrew to stimulate the heart he died within a very few minutes without regaining consciousness. A tragic business. I was more affected than I can remember. We had been friends for thirty years, you see."

Solar Pons nodded.

"And the post-mortem confirmed your earlier findings?"

"Undoubtedly, Mr Pons. His condition had worsened considerably during the past year or so to an extent which even I had not realised."

"Just so. Tell me, doctor, what was the condition of the room and the window when you arrived?"

"I don't think I quite follow you, Mr Pons. Mr Boldigrew was lying near the window and I had him very carefully carried to a divan at the far end of the room. The three of us carried him there. What else was it you mentioned?"

"The condition of the room and the window."

"The study was in some little disorder. If I remember rightly a chair was overturned and there was a jumble of papers on the desk. I cannot be certain but I think the window was uncurtained."

"It was not unlocked so far as you know?"

Dr Sherlock stared at Pons in astonishment.

"Good gracious, Mr Pons, I had no time for that. My first concern was for my patient. I had no time for the window."

"Certainly," said my companion imperturbably, continuing to eject gentle plumes of smoke toward the ceiling.

"So you discount this story of a face entirely?"

The doctor shifted on his chair.

"I am not saying there have not been some ugly practical jokes in the neighbourhood in the past. But I think the whole thing has been blown up out of all proportion by the sensational press and by some interviews given by the Police Inspector. Of course, I am not blaming Mr Balfour here. He heard Mr Boldigrew's dying words and I did not. But I cannot help feeling that it was unfortunate that he repeated the words; first to the police and then to the Press."

I was about to open my mouth but closed it on seeing the expression on Pons' face. Young Balfour looked uncomfortable but Solar Pons tactfully closed the subject.

"Thank you, doctor. You have been most helpful."

"Good night, gentlemen. No thank you, Mr Balfour, I can find my way. I will look in again in a day or two. Goodnight."

Mrs Bracegirdle appeared as soon as he opened the door and the visitor had no sooner disappeared than Pons shot a sharp glance at our host.

"So you did not tell the doctor that you had yourself seen the face, Mr Balfour."

The young man shook his head.

"Certainly not, Mr Pons. There has been enough talk in the village and I know Dr Sherlock's views on the matter. The whole thing seems fantastic now that I look at it. Perhaps I have exaggerated everything, and the Police Inspector has blown it up out of all proportion. After all, I was the only one to hear my uncle's dying words."

Solar Pons shot our host a sympathetic glance.

"Come, Mr Balfour. You are not yourself this evening. You were convinced of the truth of your statements when you visited us at Praed Street. Many people have seen this apparition, including yourself and your own gardener. This is no joke, believe me. And if your uncle's death was purely heart disease, then it was precipitated by shock, which is tantamount to murder. There is something devilish here, mark my words."

He took his pipe out of his mouth and looked once again into the heart of the fire.

"Even so, we must tread carefully. You have not told the police of this latest happening and we must not antagonise the local force. We must see the Inspector, question the gardener and find time to cultivate the acquaintance of Mr Ram Dass."

He smiled at me ironically.

"It looks like being a busy day tomorrow, Parker."

6

"Well, sir, it gave me the fright of my life!"

It was a cold, frosty morning and Stevens the gardener, a decent, kindly old man with silver hair which looked as though he were himself powdered with frost, stood at the door of his potting shed in the grounds of Bredewell House and blinked at my companion.

Both Pons and I were clad in our warmest overcoats and scarfs but even so the cold penetrated almost to the bone and Pons' breath smoked from his mouth as he made reply to the man he was interrogating.

The old man, who seemed impervious to the cold, was evidently mindful of our situation for he suddenly said, with an embarrassed stammer, "If you'll step into the glass house yonder, gentlemen, you'll no doubt find it more comfortable."

We followed him readily enough and I was astonished to find the edifice in question not only filled with a wide variety of plants and fruits, but warmly heated by steam. Stevens' eyes glistened as we came in through the entrance porch and closed the outer doors behind us. Once through the inner doors the heat came up damp and cloying and after a minute or so we were both glad to remove our outer garments.

"You were speaking of this apparition, Stevens."

"Yes, sir. I have never been more terrified, yet I am a fairly steady sort of person."

Solar Pons sat indolently on a wooden bench at our back and turned his empty pipe over in his hands. His deep-set eyes were fixed intently on the riot of green and crimson beyond the old man's head, where an unseasonal display of flowers made a mockery of the iron-frost and thin mist that was coming up across the marshes, so that even the solid form of Bredewell House only a few hundred yards away beyond the bare hedge, was already dim and insubstantial.

"Just tell me exactly what happened that evening."

"It was on a Thursday night, Mr Pons. I had forgotten my wages or, rather, because I had to go into Tidewater in the afternoon to order some materials for the garden, I had missed my turn, as it were. Mr Balfour had kindly sent word by one of the men who works on the farm and who lives in the cottage next to mine, that he would open the estate office to pay me if I liked to come back that evening."

"Why was that?"

The old man looked embarrassed.

"Well, sir, I'm always a bit short at the end of the week and as the shops keep open late on Thursdays, I usually get my groceries and pay a few bills on Thursday nights. What with my work I don't get much chance otherwise, during the week. Being a widower, sir, it throws a good deal on me, one way or another."

"I see. So you collected your wages."

"Yes, sir. I stayed chatting to Mr Balfour for a few minutes. He's a very agreeable gentleman, sir."

"Indeed," I put in.

"When I left the office, instead of going the long way round by the kitchen garden entrance, I walked down the main drive. I was keeping on the verge, thinking of nothing in particular when something came at me out of the shrubbery. It was a horrible face, Mr Pons, all green fire, with glowing red eyes. It was a terrible sight."

"But Pons . . ." I began, when I was stopped by a warning glance from my companion.

"What did you do, Stevens?"

"Well, when I got over my shock, I made as though to grapple with it but it sort of retreated into the shrubbery and seemed to disappear. It can't say I was sorry, really."

"A frightening experience indeed," mused Solar Pons. "Why did you tell Mr Balfour a different story?"

The old man looked surprised.

"Ah, you have already heard that! A white lie, sir, I am afraid. Old Mr Boldigrew was so frightened of these stories about the village and he'd been a recluse for several years, that I didn't want to make things worse. I said the thing had appeared at the window of the potting shed, which is a long way from the house. I felt I had to warn Mr Balfour that there was something terrible hanging about the grounds. I did, in fact, go to the potting shed to collect my pipe on my way back to Tidewater, so it was only a white lie, sir, like I said."

"I see, Stevens. You have no objection to my telling Mr Balfour the truth now?"

The old man shook his head.

"None at all, sir, providing you make it clear to Mr Balfour that I had no intention to deceive."

"I shall certainly do that. Thank you, Stevens. You have been most helpful."

Resuming our outer garments we again braved the bitter conditions outdoors, Pons leading the way down the drive and turning on to the road that would take us to Tidewater as though he had known the locality all his life.

"It is certainly a rum business, Pons."

"Is it not, Parker. You have seen the significance of this appearance?"

"Well, it seemed as though the thing was again near the study window and the gardener surprised it."

"Excellent, my dear fellow. You really are improving most remarkably."

The mist was already crouching at the edges of the road which ran across the low marsh country and our footsteps echoed on the frosty surface unnaturally loudly. Pons lit his pipe, shovelling fragrant blue smoke back over his shoulder.

"But you really must learn to control your exuberance."

"I do not understand you, Pons."

"You were about, if my instinct is aright, to blurt out to Stevens that the thing he saw differed widely from the description of the face young Balfour saw at the study window that night."

"You are right, Pons. I am sorry. I am afraid I did not think."

My crestfallen expression brought forth a reassuring smile from my companion.

"Let us just have your theories on the matter, Parker."

"I do not know what to say, Pons. It is inconceivable that there can be two phantoms lurking about Tidewater."

"Especially when one is quite enough," said my companion drily.

And he said nothing further until about twenty minutes later when a bout of stiff walking had brought us in sight of the dim outlines of the village of Tidewater, whose smoking chimneys added to the mist and imparted an acrid flavour to the air we breathed.

Lights showed blurrily from the shops in the centre of the village, which presented a pleasantly animated appearance for such a small community.

To my surprise, now that we had reached the village, Pons showed little inclination to seek out the police station but, instead, sauntered along as though he were on holiday, showing inordinate interest in the contents of the shop windows.

I was just about to make some remark when he suddenly stopped and took me by the sleeve.

"Ah, Parker! Just the place I fancy."

I gazed at the window in astonishment.

"A toyshop, Pons? What can you possibly want here?"

Solar Pons put his finger to the side of his nose in a mischievous manner, a thin smile playing about his lips.

"Information, Parker. Possibly a return to childhood. There is something admirable about the atmosphere of such a shop, don't you think?"

"It may be, Pons," I said cautiously. "Though I do not see why you should wish to waste time in this fashion."

"Time so spent is not wasted, Parker," said Solar Pons severely, opening the door of the establishment.

The sharp ping of the bell announced our entrance but as there were several other customers, including a number of children, already in the shop, the proprietor, a short, bearded individual merely glanced up in our direction and then turned to the counter again.

I followed Pons, slightly puzzled, as he traversed the dusty aisles of this dark and curious old shop. There were odd corners piled with furry animals; boxes of lettered alphabet bricks; Meccano sets and clockwork trains, with here and there an entranced youngster holding some treasured item.

Pons paused by a heap of tin kettledrums and peered intently at the ranks of scarlet model soldiers with their bearskins and rifles at the ready.

"One could write a treatise on this sort of thing, Parker. It really is fascinating."

"I admit that, Pons, though I fail to see . . ."

But Pons had already moved on. He picked up a humming top, as though intent on nothing else; his eyes skimmed over the wooden and metal hoops; and alighted on a rack of gyroscopes in their gaily hued boxes.

"This is more like it, Parker."

I gave a start as I noticed the items which had already caught his attention. I followed quickly as he strode into an area of unexpected fantasy.

"Carnival masks, Pons!"

"Exactly, Parker," Solar Pons chuckled, his intent gaze running across the grotesque and soulless *papier-mâché* masks which leered at us from shelves and danced slowly in the eddies of air as they hung suspended from the ceiling. I jumped as a hideous green-hued face with red eyes lurched at me from round the corner.

"Well, young man, you have certainly achieved your purpose!" Solar Pons chuckled, as a blond-haired child with a sly expression emerged from beneath the mask.

"Why, Pons, that is exactly . . ." I began.

"Is it not, Parker?" Solar Pons interrupted calmly, as he caught the eye of the bearded proprietor.

The boy scampered off and the knots of customers at the counter clearing, the owner of the shop advanced toward us.

"I have a nephew some twelve years old and am looking for a suitable present," my companion began, to my astonishment.

The bearded man grinned.

"Well, there's an excellent choice here, gentlemen."

Solar Pons looked beyond him to the carnival masks.

"Sell a lot of these, do you?"

The man looked casually at his stock.

"A fair amount for a small place like this. Fireworks Night, fancy dress parties and that sort of thing. The youngsters like putting these on and scaring folk."

"What about this one, for instance?"

Solar Pons reached out a languid hand and pulled down one of the green masks with the red eyes.

"Funnily enough, that's been a fairly popular one this winter, sir. Sold a lot of them from October onwards. As a matter of fact, I had to order fresh stock. These only came in this morning."

"Indeed. You sold them all to children, I suppose?"

The unclouded eyes above the beard looked innocently enough at us.

"A few adults, too. Parties and practical jokes, I suppose. There's only one thing wrong with them for a shilling."

"And what might that be?" Pons asked, as though he had no other interest in the world but carnival masks.

"They tear too easily. See?"

The proprietor reached one of the hideous things down. He exerted a little pressure at the top of the mask with his fingers and a minute crack appeared in the material in the area of the hair-line.

"Well, thank you. You have been most helpful, Mr . . . ?"

"McMurdo," said the bearded man shortly. "Take your time, gentlemen. If you don't see what you want come back another day."

He returned to the counter as several more children trooped in.

"He seems a most amiable fellow, Pons," I observed.

"Does he not, Parker," said my companion, looking sharply through the gloom at the proprietor.

"You don't think he could have been responsible, Pons? That hideous mask is absolutely the same as the face seen by the gardener!"

"You are remarkably observant, my dear fellow. And as for friend McMurdo I am reserving judgment. But the presence of this shop in the village raises interesting possibilities."

And he looked thoughtfully at the leering monstrosities about us.

7

"Mr Solar Pons, sir! This is an unexpected honour."

Inspector Horace Cunliffe's grizzled features were suffused with pleasure as he held out a massive hand for my companion to shake. He sat in an old-fashioned office of the local police station with a big fire roaring in the grate and a sheaf of official-looking documents on the battered old desk in front of him.

"Don't tell me this phantom business brings you to this corner of Essex."

Solar Pons smiled faintly and dropped into a seat near the fire. The Inspector pulled up another chair for me and we sat toasting ourselves for a few seconds.

"It has brought you from Colchester, apparently, Inspector."

The officer looked at my companion shrewdly.

"*Touché*, Mr Pons. I see that your reputation for sharpness has not been exaggerated."

"There must be some reason for your staying on here, when you have other important duties in the county. You evidently do not think it just a village joke, as some people would have me believe. Despite your reported words in the public press."

The Inspector blew out his cheeks once or twice and looked at Pons with a shrug.

"Ah, there you have me, Mr Pons. You have seen through my little stratagem. I hoped, through the reports I disseminated via the Press, that I would allay this fellow's suspicions and that he would strike again."

Solar Pons looked at the police officer approvingly.

"You will undoubtedly make your mark in the force, Inspector."

The Inspector's open face flushed with pleasure.

"There is something markedly wrong in the matter and I mean to get to the bottom of it."

Solar Pons produced his pipe and turned it over absently in his fingers.

"Ah, you have noticed that, have you?"

The Inspector nodded, his grey eyes fixed on a corner of the mantelpiece.

"Instinct, Mr Pons. I have been in the force for fifteen years now and it has never led me astray before. Faces do not appear at windows fortuitously and heart or no heart attack Mr Boldigrew died as a direct result, if we are to believe the nephew."

"And you do believe the nephew?"

Cunliffe's eyes moved from the mantelpiece to take in my companion's face.

"I am a good judge of character, Mr Pons. Until something comes up to disprove my theories, I believe Mr Balfour's story."

"Excellent, Inspector. I am sure we shall get on well together."

"Ah, then you have been retained by the nephew?"

Solar Pons nodded, his deep-set eyes observing the thickset police officer sharply.

"It will be a pleasure to work with you, Mr Pons. I will be open with you and I am sure you will let me know if you come across anything."

Cunliffe paused and looked at my companion almost apologetically.

"I have my methods, sir, and would prefer to keep my own counsel for the moment. Tidewater is a terrified village and many people have been frightened by this thing. Therefore, I shall not return to Colchester until I have satisfied myself about the so-called face and the circumstances of Mr Boldigrew's death."

The Inspector broke off and looked at Pons with twinkling eyes.

"I rely on you to keep me informed, Mr Pons."

"I can assure you of that."

Solar Pons stood up, a tall and commanding figure in the little office.

"You think this phantom figure will strike again?"

"It seems likely, Mr Pons. I am sure I need not underline my reasons for thinking so. In the meantime I watch and wait."

"An excellent dictum, Inspector. I will be in touch. I wish you well in your investigations. Come, Parker."

"Well, Pons," said I, as we regained the misty street, "the Inspector seems to have his head screwed on tightly enough."

Solar Pons smiled thinly.

"As I surmised before we ever came to Essex, Parker, he is an extremely shrewd and capable officer. I think we can safely leave the general run of affairs to him."

"But you have already formed some conclusions, Pons?"

"Tentatively only, Parker. I would prefer to wait a little longer before coming to any definite opinion."

I nodded, following the spare form of my companion as he threaded the attractive winding streets of the village.

"You seem to know your way remarkably well, Pons?"

My companion stopped in a doorway, his eyes bright as he lit his pipe. He contentedly puffed out smoke over his shoulder.

"I have had the advantage of examining Balfour's large-scale map of the area before you were up this morning, Parker. We have only some half a mile to go."

"The residence of Ram Dass, Pons?"

Solar Pons smiled, his head thrust down into the collar of his warm coat, the stem of the pipe clamped between his strong teeth.

"The Grange it is, Parker. I think we shall learn something there to our advantage."

"Do you not think, Pons," I said, "that this business may have been exaggerated? These children, for example. With these green masks might they not have been playing jokes?"

Solar Pons shook his head, strange lights glinting in his eyes.

"You confuse cause with effect, Parker. You are taking things the wrong way round."

"I do not understand, Pons."

Solar Pons chuckled, taking the pipe out of his mouth, as we turned a corner and left the village behind us. The mist was down close to the road now, masking the fields and the surrounding marshland.

"It is my conviction that the man responsible for Boldigrew's death took advantage of the popularity of this mask in the district. It was a question literally of a mask sheltering behind a mask. You heard what the man at the shop said. Draw your own conclusions."

"I am all at sea, Pons."

Solar Pons cleared his throat as though expressing exasperation.

"It is as clear as day, my dear fellow. He was forced to change his tactics."

My brow cleared.

"The shopkeeper, Pons?"

Solar Pons had a mocking smile on his face as an impressive Edwardian building of red brick began to compose itself from out of the mist in front of us. The large iron gates to the gravelled drive stood ajar and on the topmost stone of each of the red-brick pillars which flanked the gates, the legend: THE GRANGE was chiselled.

Our footsteps set birds scuttering in the undergrowth as we walked down the front drive to the great pillared entrance porch. The front door was opened at our ring almost immediately, and a bearded Indian servant with a gentle, melancholy face above his sober black frock-coat ushered us into a tiled hall. The mournful sound of a flute sounded from the depths of the house and there was a faint smell of incense in the air.

Pons had sent in his card by the servant who returned almost immediately to bid us to follow him. He took us through a suite of three interconnecting rooms, each furnished sumptuously with many rugs, Oriental carpets and with carvings on the walls; each with a profusion of brass ornaments and bamboo furniture. It was all too florid for my taste and my expression must have shown my feelings all too well for Pons gave me a brief, ironic smile.

The servant tapped on a mahogany door in front of us and ushered us into a study containing many leather-bound books; a bright fire burned in the grate of the carved chimney-piece and there were many weapons hanging on the walls not occupied by books. I noticed kukris, swords whose handles were ornamented with precious stones; and a rack containing blowpipes and darts tipped with bright birds' feathers.

"Heavens, Pons!" I mumbled. "This place is like a museum or armoury."

"Is it not, Parker," said Pons, looking around him with evident interest and pleasure.

The owner of The Grange had been sitting at a desk near the fire, evidently writing, for he now rose and put down the pen in his hand and stood waiting near the fireplace to receive us. A tall, impressive-looking gentleman with a black beard and cruel eyes which looked like a hawk's in his brown features, he was yet courteous and reserved. With his impeccably cut tweeds he could have been mistaken for an English country gentleman at a distance. His voice, when he spoke, was low and cultured.

"Good morning, gentlemen. This is an unexpected honour."

"Ah, you have heard of me, then?"

Ram Dass bowed gently from the waist, extending a slim, well-manicured hand toward us.

"Who has not, Mr Solar Pons?"

"You are too kind, Mr Dass."

The tall man smiled ironically as he shook hands with us in turn.

"Please be seated but I am afraid your visit has been wasted, Mr Solar Pons."

My companion's eyes were bright as he stared at our host.

"In what way?"

"Come sir. It is obvious. There have been strange happenings in the village of Tidewater. Mr Boldigrew died under mysterious circumstances. I had had numerous rows with his bailiff and it is no secret that my household is regarded with some hostility in the neighbourhood. I have expected the police before now. So when your card was brought in I was not surprised."

"You are frank at least, Mr Dass," said Solar Pons.

He looked at the tall man as he re-seated himself at the desk.

"It is my upbringing, sir."

Ram Dass bowed ironically.

"You also sound rather bitter, if I may say so," said Pons.

The Indian's eyes held a strange expression.

"Ah, you have noticed that."

"It is not difficult to read it, Mr Dass."

"I have learned to school my emotions but you are very perceptive, Mr Pons. And I will anticipate your next question by saying that I am not at all related to the gentleman who lost his money in my native country."

"Ah, you know that story. I had not supposed for one moment that you were."

Our host seemed nonplussed and stared at my companion with unconcealed surprise.

"Then why are you here, Mr Pons, if it is not an indiscreet question?"

"It is merely that I wish to see everything for myself, Mr Dass," said Solar Pons easily.

"And now, we have taken up too much of your time altogether."

He rose from his seat and I followed suit, looking blankly from one man to the other. The Indian had a fixed smile on his face and his eyes were glittering in a rather sinister manner, I thought.

"If I may presume to give advice to such a gifted criminologist . . ."

Solar Pons bowed.

"By all means."

"My advice, Mr Pons, is look closer to home!"

Pons smiled somewhat grimly.

"I take your point, Mr Dass. Good morning. Come, Parker."

We followed the silent servant out through the interconnecting rooms again.

"Well, Pons," I said sotto voce. "He is a cool one."

"Is he not, Parker."

"Did you see all those blow-pipes and other weapons, Pons? He seemed rather too prepared for our visit. And what did he mean by telling you to look nearer home?"

Solar Pons smiled enigmatically.

"It is all of a piece, Parker. It really has been a most instructive morning."

We were being ushered out the front door by this time and I had to descend the steps at a rapid trot to keep up with my companion.

"Then you have learned something?"

"By all means, Parker. But in my turn I do not understand your talk about blow-pipes."

"Well, the atmosphere is most sinister, Pons."

Solar Pons looked at me with a mocking smile as we strode on through the thickening mist.

"Hardly grounds for suspicion of murder, Parker. You will have to do better than that."

"Blow-pipes have been used for murder before, Pons."

My companion stared at me incredulously.

"But the window was closed and locked, Parker. And the post-mortem findings . . . Nevertheless, you have stumbled upon an interesting point, however inadvertently."

I felt my face growing red.

"It was just a suggestion, Pons."

"You really must learn to use your brain-power to greater advantage, Parker," said my companion reprovingly. "Now, in a few minutes we shall be back in Tidewater and should have time for just one more call before lunch."

"Where might that be, Pons?"

"At George Sainsbury's office in Tidewater High Street, Parker."

I looked at Pons uncomprehendingly.

"Sainsbury?"

"He is Boldigrew's family solicitor, Parker. I received this note from him by messenger this morning. We have been so busy I have not had time to mention it until now."

He passed me the sheet of legal notepaper; it was headed, 3 Milton Buildings, High Street, Tidewater. Written in longhand, it merely said: "Dear Mr Pons, I should appreciate an urgent consultation with you. Would midday today suit you, at my offices? Please confirm by return. Yours, George Sainsbury."

I passed back the sheet to Pons.

"What do you make of it, Pons?"

"Well, it is obvious, Parker. It is something to do with Boldigrew's will."

His face clouded and he looked extremely thoughtful as he carelessly thrust the note back in his pocket.

"The old man's estate is obviously a key to this enigma, Parker. I had intended to see the solicitors at the earliest opportunity and this appointment is timely. It wants but a quarter to twelve now and we shall be there within a few minutes."

We pressed on into the thickening mist but had not gone more than a few yards before we heard the wild clamour of bells coming through the dense blanket ahead. There was a strange glare in the sky as we hurried on.

"There is a fire, Pons!" I cried excitedly.

"Is there not, Parker," said my companion, gazing sombrely ahead to where an angry orange glow was becoming more strongly visible every moment. We hurried onwards, as though compelled by some strange sixth sense of disaster. As we gained the outskirts of Tidewater it was obvious that the fire was serious indeed.

Dense clouds of black smoke, acrid and choking, came down wind toward us and the glare of the fire grew; now we could hear the strong crackling and cries of alarm as people hurried through the streets.

I elbowed my way through the crowd after Pons. The heat was intense and it was obvious that the large red-brick building which was the heart of the fire was doomed. A murmur was passing through the crowd.

"There's someone in there!"

"The gentleman couldn't get out in time."

A large fire appliance with a brass funnel was slewed across the entrance of the street and icy cold water cascaded off the façade of the burning building in showers of sparks amid an angry hissing, while pools overflowed in runnels which swilled down the gutters. The crowd parted as someone came through, removing his hat, and I recognised the strong, capable figure of Inspector Cunliffe.

He and Pons were already in conversation and I was separated from them by a knot of people when an extra loud outburst from the crowd was followed by the dreadful hush that always follows in the presence of tragedy. The heat was tremendous now and a group of firemen, their oilskins gleaming with water were staggering from the building with a recumbent figure. There was a sickly aroma in the air which is peculiar to burning flesh.

I broke through into the cleared space as someone placed an oilskin over the charred remains. Pons' clear-minted features were grim as he conferred with Cunliffe in low tones. A man in a dark overcoat was already at the sheeted figure and he turned an anguished face toward us, shaking his head.

"There is nothing I can do, I am afraid," said Dr Sherlock in a trembling voice.

"It is Mr Sainsbury, is it?" said Cunliffe, looking swiftly about the crowd.

Sherlock nodded.

"The features are unrecognisable, I am afraid, but I can identify his pocket watch. The seals on the chain there are unmistakable."

He pulled back the edge of the waterproof to disclose the partly melted object in question and Cunliffe nodded, his dogged features grim and brooding.

"I had an appointment with him," said Pons, producing the letter from his pocket.

Cunliffe ran over it quickly, rubbing his chin in perplexity.

"This could have been important, Mr Pons," he said quietly, handing the sheet back.

We had walked a few yards away now and, bidding goodbye to Dr Sherlock, quitted the tragic scene. A hundred yards away, in clearer air and with the intervening houses between, the death of Sainsbury seemed like an unreal nightmare.

"You realise the significance of this, Inspector?"

The big man nodded.

"You give me much credit, Mr Pons, but I'm your man. Mr Balfour's estate is the key to this business, if I read things aright."

Solar Pons nodded.

"I have said it before and I will say it again, Inspector. You will go far. I had hoped to hear from Mr Sainsbury himself some of the conditions of the late Mr Boldigrew's will."

"Mr Balfour has not told you himself?"

Pons shook his head.

"For the simple reason that the will had not been read. From what my host told me this morning the ceremony was due to take place next month."

"I see."

The Police Inspector rubbed his chin again.

"All gone up in smoke now, Mr Pons?"

"It would appear so, Inspector," said Pons smoothly.

"This doesn't look like an accident to me, Mr Pons," said Cunliffe grimly, looking back over his shoulder at the great pillar of black smoke which towered upward, staining the mist.

"Like you, Inspector, I strongly suspect murder," said Pons, his eyes like ice. "But it will be rather difficult to prove, I fear. Fire is a great destroyer."

"Too true, Mr Pons," Cunliffe muttered. "Someone in this village is badly frightened. He may betray himself before long."

"That is my hope also, Inspector. I am afraid we must leave you now. There is much to do after lunch. Come, Parker."

And he led the way back at a brisk pace in the direction of Bredewell House.

8

"Now, Parker, let us just have your thoughts on this affair."

Solar Pons fixed me with piercing eyes and leaned back in his chair by the fireside. It was early afternoon and Bredewell House was quiet. Mrs Bracegirdle was going about her duties in the mansion and earlier Balfour had gone out to his estate office in the grounds. He had turned a deathly white when I had informed him of the death of the lawyer and the circumstances surrounding it, but had volunteered no comments on the matter and Pons had not asked for any.

Now he sat with the smoke from his pipe curling toward the ceiling, his thin, sensitive fingers vibrating on his knee like the antennae of an insect. Outside, oily wreaths of clammy fog hung at the windows and Bredewell House seemed isolated at the edge of the marsh. My own thoughts were little less gloomy and I stared at my companion while useless possibilities chased themselves about the recesses of my mind.

"About the phantom, Pons?"

"About the whole situation, Parker. You are becoming an excellent catalyst."

"Good of you to say so. But this business of the will has set me thinking, Pons."

"Well?"

Solar Pons' lean, feral face expressed only polite interest as he stared at me through the dancing plumes of pipe-smoke.

"It came to me at the toy-shop, Pons. It would be so easy for anyone to buy one of those masks with which to frighten old Mr Boldigrew. He had a heart condition, as we know."

I paused, conscious that Pons was looking at me with intense interest.

"Excellent, Parker! Little escapes you."

"You do me honour, Pons. I hardly dare to suggest it but it has occurred to me that young Balfour himself is the chief beneficiary of the old gentleman's will. What if he himself . . ."

I paused, hardly daring to venture the suggestion aloud. Pons' eyes were very bright now.

"Go on."

"It is only a supposition, mind, Pons. But if he had started out by donning the mask and frightening people in the neighbourhood . . . That would have provided a red herring, as it were. Then, when he struck at his uncle . . ."

"It really was an extremely tragic business, Parker," said Pons in an excessively loud voice.

I stared at him in rising irritation.

"Did you hear a word of what I was saying, Pons?"

Pons stabbed the air with the stem of his pipe.

"I don't understand, Pons."

"Naturally," my companion went on, as though I had not spoken. "Such a fire is almost impossible to stop once started. You wished to see me, Mrs Bracegirdle?"

I started and looked back over my shoulder. The housekeeper stood in the shadows near the doorway and I had not heard her come in. Now she advanced toward us with a strange, almost furtive expression on her face.

"The fog is thickening, Mr Pons. I am naturally a little worried about Mr Balfour, sir. I wondered whether you gentlemen mightn't join him at the estate office."

The interest on Pons' face quickened.

"You fear something, Mrs Bracegirdle?"

The housekeeper hesitated.

"I am obviously concerned, sir. I hope you did not mind me mentioning it."

"You think this thing will appear again?" I asked.

The housekeeper licked her lips, turning to me.

"It is possible, sir. I do not know what to expect now. These strange Indians . . ."

"I have been to see Mr Dass," said Solar Pons crisply. "And I have formed an opinion on the matter. I also think that Mr Balfour has little to fear during the daylight hours, particularly in the busy atmosphere of the estate."

He looked at Mrs Bracegirdle curiously.

"Tell me a little more about that night old Mr Boldigrew died."

Mrs Bracegirdle clasped her hands together in front of her and looked at Solar Pons sharply.

"I have already told everything I know, Mr Pons."

"It would not hurt to tell it again," said my companion gently. "Sometimes small details get overlooked."

The woman hesitated, her eyes never leaving Pons' face.

The Adventure of the Phantom Face 103

"There was something, sir, the night Mr Boldigrew died. It was so trivial I never mentioned it."

"It is the trivial which often has the greatest significance," said Pons, tenting his fingers before him.

"Well, sir, it was something I did merely for form's sake."

"And what was that, Mrs Bracegirdle?"

"It was at that dreadful moment when Mr Boldigrew died, Mr Pons. Mr Balfour rushed outside and I was left alone with the dying man for a minute or two. I raised him up and tried to give him air. It was then I noticed a thin trickle of blood on his neck."

"Indeed."

It seemed to have grown very quiet in the room and the crackling of the fire came to me unnaturally loud. Solar Pons ejected a plume of blue smoke from his mouth.

"To what did you attribute this bleeding, Mrs Bracegirdle."

"I did not pay it much attention, Mr Pons. I thought my employer may have injured himself in falling or he may have cut himself in shaving that morning. The cut was low down, near his collar, you see. So I got my handkerchief and cleaned his neck, to tidy him up before the doctor came."

"You did not tell Mr Balfour or the doctor of this?"

The housekeeper shook her head with a worried expression in her eyes.

"It did not seem important, Mr Pons. But thinking back and knowing what a wonderful way you have of reading things in tiny details I felt I ought to mention it."

"You have acted wisely," said Solar Pons slowly. "And no blame attaches to you. It may be of no importance but it has given me an inkling of the truth where all was dark before."

The housekeeper shook her head.

"The whole of Tidewater seems to be going mad, Mr Pons. Not only this new tragedy of Mr Sainsbury but in so many little things."

"In what way, pray?"

"Mrs Mackney's boy, for example. Johnnie is such a truthful lad and I believed him though his mother was angry as she thought he had lost them. The pistol especially was expensive too."

"I am afraid I do not follow, Mrs. Bracegirdle," I mumbled.

Pons shot me an amused glance and Mrs Bracegirdle flushed.

"I am not telling it very well, Mr Pons, I know. Mrs Mackney is an acquaintance of mine, who sometimes visits here. She was telling me some weeks ago of Johnnie's untruthfulness. He told her his carnival mask had been stolen. And then when his expensive air pistol disappeared, she lost her temper. She was of the opinion the boy was lying, and that he had lost them."

"Thank you, Mrs Bracegirdle!"

I was astonished at Pons' reaction. He hit his thigh with the flat of his hand, making a cracking noise like a gun shot and his eyes were alight with excitement.

"You say this was some weeks ago? Before Mr Boldigrew's death?"

"Oh, yes, Mr Pons."

"And the boy never found the mask or the air pistol?"

"No, Mr Pons."

"And these rather strangely assorted articles disappeared on the same occasion or on two separate occasions?"

"On two different occasions, Mr Pons, to the best of my recollection."

"Excellent. Now, where could the boy have lost them?"

"He swore they were stolen while he was playing, Mr Pons, but his mother wouldn't believe him."

"Does Mrs Mackney work for a living?"

"Yes, Mr Pons. She does some cleaning work about the village. In shops and at the homes of professional gentlemen."

"Including Mr Sainsbury?"

"Why, yes, Mr Pons. So I suppose Johnnie could have lost his toys anywhere."

"Exactly."

Solar Pons was silent for a moment, his fingers pulling at the lobe of his left ear, often his habit when thinking. Presently he looked up.

"Thank you, Mrs Bracegirdle. You have given me a good deal to think about. I think we will join Balfour at the estate office, Parker. I have the germ of an idea."

9

"Must you go, gentlemen?"

There was dismay on Michael Balfour's face.

The Adventure of the Phantom Face

"It is only for a day or so, Mr Balfour. I have urgent business in London that cannot be put off, I am afraid. And Dr Parker must arrange for a fresh locum."

"I quite understand, Mr Pons, but it is naturally a disappointment."

It was dusk now and lights from the farm buildings round about pricked the darkness through the windows of the estate office.

"This business is taking longer than you thought, Pons."

Solar Pons nodded.

"It is a question of catching our man off guard, Mr Balfour. Which is why I want you to be careful and adhere strictly to my instructions when we are gone."

"I will do that all right, Mr Pons."

The smoke from my companion's pipe rose in a thin spiral to the ceiling as he gazed almost dreamily out of the window. There came a tapping at the door and Stevens the gardener poked his head in.

"You wished to see me, Mr Balfour?"

"Yes, Stevens. You are going home shortly I suppose? I wondered if you would be good enough to take the pony and trap in with you and deposit Mr Pons and Dr Parker at the station. You can leave the equipage at the livery stables overnight and that will be your transport back in the morning."

"Delighted, gentlemen."

The gardener's face was frankly curious.

"Not leaving the district, sir?"

"For a few days only. I have to be back in London on urgent business."

"I will just harness the trap, sir, and will be at your disposal in a quarter of an hour."

"Bring it to the front door of the house, would you. Dr Parker and I will just have time to throw a few things into a holdall."

Stevens saluted and closed the door.

A few moments later we waited in the bitter air while Balfour locked the estate office behind him. We walked across the courtyard in the gathering dusk, thin wisps of mist already eddying eerily in the distant trees and blurring the outlines of the surrounding countryside.

"Lock your doors this evening and follow my instructions implicitly," said Pons as we stood in the hall waiting for our conductor.

Mrs Bracegirdle looked as surprised as Balfour at our sudden departure, I thought, but she kept her own counsel. A few moments later the grating of iron-bound wheels in the driveway announced the arrival of Stevens and with the briefest of goodbyes, we were soon whirling effortlessly in the direction of Tidewater.

Stevens kept his thoughts to himself, hunched over the reins and the horse picked its way instinctively through the fog. Pons smoked in silence and I must confess my own thoughts were heavy. We seemed to be hopelessly enmeshed in an evil atmosphere down here on the marshes and I could not possibly see a way clear in the impenetrable morass which surrounded us.

It was quite dark when we reached the outskirts of Tidewater and I was surprised when Pons put his hand on the driver's shoulder and jumped lithely to the ground.

"This will do nicely, Stevens."

"Do you not want the station, sir?"

"Our train does not leave for forty minutes," said Pons carelessly, "And I prefer to walk a while for the exercise, rather than sit about in a draughty waiting room."

"As you wish, sir. Goodnight."

He made a little salute in the air with the lash of his whip and jogged on into the murk. To my surprise Pons had turned aside and was walking up an alley lined with elegant small houses of red brick, with neat, white-painted windows.

"Ah, here we are, Parker. Jasmine Cottages. Number six. This is the house, I fancy."

He turned to me, his lean, feral face alive with urgency beneath the mellow gaslight.

"If you would not mind waiting, Parker, I shall hardly be a minute or so."

"As you wish, Pons," I mumbled.

I took a turn up and down the road while Pons was inside the house, completely lost now as to my companion's motives. He emerged within five minutes, rubbing his thin hands together with barely suppressed excitement.

"Excellent, Parker. Mrs Mackney was most helpful."

"Mrs Mackney, Pons? The woman whose son lost the air pistol. I hardly see . . ."

"No doubt, Parker," said Solar Pons rudely, taking his holdall from me and stepping out at a fast pace. As we turned into the High Street we almost ran into the bearded figure of

The Adventure of the Phantom Face

the toyshop proprietor, McMurdo, who was just putting up the shutters for the night.

"Ah, Mr Pons. Inclement weather, sir."

He looked sharply at the bags we were carrying.

"I heard you were leaving. Not too successful this time?"

"Perhaps, perhaps," said Pons languidly. "Goodnight to you."

I stared back over my shoulder as I followed my companion down the street.

"How did he know your name, Pons? And why did he know we were leaving? This all sounds very suspicious to me."

Solar Pons chuckled.

"These things have a habit of getting around small villages, Parker. Stevens, perhaps, or one of the estate workers."

"I do not know why we are leaving at all, Pons," I continued. "I thought you had formed some strong conclusions."

"And so I have, Parker, so I have. Ah, here is the road leading to the station if I mistake not."

As we gained the gaslit entrance I was astonished to see the sturdy form of Inspector Cunliffe waiting beneath the canopy.

At his side stood Dr Sherlock holding some books and a buff envelope in his hand.

"Good evening, Mr Pons!"

The Inspector raised his hard hat, a beaming smile on his face.

"The fact that we are returning to London seems to have become public knowledge throughout the whole town," I said somewhat bitterly.

"Indeed," said Inspector Cunliffe heartily. "Difficult to keep these things secret down here."

"Just what I was telling Parker," said Solar Pons smoothly, taking the buff envelope from Dr Sherlock.

"Good of you to remember, doctor."

"Oh, think nothing of it, Mr Pons," said Sherlock carelessly. "Glad to have been of assistance. Though I don't think you'll find much there."

Pons drew out the Sainsbury post-mortem report, perused it keenly and passed it to me.

"Death by asphyxiation, of course," I grunted, passing it back somewhat ungraciously to my companion.

"If you will excuse me I will just purchase our tickets," said Pons. "I am sure you can make small talk for a few minutes, Parker."

"I am afraid I must be off," said Dr Sherlock, raising his hat. "I have a heavy surgery this evening."

"By all means," said Pons, shaking hands. "Many thanks for your assistance."

"A pleasure."

Sherlock turned to me as Pons went over to the booking office window.

"Good night, doctor. Glad to have met you."

He bobbed away in the gathering dusk as Cunliffe and I walked through the booking hall to join Pons. We stood at the gate to the platform waiting for the train. Another had just come in from the opposite direction and the engine stood at the far platform, belching smoke and steam while the angry red glow from the firebox illuminated the driver and fireman, so that they looked like figures from a woodcut by Dürer.

A tall bearded figure came through the barrier, smiled briefly and turned aside.

"Good evening, Mr Dass!"

The Indian smiled maliciously.

"Leaving already, Mr Pons?"

"The atmosphere of Tidewater is a little stifling after that of London."

"Well, I hope you find what you are looking for."

"I am sure I shall."

The Indian smiled briefly again, his silent factotum bringing up the rear, as he walked briskly to the cab-rank at the other side of the station fore-court.

"A strange man, that," said Inspector Cunliffe heavily as he glanced after him sharply.

"But not as strange as some in Essex," said Solar Pons enigmatically. "Ah, here is our train, Inspector. You will keep alert, of course?"

"Naturally, Mr Pons," said Cunliffe politely. "You will excuse me for not coming on the platform."

My companion handed him a slip of paper.

"By all means."

The Inspector disappeared into the gloom and Pons and I were soon ensconced opposite one another in the comfort of a first-class compartment. Pons chuckled as the train drew out in long, shuddering strides.

"Now I have baited the trap, I think that most of the chief dramatis personae cannot fail to be aware of our intentions."

"What on earth do you mean, Pons?" I said.

"Oh, come, Parker!" said Solar Pons, a slight note of irritation in his tones. "You surely do not think we are leaving young Balfour alone in such a place as Bredewell House and in deadly danger of his life?"

"Then why are we going to London?"

"We are not, Parker. We are getting out at the next station and making our way back to Tidewater."

"Ah, so you only wished local people to think you were off the case?"

Solar Pons stared at me with an ironic expression in his eyes.

"Sometimes, Parker, I think you are a greater droll than even the world takes you for. Why do you think I was at such pains to let the whole of the Tidewater area know that we were returning to London?"

"I see, Pons. But Inspector Cunliffe is in the know?"

"Naturally, Parker. I am relying on his assistance if all goes as I think it might. We have baited the trap and must now wait for our man to come to us."

And with that he settled himself in his corner, belching out clouds of impenetrable blue smoke as the train thundered on through the night.

10

"Quickly, Parker!"

Pons led the way across the platform of the halt at a fast pace, so that I was hard put to follow. It was extremely dark now, bitterly cold and the fog was billowing in white swathes before our faces.

"Shall we be in time, Pons?" I asked anxiously as we hurried through the station barrier and swung to the left, on to the narrow road that must take us back to Tidewater. Behind us the glowing lights of the train we had just left were already swallowed in the murk and we could only hear its progress as it left the platform.

"If my estimation is correct we shall have ample time," said my companion imperturbably, "but I wish to be in position and survey the ground well before he comes."

"Why are you so positive it will be tonight, Pons?"

"Several reasons, Parker. Principally because he now knows we are no longer on the ground, but safely on our way to London. He thus has two clear days in which to strike. He will feel safer tonight because there is always a possibility that we might return some time tomorrow afternoon. Thirdly, the weather conditions are perfect this evening for what he has in mind. This fog is ideal for concealing his movements."

"And what has he in mind, Pons?"

"Cold, calculated murder, Parker!" said Solar Pons grimly, his chin hunched down into the collar of his overcoat, his pipe throwing a bright chain of sparks through the darkness as he strode along vigorously at my side. There was no traffic on the road, probably because of the bleak conditions and I was glad I had a bag to carry because the exercise and its weight engendered warmth.

"You do not mean it, Pons!"

"I wish I did not, my dear fellow. But this killer has already taken two lives that stood between him and a fortune. He needs only to put young Balfour out of the way to inherit old Boldigrew's estate."

"Ah, then, the will is at the bottom of it, Pons?"

"It is the key to everything, Parker. That is why the unfortunate Sainsbury was murdered and his records destroyed. He undoubtedly suspected someone and wished to inform me of something important when he was struck down."

I must confess I felt my scalp crawling at his words, uttered as they were in such hard and determined tones amid such bleak surroundings. Every step we took in this wilderness seemed to lead us deeper into the heart of an impenetrable mystery; impenetrable to me at any rate, as I had little idea of the complex thoughts that were chasing themselves through my companion's mind.

"But whom do you suspect, Pons?"

Solar Pons shook his head, a wry expression on this thin, sensitive lips.

"I would prefer not to speculate at this stage, Parker. I have nothing to go on at all but the theory I have formed. One broken or mis-read link in the chain could disprove my reasoning. Better to wait now and put it to the test. You should know the answer within an hour or two, my dear fellow."

I stared at my companion without speaking. He put his hand on my arm.

"You really are most invaluable in my little investigations, Parker. I do not know what I should do without your companionship and presence in the many crises through which we have passed."

He had never been so forthcoming before and I flushed with pleasure.

"Glad to do what I can, Pons," I stammered.

We had been walking for some ten minutes now and the exercise on the iron-bound surface of the road was beginning to dispel the deadly cold and engender some bodily warmth. Solar Pons smiled as though he could read my thoughts.

"It may be a long vigil tonight, Parker. I have taken the precaution of bringing some whisky in a flask in my pocket here. You have brought your revolver?"

"You insisted on it, Pons."

My companion nodded.

"Excellent. We may have need of it before the night is over."

He said nothing further and another twenty minutes had passed before I sensed that we were nearing our destination. My companion slackened his pace a little and touched me on the arm.

"I think we will diverge from the road here, Parker. We do not want to forewarn our man."

"What are we to do then, Pons?"

"Take to the fields, my dear fellow. Just give me a moment to check my bearings."

I did not see how he was to do so as the fog had now thickened considerably. The night was freezing too and there was an air-frost which made my ears and cheeks tingle. Pons cast about for a moment and then led the way forward without hesitation.

"Ah! I thought I was not mistaken."

He had turned into a small lane on the right; in reality it was only a cart-track whose deeply rutted surface was now bound in the iron grip of frost. Pons put his lips against my ear.

"We must be extremely careful now, Parker. We are only a few hundred yards off the farm buildings. Sound carries a long way under these conditions. And be careful how you place your feet as one may easily turn one's ankle in the dark."

"I will be careful, Pons."

My companion went on, pausing only occasionally to check his bearings. After a few minutes he opened a gate on the left that led to an open field. We walked slowly across the rough, undulating turf, the mist cold and clammy against our faces. I looked at my watch. It was so dark I had to hold my eyes only an inch or two from the dial to make out the time. It was already almost eight o'clock.

Pons only grunted when I told him and enjoined caution by putting his fingers to his lips. A moment or two later we came out on the banks of a small stream, now frozen and powdered with hoar frost. A few yards farther there was a rough wooden bridge, evidently used for cattle crossing, guarded only by simple wooden palings. We crept quietly across it and traversing the next field, the mist seemingly thicker than ever, suddenly saw lights beginning to prick the darkness.

"That is the farm, Parker," said Pons softly. "The house is occupied by the tenant farmer and he has the yard lights on this evening. That is excellent for our purpose. We must swing heavily to the left to come level with Bredewell House."

We passed the next quarter of an hour working our way round the farm and apart from a solitary dog whose barking caused us some anxiety, there was no indication that anyone knew of our presence. When Pons was satisfied he became brisker in his movements and a wicket fence, its palings looking black and sinister in the whiteness of the fog, loomed up before us. Pons found a gate and opened it carefully. We stepped through and I waited while my companion closed it behind us.

"We are only a few yards from the drive which leads from the farm area to the house," he whispered. "We must now find a sheltered spot which will command the scene of operations while affording us some concealment. I have already marked such a place but we must be extremely careful as to noise. Follow me and keep your wits about you."

We crept silently forward through the fog; it was now so thick that we were only a matter of yards away before we saw light from one of the upper windows of Bredewell House.

"Ah, this is the place, Parker," Pons whispered.

He led the way into a thicket of evergreens, the icy-cold of the leaves making a harsh noise as we crept through them, they were so brittle with the frost. Pons stopped at last and I was left looking at the gloomy fog-bank.

"I am afraid this is the best we can do," said Pons. "At least we should be able to hear our friend if he comes."

I pulled my coat-collar more tightly about my neck.

"How long are we likely to be here, Pons?"

"Oh, at least two hours," my companion rejoined casually. "Do take some whisky for inner warmth. And you will find these sandwiches excellent."

We made a simple supper crouched in the lee of a large yew tree whose trunk afforded shelter, and I must say things began to seem a little better once the warmth of the raw spirit began to permeate my system. I shifted my position, biting into a fresh sandwich.

"Where are we, Pons?"

"About midway between the farm buildings and the main gate of Bredewell House, Parker. If it were not for this fog you would find us almost opposite the study window."

"Ah, then we are on the small side-drive which loops round to rejoin the main carriage-way near the front door?"

"Exactly, Parker. I do not know whether he will be approaching from the farm or from the village. This way we should be able to cut him off if young Balfour is in danger."

"It is by no means certain he will come, Pons."

Solar Pons smiled thinly, his face dimly visible through the fog though he was only a foot or two away from me.

"You are becoming quite a philosopher, Parker. As you point out, nothing is certain in life. But as I have already indicated, I am convinced that our man is desperate and that he will strike soon. And this is the best method; to bring him to us and catch him in the act. So we must be on the alert, despite these inclement conditions."

I said nothing further but finished my *al fresco* supper and composed myself with what patience I could muster to sit out the hours. It seemed an inordinately long time, strained as my nerves were. The bitter cold; the fog; the strange surroundings and the bizarre errand which had sent us to this bleak, lonely spot in Essex all combined to arouse a darkness in my own mind; and the cramped conditions, for we could take no exercise without signalling our presence, made me miserable indeed.

It seemed as though the long night itself must have worn away though in reality only some two hours had passed, when Pons stirred at my side and put his finger to my lips.

"Have your revolver ready, Parker," he whispered. "Unless I am much mistaken someone is approaching."

I roused myself, a thin finger of ice tracing out my spine. A moment later I caught the sound which had attracted his attention. The faint, almost imperceptible echo of footsteps on the drive.

"Be extremely careful, Parker. Absolutely no noise."

Pons stood up under the shadow of the tree and I joined him, almost falling because of the cramp in my limbs. He caught me by the arm and steadied me. The sounds, though unpleasantly furtive, were now more audible. Then they ceased altogether.

"He has crossed the grass, Parker. Unless anything unforeseen occurs, we have him."

I took my revolver from my overcoat pocket and eased off the safety catch. I held it before me, muzzle pointed at the ground, as we went forward, step by step in order to make no sound.

We were on the verge at the edge of the drive now, our progress muffled by the mat of frozen grass stems. There was a sudden lightening of the mist ahead.

"That will be the study window, Parker," said Solar Pons exultantly. "And our friend has not passed on, so this is no late straggler from the farm using the drive as a short-cut."

As he spoke there came a low, urgent rapping noise from within the blanket of mist. In three paces we were across the drive; I paused by Pons, my heart thudding in my throat.

"What is it, Pons?"

"He is tapping on the window to attract attention, just as he did in the case of Boldigrew."

Almost as he spoke the blanket of mist was broken by a pale lozenge of yellow light.

"He is following instructions perfectly, Parker. Young Balfour has drawn back the window curtain. Ah! Now we have him."

As he spoke I saw what his keen eye had already picked out. The silhouette of a thin, muffled form, outlined against the whiteness of the mist. It was joined by a second figure which could only have been Balfour at the window. There was the sound of the casement being raised as we crept closer. Then the figure outside the window disappeared and when it rose from below the edge there was another silhouette in the right hand which could only have been a pistol.

"Quickly, Parker! Fire into the air!"

There was such urgency in Pons' tones that my reaction was instinctive; as the explosion, magnified tremendously by the mist, split the silence, the furtive figure turned with great rapidity. We were up to the window now and Balfour gave a cry of fear, staggering back in bewilderment. I saw a hideous yellow face which was so close that it seemed thrust into my own and then the thing had disappeared into the darkness and the fog.

"What was it, Pons?" I stammered as I became aware of other noises; dogs barking; a cry of alarm from the housekeeper; and Balfour asking incoherent questions of my companion.

"All in good time, Mr Balfour," said Pons incisively. "There is nothing further to be feared. Quickly, Parker! Before he gets away."

He set off running into the mist and I had difficulty in keeping up with him. Pons led the way without hesitation, back in the direction from which we had come. We crossed the fields, the breath sobbing in my throat and in a remarkably short while came to the lane we had traversed earlier. We had not gone far along it when Pons gave a sudden exclamation.

"We are in time, Parker. There is no hurry now."

The hooded form of a motor vehicle loomed from out of the mist; Pons glanced in at the driver's door. The interior was empty and he busied himself near the ground, peering intently at the licence plate.

"I think we will re-trace our route, Parker. Unless I miss my guess he has hidden among the farm buildings until things quieten down. He will have to come across these fields to regain his car and I do not think he will want to hang about here any longer than need be."

"Why is that, Pons?"

Solar Pons glanced at me with grim amusement.

"Because he has been badly frightened, Parker. And also because he would fear an organised search."

He glanced at his watch.

"I am certain of his identity now but I would prefer to catch him on the ground."

We had crossed the second field and were passing a small copse when Solar Pons caught me by the arm. The mist was thinning a little and a moment later I saw the dark, recumbent figure on the grass. In two strides I had reached it and turned it over. Dark trousers and a thick jersey of black wool enclosed the legs and body. I was prepared for it but the face gave me a shock; the same leering yellow monstrosity I had glimpsed earlier.

It was not until Pons had leaned forward to rip it from the features that I saw it was knitted yellow wool, embellished with details taken from a carnival mask similar to those I had seen at the shop in Tidewater. I gasped as the blue, cyanosed face came into view.

"Dr Sherlock! It seems impossible, Pons."

Solar Pons shook his head.

"There is your phantom, Parker. When a medical man goes wrong he can go very wrong indeed. But I fear from the rictus and the set of the features that he is beyond human justice."

I swiftly felt the region of the heart and then the pulse.

"You are right, Pons. It appears to me as though he has suffered a fatal heart seizure."

Solar Pons smiled grimly as he stood up. He held a gleaming silver gun in his hand.

"Young Mackney's air pistol if I am not much mistaken. The biter bit, Parker. Ironic, is it not, in view of his findings on young Balfour's uncle?"

He glanced round swiftly.

"There is no time for explanations now. We must get back to Bredewell House and then telephone Inspector Cunliffe. This matter must be handled discreetly and there has been sensation enough for one night."

11

"Yes Mrs Bracegirdle, I will have another cup of coffee, thank you."

Solar Pons chuckled and looked bright-eyed round the room. Michael Balfour sat opposite us at the circular table with Inspector Cunliffe next to him. I sat on Pons' right and at our insistence Mrs Bracegirdle sat between my companion and her employer, where she presided at the coffee pot. A week had passed since the terrifying events of the night on which Sherlock met his death and much had happened since. Young Balfour passed a hand through his rumpled hair.

"Even now, Mr Pons, though much has been explained I am still not certain why Dr Sherlock would want to murder his best friend and then make an attempt on my own life."

The Adventure of the Phantom Face

"Human nature is dark and mysterious," said Pons. "Events may turn the strongest brain and Dr Sherlock was desperately short of money."

"That is true, Mr Pons," said Inspector Cunliffe. "Our investigations have shown that Sherlock had speculated unwisely. He lost not only his own money but that of his partners in his previous practice and he left under a cloud."

Solar Pons nodded.

"Which is why he came to Tidewater. I should guess that racing was his real downfall."

Inspector Cunliffe looked sharply at Pons.

"That is correct enough, Mr Pons. He was in for thousands and was desperate for money."

"I cannot see, Pons . . ." I began, when my companion gave a short laugh.

"It was merely an inspired guess, Parker. When we met Dr Sherlock at the station that night, he carried some books as well as the medical report. I noticed that one of them was Ruff's Guide to the Turf. When I learned from Mrs Mackney that Sherlock's waiting room was filled with sporting and racing magazines I must confess my mind was turned to that direction."

Pons leaned forward at the table, the library fire on this bitter evening casting strange shadows over his lean, ascetic features.

"Let us just recapitulate, Parker, if you would be so good."

"Well, Pons," said I. "We had a rather strange old man, who was abnormally reclusive and worried; who literally bolted himself into his house after receiving threats. He dies after seeing a horrible face which had been haunting the neighbourhood; and his nephew, Mr Balfour here, who asks your help, is the heir to Mr Boldigrew's considerable fortune."

"Exactly, Parker. Most succinctly put. I could not have paraphrased it better. It became obvious to me that this was no random haunting of the village; neither was it a joke or even less a genuine phantom. It was clear from early on that Mr Boldigrew was literally scared to death, which left Mr Balfour as the only person between the murderer and a considerable fortune. You may remember, Parker, I was particularly careful to enquire into the circumstances of the other so-called 'hauntings' in the village."

"Why was that, Pons?"

"Because a brief analysis of the circumstances in each case revealed that the phantom was seen only through glass and that all the people who saw it were getting on in life."

"I am afraid I do not see the significance, Pons."

"That is because you are not using your ratiocinative powers, my dear fellow. The phantom appeared only outside windows and in the dark and then only very briefly because the hoax would have been obvious without these aids to flight. Similarly the people to whom Sherlock appeared in his disguise were elderly and either too terrified or simply not physically capable of running after him quickly. He needed time and distance to get away. The point being, of course, to establish that there was a ghost in Tidewater, before he struck at Boldigrew."

"But why not strike at my uncle first, Mr Pons?" said young Balfour, bewilderment on his features.

Solar Pons gently shook his head.

"That would not have done at all, Mr Balfour. It would immediately have thrown a spotlight on the solitary crime. Sherlock wanted to avoid this at all costs. Firstly, by establishing a veritable reign of terror in the neighbourhood. Then, when your uncle died of a heart attack after seeing the face, it would be one of a series of unconnected incidents. The last thing Sherlock wanted was to emphasise the aspect of the will."

Balfour turned worried eyes upon each of us in turn.

"I am still not sure that I understand, Mr Pons. Surely Sherlock could not go openly to the shop in the village and buy such things as carnival masks."

"Naturally not, Mr Balfour. That was where his waiting room came in so useful. His patients naturally included young children from time to time. With the craze for carnival masks and other toys in the district, they sometimes brought such items with them to his surgery. We can now never know for certain, Sherlock being dead, but it is obvious that both the carnival mask and air-pistol were abstracted from the waiting room when the young Mackney boy visited there as a patient. His mother told me the circumstances, which was when I found my thoughts on the matter becoming crystallised."

Solar Pons turned to me.

"You will remember, Parker, that the shopkeeper was at some pains to demonstrate that the green carnival masks were flimsy and did not last. In other words, they tore easily and this Sherlock soon found; having used it on several occasions to spread alarm in the neighbourhood it became worn so he undoubtedly destroyed it. You may remember, Parker, that I drew your attention to the significance of the shopkeeper, McMurdo, running out of the green masks. So Sherlock obviously had to improvise his own."

"Which accounts for the fiend with the yellow face appearing, Pons!"

My companion turned to me with a reproving look.

"Somewhat picturesquely put, Parker, but basically correct. Sherlock then constructed his own mask, as we have seen. The stage was now set for the murder of your uncle, Mr Balfour, who incidentally had nothing wrong with his heart at all."

"Nothing wrong, Pons?"

Solar Pons shook his head.

"The exhumation of Mr Boldigrew's body and the subsequent post-mortem by the County Pathologist, has established that conclusively. It was a fiction conveniently fostered by Dr Sherlock for reasons of his own."

Balfour passed his hand across his eyes.

"Then Uncle Charles did not die of a heart attack brought on by fright, Mr Pons?"

"Of course not, Mr Balfour. Naturally, no-one was to know this at the time as Dr Sherlock himself performed the original post-mortem and signed the papers so there was no reason to suspect him."

"And when did you suspect him, Pons?"

Solar Pons turned shrewd eyes to me, ejecting a thin plume of fragrant blue smoke from his pipe. He looked at Mrs Bracegirdle thoughtfully.

"The very evening we reached here, Parker. I felt that the doctor arrived a little too pat upon the scene. He played his part superlatively well, so that I could not be sure, but with my arrival in Tidewater he needed to know exactly what was going on; what my client suspected; and he required to be on the spot himself to obtain his information at first-hand."

"He did not get very much, Pons," I interjected. "But if Mr Boldigrew was murdered, Pons, then how on earth was it done?"

"By a very simple but at the same time very clever plan, Parker. You may remember that the young Mackney boy also missed one of his favourite toys, an air pistol, shortly before Mr Boldigrew was murdered. This was one of the last pieces I needed to make the whole scheme clear in my mind. You will recall, Mr Balfour, that I was particularly interested in Mr Boldigrew's rather strange custom of securing his house from intruders but himself going to the window at night and opening it when particular friends called and tapped upon the glass. It is now obvious that the ruin of the Indian venture and the loss to his partner preyed on his mind and Sherlock took advantage of that, even to the extent of sending him threatening letters."

"The threatening letters, which Sherlock undoubtedly cunningly timed, had a cumulative effect upon poor Boldigrew. They not only added to his remorse over the suicide of the Indian partner but turned him into a grim, frightened recluse who transformed his house into an almost impenetrable fortress. But, with the strange aberrations to which human nature is vulnerable, he left a loophole which Sherlock immediately seized upon."

"His odd habit of opening his study window to callers, Pons."

"Exactly, Parker. I will refer to the window again in a moment but something immediately struck me about the situation. You will recall, Parker, that I told you that the figure of the apparition could be seen only through the central pane of the turret window. If the figure had appeared at the side windows it would have been obliterated by the reflection of the room lights on the glass. That was of the utmost significance."

"Significance, Pons?"

"Of course, Parker. It told me at once that the 'phantom' could only have been someone who was familiar with the room; in other words, someone who had already been inside the house. That narrowed down the possibilities considerably."

"Brilliant, Mr Pons," said Balfour, open admiration on this face.

My companion shook his head.

"Elementary to a trained investigator, Mr Balfour. To return to the window. This seemed to me to be the crux of the matter and I soon discovered a number of very interesting points. One was the patent window lock and the fact that the window glass itself intervened between the murderer and his victim. I came to the following conclusion and though it is not now provable I am convinced it is the true explanation. The night of your uncle's death Sherlock came here in his motor vehicle and left it on the remote road beyond the farm. It was a bitterly cold night and there would have been no-one about.

He wore the same costume as on the night of his death, carrying the mask in his pocket. He saw the light in your uncle's study and tapped on the glass."

"Your uncle drew back the curtains, opened the window and spoke to the doctor. On some pretext Sherlock withdrew into the darkness, donned the mask and came back into the light to fire the air pistol that originally belonged to the Mackney boy."

Pons turned to Inspector Cunliffe.

"As we have already seen, Inspector, Sherlock had adapted the weapon to fire sharpened darts; small pieces of wood like splinters which were coated in a substance which rendered the victim unconscious in a short space of time. He then drew the window down, automatically locking it."

"I got on to this only through Mrs Bracegirdle mentioning that her employer had a cut upon his neck. I instantly surmised it to be a small wound or puncture, and the idea of a dart came into my mind. Sherlock removed it on arrival, of course."

Pons turned to the housekeeper.

"I am not, of course, blaming Mrs Bracegirdle for this but her cleaning the wound immediately erased my initial suspicions of Sherlock as my mind was already in that direction and I wondered why he would not have reported such a puncture. Of course, I had already established that the window could be closed and locked noiselessly and the same was obviously true from outside the house. Sherlock had time to draw the window down and automatically lock it before the nephew ran in."

"I see, Pons!" I interjected. "He got in his car and quickly drove home, only to be summoned back to Bredewell House."

"Exactly, Parker. Then, with great cold-bloodedness, he sent Mrs Bracegirdle and Mr Balfour out of the room while he supposedly revived the dying man, only to give him a lethal injection."

"There is no doubt about that," said Inspector Cunliffe. "The County Analyst tells me that there was a quantity of a deadly poison found in the remains, which had undoubtedly been administered intravenously."

Mrs Bracegirdle had listened with an ashen face and now she turned toward Pons, her eyes seeking his face.

"But what was the point of all this, Mr Pons?"

"You forget that Dr Sherlock was Mr Boldigrew's oldest friend. Greed and desperation had distorted his nature. It is as clear as day. The doctor was the chief beneficiary of the will in the event of Mr Balfour's demise. No doubt he had played on Mr Boldigrew's fears over the past few years by saying he had heart disease and had gained an ascendancy over him."

Young Balfour shuddered.

"It is absolutely horrible, Mr Pons. I would have rather given up the money than have all this happen."

My companion shook his head.

"Your sentiments do you credit, Mr Balfour, but we must take the world as we find it. It is a very imperfect one."

"And poor Mr Sainsbury?" put in Mrs Bracegirdle.

"Murdered by Sherlock because he alone knew that the doctor was the beneficiary of the will," said Pons. "It was obvious that he wished to tell me something but that the doctor, guessing what was in the wind, found him alone in his office, knocked him on the head and set the place on fire."

The Inspector nodded grimly.

"The Sainsbury post-mortem has established skull damage, despite the heat of the fire. Sainsbury's secretary has told us Sherlock had an appointment with him earlier that morning, though she did not see him at the office."

"Of course," went on Solar Pons, "the fact that Sherlock was the ultimate beneficiary in the event of Mr Balfour's death would have come out eventually. But as you know, if Mr Balfour had been murdered in the same way as his uncle the will would not have been published for a year or so, as is the normal custom. It is my belief that Sherlock would have been agreeably surprised at the news and as Sainsbury was safely out of the way and the copies of the will in his office destroyed, there would have been no-one to suspect him."

"It was a good thing you put me on to Somerset House, Mr Pons," said Inspector Cunliffe.

Mrs Bracegirdle turned a worried face to Pons.

"I am afraid I have misled you, Mr Pons, with my suspicions regarding Mr Ram Dass. I am so ashamed now."

Solar Pons chuckled.

"It was a natural assumption to make, Mrs Bracegirdle. But one completely unsupported by the facts. It took only a brief interview with the gentleman concerned to eliminate him entirely from my inquiries."

"Why was that, Pons? He looked extremely suspicious to me."

"That is because you were entirely superficial in your approach, Parker."

I must have looked nonplussed because my companion smiled winningly.

"Oh, come, Parker, it is not so very difficult, Mr Dass was a rather strange, colourful character in the district. Sherlock evidently banked on him being a prime suspect if murder was ever suspected, as he and the Boldigrew estate had already had a boundary dispute. I largely discounted this possibility even before we visited Mr Dass but I had to eliminate him from our inquiries. What possible motive could he have had? Money is one of the most powerful motives known to mankind. Yet Dass could not possibly benefit by Boldigrew's death. And people rarely murder over relatively trivial boundary disputes and as I had already learned that the two men had had no personal contact in the matter I swiftly put the possibility from my mind."

Solar Pons turned back to the Inspector.

"We had already established that Dass had nothing to do with the man who lost money in the Indian speculation, so I had to turn elsewhere for my culprit. Dr Sherlock was the only man who was in a position to pull the strings in the case; he was Boldigrew's oldest friend and knew most about him; he had performed the post-mortem; and, most importantly, he had the opportunity to purloin both the mask and the air-pistol from his own waiting room as my interview with Mrs Mackney made clear. The only thing missing was the motive and I saw my way to that with the death of Sainsbury, a check with Somerset House revealing the identity of the beneficiary."

"It was a clever plot," Inspector Cunliffe observed. "The air pistol had been cunningly adapted to fire the darts."

Solar Pons fixed his deep-set eyes upon his client.

"I am only sorry I had to use you as a tethered-goat in the outcome, Mr Balfour. My case rested upon pure theory and needed the corroborative factor that only the circumstance of catching the culprit in the act could give."

"But supposing the dart had been discovered?" I said. "Or it had fallen to the carpet? Surely the police might have suspected Sherlock."

Solar Pons shook his head.

"Hardly the police doctor, Parker. He had Ram Dass picked out as a ready suspect for that. As we know, he was not liked in the neighbourhood and you yourself drew attention to the blow-pipes and other weapons on his walls."

"But I am still puzzled about one or two things."

"For example?"

"The appearance of the apparition to Stevens, the gardener."

"That was entirely fortuitous, Parker. Sherlock was obviously on his way to make an attempt on Boldigrew's life but his accidental encounter with the old man frightened him. In the event he did not make his second, and fatal attempt, until the following week."

"But why did he appear in that strange way to Mr Balfour, on the first occasion, Pons?"

Solar Pons smiled wryly.

"Ah, that can only be conjecture now, Parker. He would not have been attempting to frighten Mr Balfour. He had already established his reign of terror and after his mishap with Stevens he had become more cautious. It is my contention that he was merely peering into the room, trying to make sure whether Mr Balfour was alone and carrying on with his uncle's habits. I understand from Mrs Bracegirdle that the elder man's eyesight was not so good. At any event Mr Balfour immediately spotted him and frightened him off, thereby saving his own life, for the upshot was that he came to us."

"But why was he wearing that horrific mask, Pons?"

"For the simple reason, my dear fellow, that it would disguise him. He could not simply appear at the study window in his own persona at that stage. But as soon as we appeared on the scene he realised he had to act quickly."

"That still does not explain why he tapped on the window that last time, Pons. He could not be sure that Mr Balfour would behave in the same manner as his uncle."

"That is undoubtedly true, Parker. But no-one would be afraid of Dr Sherlock. This he banked on."

Young Balfour smiled grimly.

"That is perfectly correct, doctor. When he tapped at the window he wore no mask. I was surprised to see him there but not at all suspicious. I thought perhaps you had sent a message by him. It was only when he disappeared while I was raising the window that the truth dawned upon me. Then Dr Parker's shot sounded."

"I must apologise to Dr Parker for our little deception, but he is so transparently honest and secrecy as to our true intentions was so essential that I did not take him into my confidence."

"Which is why you put it about that you were leaving Tidewater," said Balfour. "I understand now. But I was in no danger, Mr Pons. I followed your instructions implicitly. Though shocked and appalled by the sight of that dreadful face I realised you would not be far away. I was already ducking and closing the window as he raised the pistol."

"Nevertheless, Pons," I said. "Mr Balfour showed considerable courage. And you have brilliantly handled the case."

Solar Pons shook his head.

"I fear it will not go down in your annals as one of my more sparkling efforts, Parker. The affair has been conducted in a mental as well as physical fog."

"Nobody in this room but yourself would agree, Mr Pons," said young Balfour with an open smile.

"It has been a lesson, Mr Pons," said Inspector Cunliffe. "An honour to work with you, sir."

He shifted awkwardly and cleared his throat.

"I have no doubt that your reconstruction of events is substantially correct, Mr Pons. We have already found damning evidence at Dr Sherlock's home. The remains of a green carnival mask in a locked cupboard; more of those darts for the air-pistol; and a certified copy of Mr Boldigrew's will, discovered only this morning, and which corroborates our own information from Somerset House. I have seldom met a more fiendish set of circumstances involving murder. And in the end suicide was the only way out."

"You may well say so," said Pons grimly. "And it is to your own credit that you stayed on the spot, when less keen-witted officers would have returned to Colchester. Which is no doubt why you had Mr Boldigrew's inquest adjourned without a verdict being returned. Both Parker and I were puzzled why no cause of death was given. You immediately seized on the salient points; realised that the set of events involving the so-called phantom face had significance far beyond their surface appearance; and waited for further developments. Instinct is a major factor in the process of crime detection, my dear Inspector, and you have it in high degree."

Inspector Cunliffe flushed with pleasure.

"It is very kind of you to say so, Mr Pons. A word from you to that effect in the ear of my superiors would not come amiss."

"You may rely upon it," said Solar Pons gravely.

Then, turning to me, "If you would be so kind as to pass me the sugar, my dear Parker, we must see about getting back to London. Without disrespect to our host I think we have both had enough of Essex for the time being."

And he drank his coffee with great contentment.

DEATH AT THE METROPOLE

1

"A FINE MORNING, Parker!"

My friend Solar Pons walked into our cosy sitting-room at 7B Praed Street early one day in April to find me already at breakfast. It was indeed a fine morning and the sun was so warm and shining so brightly that I had been lulled into thinking it summer, even to the extent of slightly raising our sitting-room windows to allow the air to penetrate.

I gave him a piercing glance.

"You look as if you have been up all night, Pons."

"I have indeed, Parker. A somewhat wearying affair down Greenwich way but I think I have brought it to a successful conclusion."

"I am glad to hear you say so, Pons. I will just ring for Mrs Johnson and ask her to bring you some eggs and bacon."

"Pray do not put yourself out, Parker. I have already seen our amiable landlady on my way in and she has my requirements in hand."

I sank back into my chair again and reached for the silver-plated coffee-pot.

"You have had a disturbed night yourself, I see."

"Eigh?"

I looked at Pons, somewhat startled.

"You were called out and returned only within the hour."

I turned astonished eyes to the smiling face of my companion.

"How can you possibly know that, Pons, unless you saw me come in?"

My companion shook his head.

"It is not so very difficult to deduce, Parker. When I see a meticulous gentleman of sober habit sitting at breakfast unshaven, yet fully dressed but with his tie tied lining outwards and quite awry, the chain of events becomes obvious. Ergo, you were called in the middle of the night, rose hastily, dressed with extreme speed and went out. When you came back it was too late to go to bed. You have not yet shaved but sat down straight away to breakfast. Therefore, you have returned within the hour."

"Accurate in every detail, Pons," said I. "As always the matter is simple once you have pointed it out. I was called at three. It was old Mr Stedman. He had another heart attack. I dealt with him, called an ambulance from a public phone box, got him into hospital, saw the crisis past and have returned here within the past half-hour."

Solar Pons chuckled, sinking down in the chair opposite me.

"Admirable, my dear fellow. I fancy we have both been assisting our fellow man, each in his own way, during the past night. Ah, here is Mrs Johnson!"

The bright, well-scrubbed features of our good-natured landlady were now visible in the open door. She was bearing a tray of covered dishes which gave off an agreeable aroma.

"There we are, gentlemen! You look as if you could both do with a good meal and a long sleep."

"I am already enjoying a good meal, Mrs Johnson," I replied. "I shall make up for the sleep tonight."

Mrs Johnson smiled warmly, turning a twinkling eye on each of us in turn.

"If I did not point out these things, gentlemen, I don't know what would happen to the both of you."

"I dare say you are right, Mrs Johnson," said Pons equably. "For you certainly look after us incomparably."

After setting out Pons' breakfast our amiable hostess had gone over toward the window to place the tray on a table there when she gave a sudden exclamation.

"Well I never!"

"What is it, Mrs Johnson?"

Pons was at her side in a moment.

"Down there, Mr Pons. I have never seen an old fellow behave in such an odd way."

"Yes, he does look rather peculiar, Mrs Johnson," said Pons casually, turning his eyes down toward the street.

"I presume you are referring to the retired Willesden plumber with the glass eye who now runs messages for the Metropole Hotel in the Strand."

"Mr Pons!"

Mrs Johnson stared at my companion awestruck.

"How could you possibly know that, Pons?" I exclaimed.

Solar Pons burst out in an explosion of laughter.

"I am just having my little joke, Parker. I am sure Mrs Johnson will forgive me. You are incorrect in saying I could not have known it. I could not have deduced it, certainly."

I stared at Pons with mounting bewilderment.

"Then you know the man, Pons?"

"Of course, Parker! He is a retired plumber from Willesden who is now working as a porter at the Metropole. I recognised the uniform immediately. I did not know he had a glass eye but from the way he keeps bumping into people in the street and swivelling his head to the right I would certainly say that he either has lost the sight of that eye or has a glass one, which comes to the same thing."

Mrs Johnson was all smiles now.

"Really, Mr Pons," she said in mock-reproof.

"Even I must indulge my sense of humour at times, Mrs Johnson," he said abstractedly. "Meakins is certainly behaving strangely. He is hatless, agitated and careless of where he is going. But he is almost certainly coming here."

A few moments later there was a furious tattoo upon the front door-knocker, followed by several peals at the bell. Mrs Johnson was already on her way downstairs. A short while later she ushered in the old man who had been the subject of so much speculation from our window. He was indeed a pitiable sight, dishevelled and out of breath, his white hair fallen over his eyes, his dark blue uniform only half-buttoned. He peered about him uncertainly as he came into the room.

"I am sorry to intrude in such a manner, gentlemen. Mr Pons? Mr Solar Pons?"

"Come in and sit yourself down, Meakins," said Pons with a kindly smile. "It is obviously something of importance which brings you in such haste from the Metropole this morning."

"Ah, you know me, Mr Pons?"

"Indeed, you are a most distinctive figure. An old soldier, I see."

Meakins, who was just sinking gingerly into one of our easy chairs looked at Pons with amazement.

"Why, yes, sir. Though how you could possibly . . ."

"Tut, man, it is elementary," said my companion briskly. "Your bearing, the way you carry yourself in that uniform. Not to mention the wound ribbon which I perceive upon your breast there."

Meakins gave a weak smile and assented gratefully as I pressed a cup of coffee upon him as we continued with our breakfast. Mrs Johnson quitted the room as soon as she saw we had everything we required and I now had time to study our strange visitor.

He had a gaunt, rugged face in which deep lines, either of suffering or caused by some disease, ran from his nose down to the corners of his mouth. As Pons had surmised, he had something wrong with his right eye for the eyelid was all puckered down over what I suspected to be an empty socket. He evidently was aware of my scrutiny for while he was regaining his breath he shifted uneasily in his chair and looked at me with the faded blue of his good left eye.

"Though I was well over-age for the Army, I lost my eye at Ypres, doctor," he said quietly. "It is a poor substitute but I wear the ribbon just the same."

"Quite right," I said stoutly. "It was bravely earned, Meakins."

The old man smiled ironically and looked across at Solar Pons.

"I shouldn't really be sitting here, gentlemen. The manager, Mr Hibbert, asked me to bring you to the Metropole at once, Mr Pons."

Solar Pons glanced at him sharply with his deep-set eyes.

"It is a grave matter, then."

The old soldier nodded seriously, his one eye wide and staring.

"Nothing less than horrible, cold-blooded murder, Mr Pons!"

2

"Good gracious!" I said in the heavy silence which followed. My companion was already on his feet.

"Of course, I shall come at once. Though why Mr Hibbert did not telephone. . . ."

The messenger shook his head.

"It was quite impossible, Mr Pons. Mr Hibbert himself is under arrest and forbidden all communication at the moment. But he managed to whisper to me and I came straight away."

"Most singular," Pons muttered to me and then turned back to Meakins.

"Very well. I think we had best take a cab to avoid wasting further time. Fortunately, Parker, we had almost finished breakfast. Can you spare an hour or two?"

"Indeed, Pons," I mumbled, swallowing the last of my coffee. "It is my rest day today."

"That is settled, then. I think we had best hear the remainder of the story as we go along."

"If you would just give me a few minutes to wash and shave, Pons," I protested.

My companion smiled thinly.

"Of course, Parker. I think we can spare ten minutes for that useful purpose. The Metropole is a high-class establishment and we would not wish to cause a sensation on our entrance."

The old man smiled, despite the worried look on his face.

"Oh, I do not think you need worry about that, gentlemen, in view of what has happened during the night," he said.

Pons resumed his place at the table to finish his interrupted meal while I hurriedly made my toilet. A little more presentable, I soon regained the sitting-room to find Mrs Johnson clearing the table and Pons ready for our unexpected outing.

As we jolted in the cab on our way to the Strand, Meakins slumped in the corner and Pons sitting silently opposite me, smoke curling from his pipe, the old man seemed a little calmer.

"It was a gentleman who came to the hotel last night, Mr Pons. A tall, strange gentleman, with a heavy beard, dark glasses and expensive-looking clothes. It is beautiful weather, as you can see, sir, but he was all muffled up in an overcoat and scarf."

Solar Pons shot me a sardonic look.

"What do you make of that, Parker?"

I shook my head.

"You are not catching me out this time, Pons. Either he had just returned from the tropics or he wanted to avoid recognition."

"Excellent, Parker!" said Pons, tightening his strong teeth on the stem of his pipe. "You are as sharp as a razor this morning."

"I do not understand, doctor," said the old messenger, bewilderment on his honest face.

"If he had returned from the tropics he most probably had thin blood and would have felt the weather here to be cold, however much it appears warm to us."

"It is more likely to be the latter," interjected Pons crisply. "In view of the outcome. Pray continue, Meakins."

"Well, sir, he registered in the name of Mr Otto Voss of Hamburg. There were few people about when he came in some time after ten o'clock, and I was on duty in the lobby. We are rather short-staffed at the moment, so after he had registered, I carried his attaché-case up to his room, No 31. He had only the one valise, which was extremely heavy, and the small attaché-case."

"Hmm. Did you notice anything else about him?"

"He kept his glasses on and his overcoat while I was in the room and he seemed anxious for me to be gone. He had not taken his eyes off the valise all the while I was with him and when I went to put it on the rack, he darted at it and took it from me as though he was afraid I was going to drop it."

"Curious, Pons," I said.

"Indeed, Parker," returned my companion drily. "You have no doubt read something of significance into that factor."

"Undoubtedly," said I, entering into the spirit of his banter. "The ratiocinative process is a complex one but I think I may agree with you there."

Pons said nothing but little flecks of humour were dancing in his eyes as we turned down Haymarket and then left into Trafalgar Square. The pompous bulk of the National Gallery had slid by before he again broke silence.

"There is more to come, surely, Meakins?"

"By all means. I am so knocked out by this business that I have difficulty in collecting my thoughts."

We were now in the thick of the traffic joining the Strand from the forecourt of Charing Cross Station and our driver had some difficulty in turning across the flow into a narrow street running down toward the river. He stopped in front of the Metropole, a small hotel of the better sort, whose façade and appointments had an air of faded elegance. The driver cut off his engine and waited patiently until Pons' interrogation of Meakins should be completed.

"Well, sir, Mr Voss tipped me half a crown and I left him. About an hour later he rang for room service. There was no-one else about so I went to the kitchen myself and took him up a ham sandwich and a cup of coffee. He thanked me and tipped me a pound, which I thought was extremely generous of the gentleman."

"How did he seem?"

"Worried, Mr Pons. He kept glancing round the room as though frightened of something. He had the curtains tightly drawn and the window closed, though it was a beautiful warm evening."

"How did you know that?"

"The gentleman's coat had been thrown on the bed and had fallen to the floor, Mr Pons. I bent to pick it up and accidentally brushed against the curtains on that side of the bed."

"I see. Continue."

"He was wearing a thick tweed suit, Mr Pons, but still kept his glasses and the hat on."

"That is extremely curious, Parker. It suggests he did not wish his identity known."

"I follow you, Pons."

"He said nothing to you, Meakins?"

"Nothing, Mr Pons, beyond his plain 'yes' and 'no' and 'thank you' when I left."

"And his voice?"

"Very strong and powerful, Mr Pons. He spoke good English but with a heavy German accent."

"You are familiar with the German accent, of course?"

"Yes, Mr Pons. From the war. I was a guard at a prisoner-of-war camp for some time, after my wound."

"I see. And this Mr Voss has died during the night from what you tell us."

Meakins swallowed and nodded. He seemed having difficulty in articulating his words.

"Yes, Mr Pons. No-one saw him after I took him the sandwich. He was not seen this morning and after the maid had reported being unable to get into his room, the manager, Mr Hibbert took the pass-key and himself went to No 31."

"By himself?"

"By himself, Mr Pons. He came back in about twenty minutes as white as a sheet. Mr Voss was lying on his bed, strangled, Mr Pons!"

We were both silent for a moment. Pons looked absently at the faded elegance of the Metropole façade a few paces away across the pavement.

"And now Mr Hibbert has been arrested, you say?"

"Yes, Mr Pons. You see, gentlemen, the room was locked, the key was on the table and there was no other but the pass-key at the desk. So Inspector Jamison has arrested the manager . . ."

"Really."

To Meakins' evident surprise Solar Pons gave a deep chuckle and got out of the cab with astonishing alacrity. I paid the driver and joined him at the hotel entrance.

"So friend Jamison has done it again, Pons."

"It would appear so, Parker. In my experience hotel managers do not go about strangling their guests. What possible motive could the man have?"

"True, Pons," I said.

We followed Meakins over toward the Metropole entrance, pushing through the swing doors into the gold and purple interior. The old messenger led us away from the main vestibule and down a narrow corridor floored in faded red carpeting. He tapped discreetly on a door which bore the legend: MANAGER. PRIVATE in gold-painted letters. He held the door aside for us.

"Mr Pons and Dr Parker, Mr Hibbert."

I followed Pons in and Meakins came behind us to stand in front of the door as though determined to do his duty to the last. There were three men in the room; a large man with glossy black hair, dressed in civilian clothes, who was slumped in a chair behind his desk; a uniformed constable who stood guard at one side of the room; and our old acquaintance Inspector Jamison of Scotland Yard. He bristled like a terrier as soon as we had entered.

"Ah, Mr Pons! You'll not find much to engage your talents here, I'll be bound."

"We shall see, Jamison, we shall see," said Solar Pons languidly, striding past the Scotland Yard man and extending his hand to the manager.

"Now, Mr Hibbert, friend Meakins yonder tells me you are in some sort of trouble."

"It was good of you to come, Mr Pons," groaned Hibbert, a worried expression on his face. "I am accused of murder by the Inspector here. The very idea is preposterous but I must admit that the circumstances are difficult, very difficult indeed."

"You may well say so," put in Jamison acidly. "An open and shut case, Mr Pons. The room was locked and Mr Hibbert was the only person who went there; the only person who had access. The only other key to the room was upon the table."

"So I understand," said Solar Pons. "Nevertheless I would prefer to hear Mr Hibbert's story and then examine the circumstances for myself."

"I would be so grateful, Mr Pons," put in Hibbert. "If you have no objection, Inspector, I would like Meakins to order me some breakfast for I have had nothing since this terrible business began."

"By all means," said Inspector Jamison, his entire persona exuding smugness. "My constable will take the message for I have not finished interrogating Meakins yet."

"Oblige me by examining Mr Hibbert's hands, if you would be so good, Parker," said Solar Pons carelessly.

Jamison stared at Pons in amazement as I bent toward the manager.

"What am I looking for, Pons?"

"When a man is strangled, Parker, particularly if the victim is a strong, vigorous man in the prime of life, he will struggle violently. During that struggle, even if he be half-asleep as this man may have been, he might well bite his assailant on the hands and would most certainly scratch him in his attempts to dislodge the grip. In addition, there are almost always traces of flesh left beneath the murderer's finger-nails."

"I see, Pons."

Mr Hibbert was smiling and relaxed now. He put out his well-manicured hands for me to examine readily. I turned them over and subjected them to an intense scrutiny, looking for the details Pons had suggested.

"There is nothing, Pons," I said eventually. "Mr Hibbert's hands bear no traces of scratching, bruising or bites and there is certainly no extraneous tissue beneath the nails."

"Thank you, Parker," said Solar Pons crisply. "I should have been most surprised if there had been. The whole idea is preposterous. If I were you, Jamison, I would drop this business immediately. The hotel group might well sue you for defamation of character."

The Inspector's complexion went brick-red and he shifted uneasily, clasping his big hands in vexation.

"Ridiculous, Mr Pons!" he said hoarsely. "Mr Hibbert was the only person in the room; the only other key was upon the table and no-one else had visited Mr Voss this morning."

"We shall not know what has happened until we have made a thorough examination of the room and the body, Jamison," said Solar Pons, his voice bleak and his thin, wiry frame quivering with suppressed energy.

"I leave my suggestion with you for what it is worth, and I am sure you will see the sense of it. Now, Mr Hibbert, if you would be so good I should like to see the room in which Mr Voss met his lonely death. Come, Parker."

He led the way from the office at a brisk pace, leaving the Inspector standing nonplussed. My companion chuckled quietly to himself as Hibbert guided us up a thickly carpeted staircase to the second floor of the hotel.

"I fancy that will give Jamison something to think about, Parker."

I smiled.

"No doubt, Pons. The Inspector is given to rather fanciful theories I must confess."

Solar Pons shot me a shrewd glance.

"Ah, then you have seen the significance of my observations, Parker."

"I hope so, Pons," I replied guardedly.

I was spared further questions by our guide stopping in front of a polished rosewood door halfway along the discreetly luxurious corridor of the hotel, which had evidently been built in the high-tide of Edwardian opulence. But now the whole place bore a hushed and sad air; it was not only a nostalgic atmosphere of faded splendour but the ugly fact of violent death behind the façade, which I have often observed when working with Pons on his more lethal cases.

Room 31, into which we were ushered by Hibbert had the same passé elegance we had both observed elsewhere in the hotel. But we had no time for such details for all eyes were drawn inexorably to the stiffened figure which lay on the bed before us. It was clad in dressing gown and pyjamas and the disarrangement of the clothing was, the manager assured us, the result of the police surgeon's preliminary examination.

"If you would be so good, Parker," said Solar Pons softly.

He went to stand quietly at the foot of the bed alongside the manager but I was conscious, as ever, that his keen eyes were stabbing into the farthest recesses of the room.

The dead man was a strong and well-built specimen of about thirty-five or forty years. He had a heavy black beard which bristled at the ceiling as his head was drawn back in his death-agony. The features were blue and cyanosed, the tongue protruding from the parted lips like some vile and bloated sac that was on the point of bursting.

There were the heavy and classic indentations of thumbs and fingers on the throat and windpipe that follow in every instance of manual strangulation and it did not take me long to form my opinion. The man's black hair was tumbled and awry across his forehead and the dark glasses that he had evidently worn had fallen to the floor of the room in his struggles. Pons grunted when I reported my brief diagnosis.

"Curious, Parker," he said broodingly, striding to the side of the bed and making his own inspection. He bent and examined the glasses.

"The police have been over the room, I take it?"

The manager nodded.

"Yes, Mr Pons. Two officers from the C.I.D. were here before Inspector Jamison. They were extremely careful and said they would leave everything *in situ.* The Inspector said a further examination would be made later and ordered me to seal the room. Then, some while afterwards, the Inspector told me that I would be arrested."

Solar Pons gave a thin smile.

"I do not think we need take that seriously for the moment, Mr Hibbert."

He turned back to me.

"Do you not find the circumstances curious, Parker?"

I glanced at him in some surprise.

"It appears to be a simple case of manual strangulation, Pons."

My companion shot me an impatient glance.

"No, Parker, I mean the matter of the glasses."

I followed his glance to the floor.

"I do not follow, Pons."

"No matter."

Pons turned again to the manager.

"How was Voss dressed when he arrived here, Mr Hibbert?"

"As to that, I cannot say, Mr Pons, as I was not in the lobby. But I understand from Meakins that he wore dark clothes; an overcoat and trilby hat; that dark suit on the chair there; and the dark glasses."

"I see."

Solar Pons pulled thoughtfully at the lobe of his right ear.

"The curious factor is why he would feel it necessary to wear dark glasses when he was alone in the room or even while in bed."

"Perhaps he had weak eyes, Pons," I suggested.

"Perhaps, Parker, perhaps," retorted Solar Pons absently.

He bent down and took out his magnifying lens from his inner pocket. He went carefully over the floor and the area round the bed while Hibbert and I stood in silence, watching my companion's quick, alert movements. Once again I marvelled at his precise, economical actions in which there was such energy and purpose; there was a master at work here even though most of his motives and conclusions were hidden from my mind. Then he moved over to the door, examining the floor carefully and working his way back over toward the bed.

He got up with a grunt of satisfaction and dusted his trousers.

I glanced at him quickly.

"You have found something, Pons?"

He nodded.

"Whether it is of importance we shall see later. Hotel bedrooms are to a large extent public rooms, of course, and many people pass through them even in the course of a single week."

He turned to Hibbert.

"I think we have seen everything relevant, Mr Hibbert. Come, Parker."

The manager passed a hand through his disordered hair.

"But what am I to do, Mr Pons?"

We waited in the corridor while he locked the door behind us. Solar Pons laughed shortly.

"Do, Mr Hibbert? Why, nothing. Leave things to me. I fancy it will not take long to convince friend Jamison of the ridiculousness of this charge he is attempting to bring."

The manager still looked unconvinced as he glanced to me.

"I think you will find things as Pons says," I told him. "It would not be the first time the Inspector has made a fool of himself."

"Come, Parker," said my companion, with a thin smile. "You are being rather hard on Jamison. He has his uses. And now, if you please, Mr Hibbert, I would like a word in private before we rejoin the Inspector."

3

Inspector Jamison was in an unpleasant temper when I rejoined him and Pons in the manager's office. Pons had gone in first and there had been a muffled conversation from behind the heavy door which continued for perhaps ten minutes. When I was eventually admitted to the room by Pons my friend was smiling with satisfaction and Jamison was standing by Hibbert's desk frowning heavily. He had a red face and a chastened air as my companion turned to him.

"And now, Inspector, I would be obliged if you would let me have a glimpse of Voss' effects. I presume your men have already removed them from the room for there was precious little there."

"They are in a cardboard box on the desk here," said Jamison ungraciously. "You are welcome to look through them though I can't see what help they will be. The man was Otto Voss all right. We have his passport there and a number of other documents. He lived in Hamburg."

"I see he brought some newspapers with him."

Pons' sharp eyes had already fastened on two journals in the heavy Gothic-style type affected by German books and periodicals. He picked up a copy of the *Hamburger Zeitung*.

"Rather curious, is it not?"

Jamison looked discomfited.

"I do not understand you, Mr Pons."

"Both newspapers are of the same date."

"Presumably he bought them both the same day. Nothing unusual in that."

There was a sarcastic edge to Jamison's voice which Pons ignored.

"Yes, man, but these are over three weeks old. That is surely significant. I commend that fact to your attention."

He went swiftly through the newspapers, to the Inspector's evident bewilderment. I must confess that I was equally puzzled but I kept my own counsel and silently watched as Pons went on, turning the pages of the journals with fingers as nervous and tensile as the antennae of an insect. He had a satisfied expression on his face as he put them down.

He next turned to the passport, then held it out for me to look at. I could see that the photograph indeed depicted the dead man in the room above. There was no mistaking the heavy beard, and the features despite the subtle change which death always brings with it.

"There is no doubt this passport is genuine, Pons?"

My companion was already holding it up to the light. He shook his head.

"I have made some little study of the textures of paper and the like, Parker. This would have to be the finest forgery in the world and I do not think the criminal fraternity has yet reached that degree of excellence. I would stake my reputation that this is a genuine document, issued in Hamburg. It should be easy enough to check in any event. No doubt friend Jamison has already put matters in hand."

"We are in touch with the Hamburg police," Jamison said ponderously.

I had taken the passport from Pons and studied it carefully.

"What does this long phrase mean, Pons? I cannot make it out."

Solar Pons shrugged carelessly, his eyes gleaming.

"It is his profession, Parker. He was an export official."

"I see."

I stared at my companion for a few moments.

"Is it of significance, Pons?"

Solar Pons pulled gently with delicate fingers at the lobe of his ear.

"It may be, Parker, it may be. I commend it to you."

Inspector Jamison had stood apart from us all this time, resentment burning in every facet of his stiff figure. His eyes had followed Pons' moves with curiosity but it was evident that he had read nothing from my friend's comments or actions during the past five minutes. The windows of the office were open and the noises of the muffled traffic from the Strand came to us, insubstantial and far off as a dream.

We were alone in the office with the Inspector for I understood that the manager was taking a belated breakfast in a corner of the main dining room though, idiotically to my way of thinking, under the close observation of Jamison's ubiquitous constable.

Solar Pons put down the documents at last.

"And now, I think, I would like a word with the young lady at the reception desk and a glance at the hotel register."

"By all means, Mr Pons."

Some of the redness had died away from the Scotland Yard man's neck and he seemed in a more placatory mood as he led the way along the corridor and down into the hotel's main reception area.

A tall, slim girl with fair hair was sitting at the desk and she readily handed over the register to Pons. He stood for a moment, running a thumb down the margin, a frown on his clear-minted, aquiline features.

"The study of hand-writing is a much neglected one, Parker," he observed. "Oh, I give you that there have been a number of studies by people who purport to be able to read character from hand-writing, but there is a good deal more to it than that."

"Indeed, Pons."

My friend smiled rather cynically and looked from Inspector Jamison to the girl behind the desk.

"Criminal tendencies are inclined to show up in hand-writing also. I must give the matter some attention in a monograph one of these days."

"I look forward to reading it, Pons," I observed.

My companion turned back to the book and examined it intently.

"Here we are. Voss registered correctly, in his own name and giving his correct residence, as you can see clearly."

To my astonishment, after looking at Voss' signature, he went back through the register, turning to the previous page. He had produced his powerful pocket lens and went carefully over the pages, lingering here and there, as though the signatures were some exotic botanical specimens. His eyes were gleaming as he put the lens back in its case and transferred it to his pocket.

"Interesting, Parker. As I said, I must give it some more considered study in printed form. Now, what is the young lady's name, Jamison?"

"Miss Anna Smithson," said the Inspector heavily.

"Now, Miss Smithson, would it be too much trouble for you to recall the events of last night?"

The young lady smiled, revealing perfect rows of teeth.

"I am afraid I cannot help you, Mr Pons. I go off at six o'clock each evening. You want Mr Lennard, who takes over the desk at night."

"I see. Would he be in the hotel?"

"I have had him recalled for purposes of questioning, Mr Pons," said Jamison stiffly. "I will have him fetched."

He went over to the dining room entrance and signalled to his constable. A minute or two later the officer returned with a thin, sallow man with silver hair cut en brosse. He wore a faded blue suit and somehow looked all of a part with the Metropole. His gold pince-nez hung by a frayed velvet ribbon from his lapel and he peered anxiously about him as the Inspector introduced Pons and myself.

"This gentlemen is Mr Solar Pons," Jamison began pompously. "He would like to ask you a few questions."

"Certainly, Mr Pons," said the silver-haired man, looking uncertainly about him and moving his hands together restlessly.

"I understand you came on duty last night at about six o'clock, Lennard."

"That is correct, sir. It was just five minutes to. I always believe in being prompt and punctual."

"An admirable trait," said Solar Pons smoothly. "Which extends apparently to even being before your time. Something that must have stood you in good stead in your previous occupation."

"Eigh?"

The night receptionist looked slightly discomfited and moved his feet uneasily on the carpeting. This, combined with the restless weaving motions of his hands suddenly made him look uncertain and unreliable.

"You have been a book-keeper unless I miss my guess," said my companion decisively. "Your desk was in front of a window and you sat at right angles to it. I would further infer that you have been employed by the Metropole Hotel for only a short time; say a fortnight at the outside."

"This is astonishing, Mr Pons!" burst out the man being interrogated, and though I was equally surprised I felt inwardly amused at the expression on the faces of Inspector Jamison and the young lady receptionist.

"Tut, man, it was obvious," said Solar Pons crisply. "The weather has been extraordinarily warm this spring. You exhibit a tan on the right hand side of your face only, the left being quite white and pallid. Therefore, in your normal occupation you sat in front of a window and as is well-known glass has the property of intensifying sunlight. I know of no other circumstance which would lead to such a construction. Your occupation here as night receptionist would not give rise to such a complexion, for we are under artificial light, a condition which must obtain at all times."

His eyes positively twinkled as he glanced at Jamison.

"Therefore, I postulate, Parker—though entirely at random—that Lennard here had been a book-keeper. He has a neat, bookish look; his right shoulder is slightly lower at the point where he leans forward to use his pen on the desk and his right sleeve there is well worn where he rests it on the wooden surface."

"Remarkable, Pons," I said warmly.

"It was self-evident, Parker."

"But how can you be so positive that Mr Lennard has been here only a short time?"

"The degree of tan in the complexion, Parker. If he had been employed by the hotel for much longer than a fortnight the tan on the right-hand side of his face would have faded. Therefore, he has been here only a short while."

Inspector Jamison cleared his throat with a harsh rasping noise.

"Very ingenious, Mr Pons," he said heavily. "And if I may say so . . ."

He was interrupted abruptly by Lennard who seized my companion effusively by the hand and pumped it up and down.

"Correct in every detail, Mr Pons! It is the most extraordinary thing I have ever heard. It is absolutely amazing. The firm failed just three weeks ago and I was lucky to find this berth at such short notice. Jobs are not easy to come by these days."

"That is perfectly true," said I. "Eh, Pons?"

"If you say so, Parker," said Solar Pons languidly, his eyes fixed somewhere up in a corner of the ceiling. "You are more in touch with the market place than I, old fellow."

His deep-set eyes were suddenly sharp and penetrating.

"Now, Lennard, let us just reconstruct the events of last night. You came on duty just before six. I want you to be absolutely precise and detailed as to the circumstances relating to the late Mr Voss."

Lennard moved his hands restlessly to and fro again.

"Well, Mr Pons, as near as I can recollect it was just a fraction after 10.15 P.M. when he came into the lobby."

I glanced at my companion.

"That tallies with what Meakins told us, Pons."

Solar Pons smiled thinly.

"It had not escaped my observation, Parker. Pray continue, Lennard."

"He was a tall, thick-bearded man with dark glasses. I was rather surprised when he kept the glasses on in the hotel and even more so to see that he was dressed in heavy clothes with a scarf on such an evening."

"Quite so. What about his voice?"

"Very guttural and hoarse, Mr Pons, as though he had a bad cold. He had a strong foreign accent but he didn't speak very much."

Pons nodded, his penetrating eyes fixed intently on the receptionist's face. The young lady had gone back to the desk at the insistent buzzing of the telephone and we now moved away down the foyer as a group of guests came in and demanded their keys.

"What happened next?"

"Nothing of any import, Mr Pons. The foreign gentleman registered as Mr Otto Voss of Hamburg, as you have already seen from the register. We are rather short-staffed as Meakins has probably told you and he himself carried the guest's attaché-case up. The gentleman carried up his valise himself. It was extremely heavy, I noticed."

"Indeed."

Solar Pons stood pulling thoughtfully at the lobe of his left ear, his eyes now fixed somewhere in space.

"What other luggage had he?"

"Nothing but the small attaché-case, Mr Pons. The last I saw of him he was walking up the stairs with Meakins in front of him."

"He did not use the lift?"

"I am afraid it was switched off at that time of the evening, Mr Pons."

My companion nodded.

"Now, I want you to think very carefully, Lennard. Your answer may be of vital importance. I want to know if you were away from the desk here at any time during the night."

A worried expression passed across the silver-haired man's face.

"I took a break for coffee and sandwiches from about half-past eleven to half-past twelve, Mr Pons. It is not exactly against the rules but the management frown on it, though they know we will not be in the lobby all evening. We can easily hear if a guest rings down or the telephone goes, for we have a large repeater bell which is easily audible in the kitchen area."

"I see. So you went to the kitchen for your meal and were away an hour?"

"That is so, Mr Pons."

"So that anyone could have come and gone from the hotel without your seeing or hearing them?"

Lennard turned puzzled eyes on to Solar Pons before glancing at the immobile figure of Jamison.

"I suppose so, Mr Pons, though I cannot see what . . ."

"That will be all, Lennard," said Pons crisply, a note of suppressed excitement in his voice. "You have given your account in an admirably detailed manner."

He rubbed his thin hands together briskly.

"I think we have done all we can here for the moment, Parker. Tell me, Lennard, before we part, is Mr Esau Thornton of Banstead, Surrey, still in the hotel?"

"Yes, indeed, Mr Pons. A most delightful gentleman. He proposes to leave tomorrow afternoon for he asked me to make his bill up for midday tomorrow."

"Excellent! Now, Parker, I think our next task is to pay a little visit to a good theatrical costumier's. There are two leading London firms close by, if I remember correctly."

We had turned away from the desk now, leaving Jamison with a baffled expression on his face. I hurried after Pons, having difficulty in keeping up.

"Theatrical costumiers, Pons? What on earth are you talking about?"

"Tut, Parker. The matter is elementary. Ah, here is a cab."

Pons jumped in quickly, giving an address I didn't catch, and I had just time to follow him before we glided away into the roaring chaos of the Strand. We paid off the cab near Bond Street and I kept hard at my companion's heels as he turned into a narrow, fashionable street. He stopped in front of a window which had little in it except wigs and grease-paint and studied it for a minute or two with what I thought to be exaggerated care. His next remark startled me.

"I thought perhaps we might have been followed, Parker. It is as well to take every precaution."

He drew me into the arched entrance of the establishment.

"Now, my dear fellow, if you will stand guard for a few moments I shall not keep you long."

He hurried into the shop and a short while afterward I saw him in earnest conversation with a tall, handsome young man with hair like patent leather. He re-joined me a few moments later, a wry expression on his face.

"It was unlikely that we should strike lucky first time off, Parker. Let us just see whether Glida and Company are our people. It is only a few steps farther down."

The next establishment was incomparably more fashionable and the window was filled with fantastic-looking military uniforms of a century or more ago, slashed with scarlet and blue and gold, the gleaming epaulettes shining like stars in the highly polished teak and chromium settings. On the windows in gold curlicue script were the legends: Glida and Company. Theatrical Costumiers. By Appointment to Their Majesties.

As before I stayed outside. This time Pons interviewed a tall, powerfully-built man whose beard was heavily flecked with grey. He appeared to be the proprietor for he sent an assistant scuttling for a heavy ledger with an imperious wave of the hand. The conversation lasted some five or seven minutes and when Pons re-joined me there was a familiar glint dancing in his eyes.

"I see you are in luck, Pons," I remarked.

"Your ratiocinative faculties are in full flow, Parker," said Solar Pons drily, drawing me farther down the pavement.

"We have been extremely fortunate in this matter in that our quarry has not flown. The only remaining problem is how to spring the trap in the most effective manner."

"I am afraid I do not follow, Pons."

"That is because you have looked only, my dear fellow, without seeing what was so plainly before you. We are dealing with an extremely ruthless and bold criminal. We must get back to the hotel at once."

And he said not a word further until we had arrived at our destination.

4

"I am immensely grateful to you, Mr Pons!"

"Tut, Mr Hibbert, I have done nothing for you as yet."

Pons and I sat at lunch with the manager in the Metropole dining room. I was extremely hungry after our morning's activities and did full justice to the excellent meal. The windows were open, golden bars of sunlight glanced in and the curtains billowed slightly with a cooling breeze. I smiled as I noticed Jamison's gloomy countenance passing the dining room doors. The body of the late Mr Voss had been removed discreetly by a back entrance less than an hour ago. Hibbert had noticed Jamison too and his nose wrinkled in distaste.

"Nevertheless, Mr Pons, I think you have managed to put that ridiculous police inspector's limited mind into another channel. The very idea of arresting me was fantastic. I do not know what I am to say to my board of directors."

Pons smiled encouragingly and I broke into the conversation.

"Jamison is not so bad when you get to know him, Mr Hibbert. He has his limitations, as you so justly point out . . ."

The manager interrupted me in his turn.

"You have not been arrested by him, Dr Parker," he said ruefully. "I think you might have a different standpoint in that case."

Solar Pons chuckled.

"*Touché*, Mr Hibbert. I think he has you there, Parker."

Then he abruptly became serious.

"But we are not yet out of the wood. I must just make sure we do not move prematurely. Have you managed to contact those taxi-drivers?"

"By all means, Mr Pons. There are six of them, all regulars on the taxi-rank here and they will be at your disposal from three o'clock onwards."

I turned a puzzled face to my companion.

"Taxi-drivers, Pons?"

"It is just a little matter, Parker, of crossing the *t*'s and dotting the *i*'s. As in most investigative work, you understand, Mr Hibbert."

"You are certainly leaving nothing to chance, Mr Pons, though what you can read into this hopeless riddle is beyond me."

"Hardly hopeless, Mr Hibbert," said Pons smoothly. "Now, as we have finished our coffee and it wants but five minutes to three I think we might make a move."

"I have asked them to come to my office one at a time, at three minute intervals, Mr Pons."

"Excellent."

I followed my companion and the manager into the latter's office, so lately the scene of the little drama when Hibbert had fancied himself under close arrest. The atmosphere at the Metropole had so far changed since Pons' arrival that the manager appeared to be in the ascendancy and Jamison himself on the defensive. The first of the drivers, a tall, thin, bearded man, was already waiting outside the door, nervously twisting his cap in his hands.

As soon as we were established in the office, the driver standing before the manager's desk, Pons put the man at his ease.

"I am concerned only with the events of yesterday. If you can recall those fares you took up from the rank outside the hotel, I would be obliged. I am looking for a tall, burly man with fair hair who would have come from the hotel."

The driver considered for only a moment and then shook his head.

"To the best of my recollection, sir, I never took up any fare of that description yesterday."

I turned to Pons in astonishment but wisely held my tongue. Pons' face expressed neither disappointment nor satisfaction.

"I am much obliged to you," he said evenly. "Here is half a guinea for your time and trouble."

We waited in silence until the next man was announced. The little scene, Pons' questions and the drivers' answers were continued until four interviews had been conducted in this manner with negative results.

The fifth man who presented himself was a little, sharp-faced person whose smart appearance and lively features bespoke intelligence and alertness. He listened in silence as my companion put to him the question he had posed to all the others.

"Yes, sir, I did," he said without hesitation. "Tall, fair man, as you say. Late in the afternoon."

Pons nodded, his eyes dancing with suppressed excitement.

"Can you remember where you took him?"

The driver rubbed his chin with the forefinger of his right hand.

"An address in Mayfair, sir. Some sort of theatrical costumiers, if I remember rightly."

"Can you recall the name?"

A puzzled expression passed across the taxi-driver's face.

"Some sort of foreign-sounding place. I'm not very good at such things."

Pons had a thin smile on his lips now.

"Would it have been Glida and Company?"

A look of surprise and enlightenment succeeded the driver's puzzlement.

"That's it, sir. It comes back to me now."

Solar Pons chuckled with satisfaction.

"Excellent. You have been most helpful. Here is a guinea for your trouble. You may tell your colleague waiting outside that he will not be needed now and give him this half-guinea with my compliments."

The man took the money as though he could not believe his luck.

"Thank you, sir. Much obliged, I'm sure."

We were silent until the door had closed behind him.

"How on earth, Pons . . ." I began when my friend interrupted me by putting a finger to his lips.

"All in good time, Parker. We have now to lay our man by the heels and must do it swiftly and with discretion if we are not to bring further scandal to the hotel."

"I must confess, Mr Pons, I am completely at a loss," interjected the unfortunate Mr Hibbert. "But if you will tell me how I may assist, every facility of the hotel is at your disposal."

"You are displaying an admirable spirit, Mr Hibbert," said my companion. "You have been greatly tried in the last few hours but unless I am much mistaken, your ordeal will be shortly over."

He had produced his pipe from his pocket and for the next few minutes he sat puffing fragrant smoke-rings toward the ceiling, his eyes half-closed as he remained in silent thought. I knew better than to interrupt him at such moments. Truth to tell I had much to think of myself, though in my case, confusion remained uppermost. I had seldom encountered such a baffling set of circumstances as confronted Pons at this moment yet it was evident that everything which appeared murky and obscure to me was crystal-clear to him.

At length he opened his eyes and addressed me in the following terms.

"We must proceed carefully, Parker. You have not your revolver with you, I take it?"

I shook my head.

"Good heavens, Pons, is the situation as dangerous as that? You did not ask me to bring it and therefore, I naturally . . ."

Pons silenced me by putting his hand on my arm.

"It is not your fault, Parker, but nevertheless we should not go into this blindfold. Our man is cunning, ruthless, highly dangerous and most probably armed. Despite superior numbers, we would be wise to meet him on equal terms. Unless I miss my guess he will fight desperately when cornered."

His eyes had passed across the office as he was speaking and had lighted on an umbrella stand in the corner.

"Ah! Just the thing. That stout walking stick yonder is yours, Mr Hibbert?"

"Indeed, Mr Pons. Do you wish to borrow it?"

"If you would be so good."

"By all means, sir."

Hibbert got up and courteously fetched the stick and handed it to my companion. He hefted it in his hand silently for a moment.

"Admirable, Mr Hibbert. I fancy it will do nicely. Properly handled it would subdue the most aggressive opponent. If you would do the honours, Parker."

I took the stick from him and weighed it in my right hand. It was indeed a formidable weapon. We were standing so when there came a peremptory rapping at the door and the sour features of Inspector Jamison were thrust into the room.

5

"Ah, I am glad you are here, Jamison," said Pons smoothly. "You are just in time for the dénouement of this little affair."

Jamison's expression became even more acid if that were possible. He coughed awkwardly.

"I have taken your advice, Mr Pons," he began.

He looked placatingly toward me.

"I telephoned my superiors at Scotland Yard. When I explained the situation they took the same view as you. The case against Mr Hibbert is dropped."

"There never was a case against him," Pons returned crisply. "Nevertheless, I am glad to hear you say so."

Jamison scratched his head and looked blankly from Pons to me.

"That's all very well, Mr Pons, but where are we to begin? Blessed if I can see how anyone could get in there to murder Mr Voss and escape while leaving the key on the table."

"That is because you are not using your eyes, Jamison. The matter is simple enough, though it presents ingenious facets. With your help I expect to have the murderer behind bars before the evening is out."

Jamison opened his mouth once or twice but was unable to articulate the words. He looked like an expiring fish and I must confess I was forced to look away into another corner of the room or my amusement would have shown upon my face. Not that I was any more enlightened than the good Inspector but I had learned to conceal my feelings a little more successfully than the Scotland Yard man.

Pons tore a leaf from his pocket-book, scribbled something on it and handed it to Jamison.

"I want a watch kept on the guest in this room, day and night if necessary. You'll need plain-clothes men, of course, and officers as unobtrusive as possible. If he leaves the hotel he is to be followed and a report made to me, through you. If he attempts to leave with his luggage he must be stopped, by force if necessary. But your men must be told, in the strongest possible terms, that he may be armed and desperate and will in all probability resist."

Inspector Jamison looked grave, but nodded his head in his best official manner.

"Very well, Mr Pons. I'll see to it personally. I have a couple of men in mind, both ex-boxers and handy in a rough-house."

Solar Pons smiled thinly at Jamison.

"Excellent."

He turned back to me. "I think that is all we need do for the moment. If I read this man's character aright he will not move until this evening, providing that he has managed the currency situation successfully."

My expression must have been blank indeed for Pons' face assumed a wry aspect.

"Come, Parker, this is not so very difficult. Just give it your undivided attention and I am sure all will be light where darkness reigned before."

"I have heard you say so on many occasions, Pons," I said ruefully. "But I have never yet met the man who could match your deductive faculties."

Jamison was about to quit the room but hesitated with his hand on the knob of the door.

"Where will you be, Mr Pons?"

My companion glanced over at the clock in the corner.

"I think it is just about the hour of tea, Parker. A pleasant occasion, especially in such a delightfully old-fashioned hotel. I think I may safely say, Jamison, that Parker and myself will be agreeably occupied in the tea-room for the next hour or so."

My companion was remarkably quiet and absorbed during the meal and I forebore to disturb him. There was tension beneath the surface, nevertheless, and more than once I noticed his clear-minted, aquiline face turn expectantly toward the door to the main vestibule as it opened to admit some new guest or staff member. But the time passed without incident and he made only one comment.

"I think we may safely leave routine matters to friend Jamison, Parker. Defective as he is in all the higher processes of ratiocination, if he is set a definite task and has a given objective to work toward there is no more dogged and better a man in his limited sphere."

As soon as we quitted the dining room Pons sought out Jamison and the two were closeted for the better part of an hour. When my companion rejoined me he took me to a small room behind the reception desk, which had been set aside for our purposes.

"I am afraid this will be rather boring, my dear fellow, but it is essential to keep alert at all times this evening."

"I am entirely at your service, Pons," I said.

I had brought in the manager's heavy stick with me and I set it down beside my chair as I perused the evening paper that Hibbert had had sent in. The hours seemed to pass with leaden slowness.

It was past nine in the evening and we had partaken of a light snack of sandwiches and coffee before anything further happened. The door opened and Jamison poked his head somewhat furtively into the room.

"Hamilton has just telephoned down, Mr Pons. Your man is on the move. He has a large suitcase and a valise with him."

Solar Pons rubbed his thin fingers together with satisfaction. He sprang to his feet like a tense spring that had just been released.

"Excellent! Just hold yourself in readiness, Parker."

"I wish I knew what this was all about, Pons," I grumbled.

"All in good time, my dear fellow," said my companion crisply, turning to Jamison who was lingering in the doorway. The Scotland Yard man still had a worried expression on his face.

"I hope you know what you are doing, Mr Pons. I am sticking my neck out in this matter and Mr Hibbert has already threatened to sue the police."

"Never mind that now, Jamison," said Pons in that omnipotent manner which I confess I sometimes find maddening. "We have more important things afoot. I will take full responsibility for whatever happens."

"Just so long as that is understood, Mr Pons," said Jamison stiffly, little patches of red standing out on his sallow cheeks.

"I must confess I have some sympathy with the Inspector, Pons," I said somewhat tartly as soon as he had withdrawn.

"Do you not, Parker," said Pons, his eyes twinkling.

"Now, we must quickly move into position. It will take our man some five minutes to reach the desk if he is using the lift; about ten minutes if he walks down. We must find a divan or chairs as near to the reception desk as possible and pretend to be hotel guests perusing the newspapers."

"Who is this man, Pons?" I asked, as we quickly quitted the room and took our seats on a long low divan to one side of and some yards from the reception desk.

"I believe I mentioned him earlier today, Parker. I was then told that he would not be quitting the hotel until tomorrow afternoon. From that I concluded he would make his move this evening, when the hotel was quiet. It seems that I have not been wrong."

Pons turned to me as the whine of the lift sounded in the quiet, almost hushed atmosphere of the hotel lounge.

"Do try and look a little more like a relaxed hotel guest, my dear fellow. Your knuckles are gleaming white on the handle of that stick."

I relinquished it with a mutter of apology and fixed my gaze on the wrought iron doors of the lift entrance as the cage neared the ground floor. My features were sheltered by the magazine I was reading and I had a clear view over the top of the pages as I was almost directly facing the lift.

Lennard was on duty at the desk and was desultorily turning over some letters destined for the pigeon-holes behind him. There was no sign of Jamison and his men but I had no doubt they were lurking near. The clock in the lobby indicated 9.15 P.M. precisely as the lift-cage clicked to a halt on the ground floor and a well-built, blond-haired man with a hard face walked toward us carrying a heavy case in his right hand and a valise in his left.

6

The events of the next few minutes remain a blur in my memory. Certainly, no more dramatic incident stands out in my mind; there have been more bizarre cases, of course, and many in which the surroundings were outré in the extreme. But none more violent or shocking played out against such a mundane background as the Metropole Hotel.

The fair-haired guest, whose eyes were shooting sharp glances to either side came straight on without hesitating, though the strain on his right arm must have been considerable, as it was obvious the case he was carrying was extremely weighty. Lennard came forward as he approached and gave him a cheerful smile.

"I would like my account, please," the tall man said, putting his key down on the desk. "The name is Thornton, Room 84."

The worried look was back on Lennard's face again now.

"The young lady has gone off duty sir. I understood her to say you were leaving tomorrow afternoon."

"I have changed my mind," the other rapped impatiently. "That was my intention originally but I have been called away on urgent business."

Lennard shrugged apologetically.

"I don't know whether she has left the bill, sir . . ." he began.

He was interrupted dramatically by his interrogator, who slammed the flat of his hand down on the reception counter with a loud bang and retorted explosively, "Well look, man, for goodness' sake, instead of standing there gawping. Unless you wish me to fetch the manager?"

Lennard cowered back behind the desk at the menace in the other's eyes.

"Certainly, sir. Straight away."

His voice was agitated, his manner flustered, as he went through into the small office behind the counter. I kept my face down to my magazine but Pons had looked up as though in casual curiosity at the angry scene. Thornton evidently felt this himself, for he bit his underlip with annoyance and controlled the nervous drumming of his fingers on the countertop. I thought he was about to make some observation to my companion but he evidently thought better of it, and instead turned on his heel to glance at the clock set above the lift entrance at the other side of the hall.

We waited in a tense silence like that for perhaps two minutes; I concentrated on the article in my magazine but the type swam before my eyes and conveyed nothing to me. I could feel the rough surface of the manager's stick reassuringly solid against the fingers of my left hand. Then we heard the hurried tread of the receptionist's feet coming back. He was flushed and nervous still but he carried a slip of paper in his hand.

"Here it is, sir," he said quickly. "I am sorry to have kept you waiting. Miss Smithson had made up the account and left it on the desk."

Thornton grunted and glanced at the document, reaching inside his coat for his wallet. It was then that Pons acted.

With a subtle gesture to me he rose quickly, put down his newspaper with a stifled yawn, and turned as though to quit the vestibule. As he passed behind Thornton and while the other's back was turned, he apparently stumbled across the case. It was cleverly done and though I knew Pons' clumsiness was only simulated I was completely deceived. Pons landed asprawl behind the thickset man.

"Dear me," he said apologetically. "I am so sorry."

The blond man gave a snarl and reached for his pocket. For once I was equal to the occasion. I had risen after Pons and was standing only a few feet away. I seized my stick and rushed forward, cannoning into Thornton. Taken off balance, he half-turned and fell heavily over Pons' semi-recumbent form. I had one glimpse of Lennard's face, frozen in horror and then Thornton had hit the floor.

He rolled over, Pons' hand clamped to his wrist.

"Quickly, Parker!" my friend snapped in unruffled tones.

I brought the heavy stick over hard, felt it crack against bone. Thornton's face turned grey and his arm hung limply. A heavy blued-steel automatic pistol bounced across the floor.

The lobby suddenly seemed full of men. Jamison had darted from somewhere behind the reception desk and threw himself without hesitation, terrier-like and determined, on to the suddenly raving figure of Thornton. Two plains-clothes men joined in and there was a wild mêlée of flying arms and legs, round which I hovered anxiously, glimpsing Pons rising and falling amid the confusion like some craft tossed in a stormy sea.

More police officers arrived and I could see Hibbert, pale and distracted in the background. Pons rose to his feet, a wry smile on his face, and dusted himself down.

"Well, Parker," he drawled. "It seems as though our little surmise has borne fruit."

"Indeed, Pons," I said, glimpsing Jamison's dogged face and the gleam of triumph in his eyes as handcuffs closed on the blond man's wrists.

"But I hope we have the right man."

"So do I, Dr Parker," Jamison snapped, straightening up, his breathing fast and shallow.

"Tut, Inspector," said Solar Pons calmly. "There is no doubt about it. The gentleman yonder, whatever his real name, is our man right enough. No self-respecting guest carries an automatic, far less being prepared to use it in a crowded hotel lobby."

He looked wryly at the anxious faces clustered round the harassed manager, as guests and staff were drawn to the boiling confusion about the blond man, now recumbent and glaring-eyed upon the floor.

"Just fetch a knife, Jamison, if you would be so good, and we will cut open that case," Pons commanded.

The Inspector hesitated but sent a constable to the kitchen. The pinioned man redoubled his efforts to escape as Pons approached the heavy valise which had been knocked over in the desperate struggle. It had three locks and, as Pons had expected, was secured. He cut a six-inch gash in the expensive leather with the razor-sharp kitchen-knife and soon eased up a triangular flap. From the gap poured several bundles of five-pound Bank of England notes.

Jamison looked stupefied. The blond man's face was set like granite as the police officers hauled him to his feet. His glittering eyes never left my companion's face.

"What are the charges, Mr Pons?" said Inspector Jamison awkwardly.

Pons smiled faintly.

"Murder and bank robbery will do to be going on with."

"Bank robbery, Mr Pons!"

My companion chuckled.

"Of course, Jamison. This case contains the equivalent of more than one hundred thousand pounds sterling, the property of the Hamburg branch of the German State Bank. If you had paid a little attention to an elementary study of languages the whole picture would soon have become clear to you."

I shook my head.

"The whole thing is far from clear to me, Pons. What you are saying is that Thornton is the man who murdered Voss?"

Solar Pons turned his deep-set eyes on me thoughtfully.

"What I am saying is that Thornton is Voss in a sense," he said. "It may seem rather complicated but it will soon be made clear."

Inspector Jamison's face was a study in bafflement.

"You mean to say he murdered himself, Mr Pons?" he said heavily, with a leaden attempt at irony.

"In a way, yes," Solar Pons replied shortly. "But I suggest this is neither the time nor the place for such explanations. I fancy you will get nothing out of Mr Thornton tonight and I am not yet in a position to hazard a guess at his true identity. I suggest that you formally charge him and then return here to Mr Hibbert's office."

"You have a full explanation then, Mr Pons?"

"I trust so, Jamison," said Pons, straight-faced. "In the meantime, Parker, I suggest we adjourn to the bar. I am sure Mr Hibbert will join us in celebrating his clearance of all suspicion, however far-fetched and idiotic such a supposition might seem to a rational mind."

And he led the way forward as the officers hurried the blond-haired man away.

7

Solar Pons lit his pipe and blew out a cloud of aromatic smoke toward the ceiling. Jamison had returned from charging his prisoner within the hour and now, flushed and breathless, sank into a chair at the other side of the table in the manager's office. A tray of drinks was before us and Hibbert himself, who was the only other person in the room apart from Pons, myself and the Inspector, was dispensing the refreshment.

"I don't know how you did it, Mr Pons," he said for the third time, "but it was quite brilliant."

"I am sure you are right, Mr Hibbert," said Jamison heavily, "and if it helps at all, I apologise on behalf of the police for the suspicion which fell upon you. But you must see how it looked to me."

"I think we can forget all that, Inspector," I put in hastily, diverting the manager's attention as the redness had mounted to his cheeks again at the Scotland Yard man's words.

"What I would like to know—and I am sure we are all agreed on this—is what this business is all about, for I have not the faintest idea myself."

Solar Pons half-closed his eyes, shovelling out blue smoke over his shoulder, taking the proffered glass the manager held out to him.

"There were a number of factors which stood out in a marked manner right from the beginning, Parker. They led to certain inescapable conclusions."

"And what might those be, Pons?"

"Obvious ones, Parker. The most striking stemming from the entrance of the mysterious hotel guest, with his heavy valise and bizarre appearance."

I turned puzzled eyes on my companion.

"You mean Voss, Pons. I fail to see . . ."

"That was because you were not looking, my dear fellow. Everything pointed toward only one set of conclusions. The man wished to draw attention to himself. Or rather, he wished to draw attention to his disguise. The heavy clothing in this warm weather; the guttural accent; the beard; the dark glasses. The man who registered as Otto Voss of Hamburg wished to create an identity."

Solar Pons paused and opened his penetrating eyes.

"The identity of the man he intended to kill."

Inspector Jamison gave a muffled exclamation.

"Am I to understand, Mr Pons . . ." he began ponderously.

"By all means," my companion interrupted crisply. "I do not yet know his real name but the Otto Voss who registered here was the man we have just arrested in the persona of Esau

Thornton. As you will have observed, Parker, they are both of the same general build and height."

"That is so, Pons. Then the man murdered in Room 31?"

"Was the real Voss, of course."

The manager had consternation on his face and opened his mouth to ask a question when Pons forestalled him.

"What is the motive for all this, you ask? Money of course. Greed. Sheer cupidity. Allied with treachery which one commonly finds among thieves of the more daring sort."

"You mentioned robbery, Mr Pons," said Jamison diffidently, his eyes never leaving Solar Pons' face.

My companion put down his pipe on the edge of a crystal tray on the table and nodded.

"And I commended to you, did I not, the study of languages. The most obvious clues were staring you in the face, in those copies of the *Hamburger Zeitung* which Thornton evidently overlooked in his baggage when he strangled Voss. Careless, but understandable under the circumstances. My knowledge of German is limited, certainly, but I read enough to realise that the principal items of interest in both issues were reports of a bank robbery in that city in which two daring robbers had escaped with almost £200,000."

"I see, Pons! And you thought Voss and Thornton were the men?"

Solar Pons inclined his head toward me.

"Obviously, Parker. I had already formed a tentative theory and I now had a possible motive, immeasurably strengthened by the weight of the valise the disguised Voss carried and by the fact that he would not entrust it to anyone else at the hotel. It was obvious too that the papers had been retained by the thieves, who wished to find out how much the police had discovered about the robbery."

"I confess I am still all at sea," said Hibbert, somewhat irritably. "I wish you would explain the matter slowly, stage by stage, Mr Pons, for I am but a layman in these matters."

"By all means, Mr Hibbert," said my friend with a faint smile. "My apologies for telling the story out of chronological sequence."

He picked up his pipe again and sat in silence for a moment or two while we waited impatiently for him to go on.

"At this stage many of my suppositions must necessarily be conjecture but I am convinced that when the true facts emerge they will differ from my conclusions only in detail. We will continue to call these two men Thornton and Voss for convenience, until such time as their true identities are established. It is on the cards that Voss is the man's real name as his passport was undoubtedly genuine and his profession vital to the plan to rob one of Hamburg's biggest banks."

Pons pulled absently at the lobe of his left ear, smiling ironically at Inspector Jamison.

"How much money was in that valise, Inspector?"

Jamison shifted uneasily in his chair.

"As near as we can make out in the brief time at our disposal, though it is only a rough estimate, something in excess of £100,000."

Pons nodded.

"Exactly. The percentage one would have expected had the German deutschmarks been exchanged through the underworld. There were only two men involved in the robbery, which took place a little over three weeks ago. The manager was held up at gun-point in his own office and forced to accompany them to the vaults. There, they were left undisturbed with the manager. They forced him to fill cases with medium-denomination currency. Then they simply walked out in conversation with the manager. The man we know as Thornton even shook hands with him on the front steps while Voss started a fast car at the kerbside."

"But how was that possible, Pons?" I asked.

"Because, Parker, Thornton was covering the man with a gun in his pocket. There is no doubt he would have shot the manager dead with as little compunction as you or I would squash a mosquito. They got clean away in a daring and simple crime that captured the imagination of the German public."

"But how do you know all this, Mr Pons?" put in Jamison.

"For the simple reason that it was all in those two newspaper stories," said Solar Pons, obviously finding difficulty in keeping the impatience from his voice.

"But how would they have got the money to England, Pons?"

"They had thought of that, too, Parker. Again, it was simple but daring. They waited three weeks until the outcry had died down. Then they travelled via Hook of Holland-Harwich."

"Your crystal ball again, Mr Pons?"

The Inspector could not keep the sneer from his voice.

"Simple commonsense, Jamison. Voss' passport was stamped Harwich. His profession gave me the answer immediately. He simply walked through Customs with the case."

"Through Customs, Pons?"

"His profession, Parker. He was an export official. No doubt he had made the same run many times previously. I counted no less than ten Harwich stamps on the passport, which was issued only last year. He undoubtedly had privileges and it is my opinion his luggage would not have been searched. The Customs of all European countries accord special privileges to such officials in their comings and goings across frontiers. But a simple telephone call to Harwich should speedily resolve the matter, Jamison."

"I will see to it, Mr Pons," said the Inspector heavily.

"We do not, of course, know exactly what led to the rift between the two men," Pons went on, "but it must be obvious to the meanest intelligence that Thornton had at some stage decided to betray his partner and seize all the money for himself. He would not have done that until the pair arrived in London."

"Why was that, Pons?"

"For the simple reason that the two men would have had to change the stolen money into English currency. Thornton would have had a difficult enough task to elude his enraged partner without having to worry about him following from Harwich to London. It is very much easier to disappear in a great city. And the hotel was carefully chosen."

"Carefully chosen, Mr Pons?"

It was Hibbert this time, who sat with his eyes intently on Pons' face, absorbing his every word.

"It is reasonably small and discreet, so that the fugitive could monitor the movements of fellow-guests. There are three means of exit; one to the Strand, another to the Embankment and a third, via a small courtyard in the rear, through which a guest, by using a service exit, could get to either area. More important still, it is within a stone's-throw of Soho."

"I do not follow you, Pons."

"Tut, Parker, it is simplicity itself. The men would need to change the money and Soho with its criminal underworld would be ideal for the contacts they wished to make. Thornton in his own persona settled in here three days ago because he knew it would take several days and the caseful of money, with a vengeful partner hot in pursuit, was literally a keg of gunpowder. As we have seen, he was successful in making his contact and changing the money; the facility would have cost him the usual fifty per cent."

"I see. But why did he simply not kill Voss on the train, Pons, without all this elaborate masquerade?"

Solar Pons slowly shook his head, a look of incredulity on his features.

"Come, Parker, Thornton was a murderer but not a fool. The last thing he would want would be a corpse on a railway train with himself aboard with a caseful of stolen German currency. It would be to his advantage to sneak away by some means leaving his partner temporarily unaware of his loss. He obviously hoped to give him the slip in London where he, a native of the country, had all the contacts and the advantages while Voss, a foreigner, and conspicuous in his appearance, would be at a disadvantage. But somehow Voss followed him and learned that he had come to this hotel."

Solar Pons smiled faintly.

"So much for scientific conjecture. Now for fact. During his flight, he had conceived a plan brilliant in its simplicity. It called for a great deal of nerve and daring, to say nothing of ingenuity, but the man we knew as Thornton had plenty of all three. Perhaps he had hoped to escape Voss altogether but he must have known there was small chance of that. His partner would obviously know of the plans for changing the money and the weight factor alone dictated a base close to the area chosen for converting the notes into English currency."

"Talking of the weight factor, Mr Pons," Jamison interjected suddenly. "I've got another puzzle on hand. My men found a suitcase full of strips of newspaper in Thornton's room when we searched it earlier tonight. That was a terrific weight too."

Solar Pons' eyes were dancing now.

"I am not at all surprised, Jamison. Obviously Thornton's first task was to leave the caseful of money at a left-luggage office, probably Charing Cross Station cloakroom, which is no great distance from here. But he would obviously have left it there for as short a time as possible. He turned up here in his own persona with a suitcase weighted down with newspaper to simulate the caseful of money, in case he were watched. He registered as Thornton, with an address at Banstead and was given Room 84. Yesterday, he again arrived at the hotel, this time heavily disguised as his partner Voss, and carrying the case containing the money, which he had retrieved from the left-luggage office."

"But what if his partner had seen him, Pons?"

Solar Pons paused and looked sombrely round the manager's office.

"That would not matter at all, Parker. It would merely strengthen the real Voss' conviction that not only was Thornton cheating him of his half-share but was laying a false trail to implicate the real Voss if the police were watching. But I doubt if Thornton was actually seen arriving by his duped partner. He would have searched the hotel registers, looking for Thornton's handwriting, albeit giving a faked name and address. In fact, this was what first gave me grounds for believing a deception to have taken place."

"The register, Pons?"

"Of course, Parker. On examining the book I made some remarkable discoveries. Although the inks were different and the hands elaborately disguised, there was no doubt that the man Thornton and the guest Voss shared basic similarities in their handwriting. When I saw that the signature and address of Voss revealed none of those Germanic qualities so beloved of that Nordic race, such as the heavy Gothic-style script taught in their schools and adopted as type-face for newspapers and books, I immediately came to the conclusion that the two men occupying those two rooms shared the same identity and that the man registered in the name of Voss was not a German. Having reached that conclusion I combined the information with the somewhat bizarre appearance of the second guest, which told me a great deal."

"Brilliant, Mr Pons!" said Hibbert enthusiastically.

"Hardly," said my companion deprecatingly. "I have made some little study of handwriting, Mr Hibbert, and the reading of such characteristics is a fairly simple matter to the skilled observer."

"Even so, Mr Pons," said Jamison heavily, "there still remains a great deal to be explained."

"I am coming to that, Jamison."

Solar Pons tented his thin fingers before him.

"As we know, the fake Voss arrived last night, elaborately disguised and carrying the heavily loaded suitcase. He made it a point to draw attention to the weight of the case and did not let it out of his possession. In addition to the heavy clothing he wore dark glasses not only to disguise himself, because the eyes are extremely difficult to conceal or alter, but further to draw attention to himself. He needed all these bizarre details so that when the body of the real Voss was discovered there should be no doubts in the minds of the hotel staff of his identity. He had at that stage known that Voss was closely at his heels and now that he had the real case of money he was at pains to draw attention to himself."

"I see, Pons."

Solar Pons smiled briefly at me and went on, as though burdened with the weight of his thoughts.

"When I examined the dead man's bedroom a number of things immediately struck me. The elaborate precautions taken by Voss, the fact that he kept his dark glasses on in the room and only spoke to Meakins very briefly. He did not speak much because he did not wish to give himself away and a disguised voice is difficult to maintain for any length of time. I realised at once that Meakins could not have known whether he had a genuine German accent or not from the brief communication he had had with him.

"But Thornton overdid matters. Though he undressed the corpse of his victim after the murder he stage-managed the thing far too thoroughly. I drew your attention to it at the time, Parker, but it was obvious to a trained eye that the real Voss would never wear dark glasses in bed. If his object were to disguise himself on arrival at the hotel what would be the point when on his own in a locked room where no-one could see him? It did not take me long to construct a theory which was further strengthened by the evidence of the hotel staff, and the dead man's possessions, particularly the two newspapers and the passport with its tell-tale Harwich-Hook Customs stamps.

"These, together with Voss' profession gave me the essential outline of the matter. We may briefly paraphrase my findings as follows. The newspapers were over three weeks old but carefully preserved. Therefore there was something in them of significance. The only two possible items which fitted were those concerning the Hamburg bank robbery. In the bedroom, I pointed out to you, Parker, that something might be read, though the traces of many people made it difficult to read indications in a semi-public place like a hotel bedroom.

"However, I made out the heavy indentations of feet behind the door and it was obvious to me that Voss had been strangled by someone concealed behind the door who had then dragged the body over to the bed. There were the distinct indentations of heel-marks quite clearly traceable in the heavy pile carpet. The police were not looking for such things; therefore they did not discover them.

"The passport was definitely genuine and definitely that of Voss; there was no mistaking the face. The question therefore that came at once to my mind was whether the man who arrived at the hotel was Voss or not. Circumstances led me to conclude that he was someone disguised as Voss. What was the point of the masquerade, then? Simply, that Thornton could not afford to have the body of a complete stranger lying about the hotel. The police might have immediately checked with the German Embassy which would have led to the embarrassing disclosure that Voss was being sought for the Hamburg robbery.

"By registering as Voss he was establishing his presence in the hotel, and hoping that the English police would concentrate on the search for the murderer rather than on checking the identity of an obscure German businessman. He needed a little time; at least another day for changing the money into English currency, when he could conveniently disappear. My guess is that he changed the money this afternoon and decided to move out tonight, when the hotel would be quiet.

"The passport was genuine, therefore Voss was genuine. But the man who arrived here was not. I commended his profession to you, Parker. He was an export official. That immediately suggested the two men merely walked through Customs with the stolen money.

"I next turned to the source of the disguise and with the statement of the taxi-driver we confirmed the West End theatrical costumiers, Glida and Company, whose proprietor gave me a description of my man which fitted Thornton perfectly when I glimpsed him later passing through the lobby."

"It was a plan brilliant in its simplicity, Pons."

"Was it not, Parker."

"That is all very well, Mr Pons," said Jamison harshly. "I have no doubt we shall find things as you say but what about the locked door and Mr Hibbert's involvement in the matter?"

"Oh, come, Inspector, the matter is childishly simple and Mr Hibbert's so-called involvement is nothing more than the behaviour of any highly-trained hotel manager on being confronted with a murder on his premises. I thought I had explained the matter even to your satisfaction. Thornton was already registered and in possession of Room 84, when he had the money under lock and key. He had laid an elaborate trail, aware that his partner was keeping him under observation. He took possession of the new room, No 31, as Voss, changed his clothes and waited.

"Though it cannot now be proved, it is my belief that the real Voss bided his time until late in the evening, perhaps sitting in the lobby, until he saw Lennard leave his post at the desk. It would be the work of a moment for him to abstract the pass-key from the number board. He would, already, of course, have ascertained the room from a perusal of the register, most likely at a busy period of the day when the receptionist's attention was elsewhere.

"But Thornton was waiting for him when he opened the door; strangled him—as we have seen he was a powerful and very violent man—and removed his clothing. He had hours to carry out the rest of his plan. When he had arranged things to his satisfaction, Voss in the bed with his pyjamas on, Thornton left the room key on the table. He let himself out, taking the case full of cut newspaper and the clothes Voss had worn."

Jamison nodded heavily.

"We have already found them in the room Thornton rented," he said ponderously.

Solar Pons looked round the table.

"When he had covered his traces, all he had to do was to go down the back stairs and out into the Strand. Awaiting the right opportunity he returned to the hotel, by the front entrance, replacing the pass-key on its hook while Lennard was still in the kitchen quarters."

"But supposing he were seen, Pons?"

"That would not matter, Parker. He was merely retrieving the key of his own room from the board and undoubtedly he would have had it in his hand for that purpose. But as we know from Lennard himself, he was not seen. It was a bold and brilliant scheme and ought, by all the laws of averages, to have succeeded."

"And it would have done but for you, Mr Pons," said Hibbert warmly. "I have never seen or heard anything so brilliant."

"You do me too much honour," Solar Pons protested. "The matter was not without its interesting aspects but must remain conjectural until friend Jamison here has established the salient facts. I fear we shall not get much out of Thornton himself. He bears all the marks of the hardened professional criminal."

"I am still puzzled about one thing, Pons," I said. "Why did not Thornton leave the hotel immediately after the murder?"

My companion gave a wry chuckle.

"Apart from the fact that he had not yet changed the money, that was just what he could not afford to do, Parker. And that was something I banked on as soon as I began to see the truth of the matter. If Thornton had left the hotel in the middle of the night it would immediately have drawn attention to him and that was the last thing he wished. Having noted the similarity between the handwriting of Thornton and Voss I learned that the former had given it as his intention of leaving the hotel tomorrow. That was very cool under the circumstances but I then hazarded a guess, rightly as it turned out, that he would leave some time this evening as even he—iron-nerved as he was—could not afford to overplay his hand. At any moment the police might have decided to turn their attention to the guests. But he had all the attributes of the real professional. Coolness and brute courage in equal measure. He undoubtedly relied on the police assuming the murderer had already left the hotel the previous night and would turn their efforts in that direction accordingly. I really would be most grateful, Inspector, if you would let me know the man's real identity should it turn up in your criminal records."

"We are on to it, Mr Pons," said Jamison, resignation in every timbre of his voice.

He rose and hovered uncertainly for a moment or two.

"Well, I must get back to the Yard, gentlemen. We have much to do."

"I am sure you have, Inspector," said Pons drily.

Jamison stepped forward, putting out his hand to the manager, his face red and troubled.

"I am sorry, Mr Hibbert, but circumstances were against you."

"Think nothing of it, Inspector," said Hibbert cordially.

Jamison shook his head, a curious expression in his eyes.

"It has been a lesson to me, Mr Pons."

"It is a wise man who benefits by experience, Inspector," said Pons equably.

He glanced over at the clock in the corner of the manager's office.

"Ah, Parker, it has been a somewhat fatiguing day. If we hurry back to Praed Street I have no doubt we shall be just in time for one of Mrs Johnson's excellent suppers."

THE ADVENTURE OF
THE CALLOUS COLONEL

1

"WHAT ON EARTH are you doing there, Pons?"
I paused on the threshold of our sitting-room at 7B Praed Street in astonishment. It was a bitterly cold morning in early February and I had just come in from a particularly fatiguing case.

On opening the door I was immediately confronted with the spectacle of my friend Solar Pons, his lean, angular figure recumbent on the carpet, his right hand holding the gleaming barrel of a revolver flat against a bolster taken from one of our armchairs. Beyond the bolster was a plaster bust of Napoleon which normally lived on top of a bookcase in the far corner.

Pons laughed and got up, dusting the knees of his trousers.
"Just indulging in a little amateur theatricals, Parker."
I glanced down at the mess on the carpet, the rich crimson firelight glinting over the pale surface of the bust. To my astonishment I saw there was a small hole in one side of it and a distinct smell of burning.

"It looks as though your services will be in demand at the Lyceum, Pons, if this goes on," I said somewhat tartly, noting that there was a hole drilled clean through the bolster.

My companion chuckled, his right hand softly stroking the lobe of his right ear.

"*Touché*, Parker. You are developing quite a pretty wit of late. I see I shall have to be on my mettle."

He looked down ruefully at the bolster and the bust.

"But you are right in one respect. I fear my little drama will not be greatly appreciated by Mrs Johnson. If you had been but five minutes earlier you would have heard the muffled explosion."

I looked at him in astonishment.

"Good heavens, Pons! You don't mean to tell me you have actually fired that thing in here?"

My friend shook his head.

"Oh, I can assure you, Parker, there was little danger. I had carefully worked out the possible impact. The bullet has just penetrated the surface of the bust, the greater force of the blow having been taken by the cushion. That explains both the crushing impact of the wound, consistent with the unfortunate man having apparently shattered his head upon the stony ground, and the lack of any sound for people who were passing the edge of the Forest only a few hundred yards away. It also had another advantage in that there was no scorching of the wound which would have given the game away in short order."

I put my medical case down on my armchair and my overcoat on top of it and drew nearer to the fire. I looked at Pons with rising irritation.

"I wish I knew what you were talking about."

"I am sorry, Parker. I sometimes forget that you are not always au fait with my cases. I was merely conducting a little experiment in ballistics. Though the characteristics of a bullet striking plaster are different from that of flesh, I fancy my theory will stand up in court. Sufficiently, I trust, to put paid to the unspeakable activities of the abominable Mr Horace Mortiboys of Epping."

His deep-set eyes looked so angry and vengeful at that moment that I was quite taken aback. Then he seemed to recollect himself and stirred as I spoke again.

"I did not realise, Pons. One of your cases, eh? I trust you have now brought it to a successful conclusion."

"I think we may say so, my dear fellow. Come and sit near the fire. Lunch will be served in a quarter of an hour or so."

"I must say I could do with it," I returned. "Just give me a few moments to put my things away and wash my hands."

When I returned to the sitting-room Pons had tidied the carpet, the bust was back in situ on the bookcase, the damaged side away from the viewer; and the rumpled bolster on one of

The Adventure of the Callous Colonel

the chairs. Pons had evidently returned the revolver to his bedroom for there was no sign of it. He sat in his own chair to one side of the fire indolently reading *The Times* as though he had not a thing in the world on his mind.

After a few minutes he put down the paper and turned his deep-set eyes on me.

"What do you know about Colonel Alistair McDonald, Parker?"

I glanced up from the fire in mild surprise.

"Not a thing, Pons," I admitted. "Should I?"

My companion shook his head, a faint smile on his face.

"Your field is altogether too specialised, Parker. You have been missing something. Explorer, big-game hunter, stalker, collector of esoteric objects, he also has regrettable criminal tendencies which have made him a good deal of money. At the present time I should class him as the third most dangerous man in Europe."

Solar Pons tented his slender fingers before him and stared broodingly into the fire.

"In fact he has twice tried to kill me, the most recent occasion being yesterday."

"Good heavens, Pons! You cannot mean it?" I spluttered.

Solar Pons shook his head.

"I wish I were not serious, Parker. A parcel came for me yesterday. If I had not been on my guard, I should not be sitting here talking to you now."

He glanced over at his desk in the far corner.

"Just take a look at that. But please do not touch the thing. I should burn it, by rights, but I am retaining the ingenious toy as possible evidence."

I got up and crossed the room to stare down at the brown-paper parcel which sat on my friend's blotter. It had been opened out and a strange wooden idol figure sat in the midst of it. It had a curiously shaped base, with a marked indentation in the front, obviously to fit the thumb of a person holding the image by the base. I saw now that there was a small steel needle protruding from the front of it.

"I do not understand, Pons," I remarked, as I resumed my seat.

"It is simple, Parker," Solar Pons commented. "I might have picked it up from the cardboard box but for the fact that I noted a minute hole in the shallow depression in front of the thing. I procured a pair of pliers with which to hold it and with the aid of a heavy ruler I applied pressure. The result was quite dramatic, the needle stabbing forward through the hole. After analysis I found that the needle, which is of the ordinary sewing variety, had been impregnated with a solution of curare, which I need not tell you is a deadly poison, which speedily produces paralysis and death."

I gazed at Pons open-mouthed.

"But why should this Colonel McDonald wish to kill you, Pons? And how do you know he sent the idol?"

Solar Pons chuckled drily.

"It has all the hall-marks of the Colonel's ingenious mind, Parker. The thing is entirely hand-made. The carving, the staining with red varnish, the glass-eyes, the skilful painting of the features, and the heavy spring-mechanism, typical of the skilled toy-maker, bear all the signs of the Colonel's ingenuity. The parcel was post-marked Putney by the bye, so he and his agents are not far away."

"I still do not understand, Pons."

"Tut, Parker, the matter is simple enough. A few months ago I was instrumental in exposing a gross public swindle, involving a non-existent housing scheme on the Riviera. The company responsible was headed by puppets, of course, but I have no doubt the Colonel's hand was behind the thing. He lives in Inverness, incidentally, and the intricate machinations of these schemes are peculiar to him. In fact I am informed by Scotland Yard that inquiries into the fraud may take two years or more, with no guarantee of conviction. The directors of the scheme are figureheads and the police have so far found no visible trace of McDonald in the affair. But I have no doubt my interference has rankled."

Pons twisted down the corners of his mouth and looked mockingly over at the parcel in the far corner.

"Just peruse his entry in that current volume of Who's Who, if you would be so good."

I brought the weighty volume to my armchair and studied it. I soon found the item I wanted. McDonald's entry was impressive indeed. He lived at Ardrossan Lodge near a small village about twenty miles from Inverness. I went down the article with increasing puzzlement.

"He is a scholar too, Pons."

"Is he not, Parker."

"Publications include, 'The Sphere and the Triangle' (1914) and 'The Dimensions of Ecstasy' (1923)," I said.

Pons chuckled drily.

"Oh, yes, the Colonel has a great deal to him. The Dimensions of Ecstasy indeed. He is as much at home among the shelves of the library and the higher philosophy as he is at a rough shoot or on one of the crags of his native heath."

I put down the volume on the table.

"You intrigue me, Pons. This business is serious."

Solar Pons looked at me sombrely.

"Serious indeed, Parker. It can only end one way or another. We have been conducting a struggle at long-distance for the past six years or so. I really must take up the challenge."

I looked at him sharply.

"You have something in mind?"

"There is a matter in train which bears the unmistakable stamp of Master McDonald," my friend went on. "I fancy he sent me the parcel because he wished to clear the decks before putting it in motion."

His eyes were fixed somewhere up beyond me at the ceiling.

"I really would give a great deal to checkmate him."

He broke off abruptly.

"Ah, there is Mrs Johnson's motherly tread upon the stair. We will take up this matter again after lunch."

2

My sick calls took me out again in the afternoon and it was not until the early evening that I once again set eyes on my friend. A thin fog was swirling about the streets and I was glad to get indoors. When I entered the sitting-room I found Pons in consultation with a tall, fair-haired girl of about twenty-five, whose pink cheeks and flashing eyes bespoke some degree of agitation.

"Ah, this is my friend and colleague, Dr Lyndon Parker," said Pons, rising from his chair and effecting the introductions. "Allow me to present my client, Miss Jennifer Hayling of Wortley Hall, Norfolk, and Inverness."

"Inverness, Pons!"

I could not resist an involuntary start and Miss Hayling paused in shaking hands, before favouring me with a brief smile.

"This is connected with Colonel McDonald, then, Pons?" I asked as I took off my overcoat and drew my chair up to the fire.

"Indeed it is, Dr Parker," said the young lady indignantly, "though I cannot prove it. But a more thorough-going rascal it has never been my misfortune to encounter until now."

I looked at her in surprise.

"I really must press upon you the necessity of telling your story again, Miss Hayling," said Pons quickly. "That is, if we are to persuade the doctor to accompany us to Scotland for I certainly cannot do without him."

My surprise grew.

"Scotland, Pons! Good heavens! It is a long way in such inclement weather."

"It is indeed, Parker," said my companion smoothly, "but it is vitally urgent that I travel there. It is a matter of life and death."

I sat looking from one to the other for a long moment.

"I will certainly come, Pons, in that case. Though what my locum will say I cannot tell."

"There will be time enough to make arrangements, Parker. We shall not need to depart until tomorrow."

"Leave it to me," I said, with a reassuring smile at Miss Hayling.

Our visitor, who was elegantly dressed in a well-cut overcoat with a fashionable fur collar, now resumed her seat at the fireside, removing her outer garment to reveal a full-fashioned figure clad in a thick jersey dress. On her head she wore a West End milliner's version of what passes in the South for a Scottish lady's tam-o-shanter with a knitted bobble.

The young lady smiled as though she had guessed what I was thinking.

"I have only just returned from Scotland, Dr Parker, and I like to give some token respect to the land of my adoption."

"Certainly, Miss Hayling," I returned. "I was thinking it most becoming."

"You are extremely gallant this evening, Parker," said Pons gravely. "But I fear these sartorial notations are coming between us and the young lady's story."

With a brief smile at both of us, our attractive visitor plunged into her tale without more ado.

"As I already told you in my letters, Mr Pons, I am an orphan, living mainly in the Norwich area. My mother was

Scottish and the family once owned considerable estates near Inverness. During the time of my parents' marriage they divided their time between Glen Affric and Norwich, where my father had business interests. Both my parents were killed in a tragic accident a little over a year ago."

A cloud passed over her face and she paused, as though the recollection were painful to her.

"I am so sorry, Miss Hayling," I mumbled, with a quick glance at Pons.

He sat with his brows knitted, as though concentrating fiercely, several sheets of paper, evidently his client's letters, spread out on the table at his side. At the girl's extended permission he lit his pipe and was soon contentedly wreathed in aromatic blue smoke.

"I would not have referred to it again except that Mr Pons seems to think the matter of some significance," the girl resumed.

"It may be, Miss Hayling, it may be," Solar Pons interjected. "There is a wealth of difference. Pray continue."

With a shy smile in my direction, our visitor went on, "You would not, of course, know Glen Affric or the terrain thereabouts, but it is, as you might imagine, hilly, with steep winding roads, often little more than lanes. The road from the main gates of Glen Affric is extremely steep and winds down through rather forbidding pine forests. It is well enough in summer but in winter, especially during icy conditions, can be extremely dangerous.

"I had often told my parents to take the car and they usually did so but they were inordinately fond of driving about the neighbourhood in a pony and trap, as my father, who was not a Scot at all, loved to pose as a laird, which caused both him and my mother great amusement."

The girl smiled reminiscently, as though she could see her dead parents' images rising before her once again in the flesh and I must say I was touched at the warmth of her expression.

"The road turns at right angles across an old stone bridge, which spans a ravine through which a stream runs. It was there, just at the bridge entrance, that the accident happened. The shafts snapped on the turn, the pony went on, but both my parents and the vehicle crashed through the wooden guard-rail into the ravine below."

Our visitor was silent as though re-living the horror of the moment and I broke the silence, tactfully, I thought.

"I see, Pons. In the wintry conditions, no doubt the horse slipped at the turn and the unwonted strain on the shafts broke the wood, thus precipitating the tragedy."

"Perhaps, Parker," said my companion softly, his eyes flashing me a discreet warning. "The point is that it was unusually mild spring weather at the onset of April last year and the road was firm and dry."

I must have sat with my mouth open for a second or two and by that time the young lady had recovered herself.

"It was after my parents' death, Mr Pons; some months in fact, when I had come back to Scotland and was going through their papers, that I found the letters from the Scottish Land Trust, signed by their President, Mungo Ferguson."

"Mungo Ferguson," said Pons through the thin banners of smoke, his voice soft and almost dreamy.

"Tell me about him again, Miss Hayling."

"He is a loathsome creature, Mr Pons. A bully and a braggart. A great, red-bearded man who thinks he can ride roughshod over other people's rights."

Solar Pons smiled, taking his pipe out of his mouth.

"He did not ride roughshod over you at any rate, Miss Hayling," he observed. "For you took a whip and showed him off the estate, did you not?"

The girl flushed and there were little sparks of amusement dancing in her eyes.

"Indeed I did, Mr Pons!" she said spiritedly, "and I believe I have adequately described the incident in my letters."

"Good heavens, Miss Hayling!" I exclaimed. "And this is the brute we are up against?"

Solar Pons shook his head, smiling at me through the coils of smoke.

"Hardly, Parker. You have surely not forgotten our earlier conversation. Ferguson is merely the cloak for something far more sinister. Let us hear something of the letters, Miss Hayling. You did send me a sample and I have in fact already checked on the registration of the company in question. The Scottish Land Trust, with Ferguson as President was first registered something over eighteen months ago and has a paid-up capital of £100."

I looked at Pons in surprise.

"That does not sound very impressive, Pons."

Solar Pons chuckled drily.

"You have not seen their notepaper, Parker. That is impressive enough at any event."

"Then you think the whole thing a swindle, Mr Pons?" said the girl impetuously. "They have offered a good price for the house and land."

"Too good, though it is genuine enough, at any rate," said my companion sombrely. "I think you would find the money forthcoming readily enough if you were to agree to their request."

"But fifty thousand pounds, Mr Pons! The whole estate is not worth a fraction of that. The house is well enough but the rest is just 300 acres of woodland, with some coarse grazing. There is not even any shooting or a trout stream or anything of the sort."

My astonishment must have shown on my face.

"Fifty thousand pounds, Pons?"

"Interesting, is it not, Parker. This is why Miss Hayling's little problem intrigues me so. Have a look at this."

My friend passed me an impressive, blue-tinted deckle-edged sheet of stationery, which had very elaborate headings in flowing script printed on it.

The legend, Scottish Land Trust, Registered Offices, Carnock House, Inverness, was followed by a list of directors whose names meant nothing to me. The letter, addressed to Miss Hayling's parents, was an offer, couched in unctuous terms, of fifty thousand pounds sterling for the estate known as Glen Affric. It was dated more than a year earlier and signed by Mungo Ferguson. I passed it back to Pons with a non-committal grunt.

"We are rather running ahead of ourselves," said he. "Just let me *précis* the situation. Mr and Mrs Hayling were made an astronomical offer for Glen Affric estate, which is worth only a fraction of that, about eighteen months ago. They refused, as they had a great affection for the place, which is nevertheless worthless from a commercial development point of view.

"Mungo Ferguson, the President, persisted with the offer, however, and said that the Trust wished to develop the property as a leisure and holiday centre and the site was the only place suitable for many miles around."

"There may be something in that, Mr Pons," the girl muttered, searching Pons' face with attentive eyes.

"A short while after the last of these letters, Mr and Mrs Hayling died in the tragic accident with the pony and trap,"

Pons continued. "Following the funeral Miss Hayling returned to Norwich and the Scottish house, with a reduced staff of three, remained in her ownership. But about six months ago the Trust's offers were repeated by letter, at the lady's Norwich address. What could be the reason behind such persistence?"

"I have no idea, Pons."

"Nevertheless," my companion returned. "It raises a number of interesting possibilities. This company seems inordinately concerned with this piece of ground. However, it is something which cannot be fully appreciated without seeing the terrain."

"You think the company genuine, Pons?"

Solar Pons tented his thin fingers before him.

"Oh, it is genuine enough so far as it goes, Parker. Miss Hayling, nothing if not a persistent young lady, has been to the Trust's headquarters in Inverness. They have a proper office there, which is open at fixed hours on five days a week, though the one clerk employed there has little to do. But I am holding up Miss Hayling's narrative. There are far more sinister overtones to come."

"You have put the situation admirably, Mr Pons," said the girl. "This was how things stood until I returned to live again in Scotland back in the autumn."

"You had been called there by your old servants, had you not?"

"Yes indeed, Mr Pons. By Mr and Mrs McRae, steward and housekeeper respectively. They are the only staff now apart from Mackintosh, the outside man and gardener."

"Something strange had happened, I understand."

The girl nodded, her eyes worried.

"Strange enough, Mr Pons. After I had received McRae's letter I thought I had better get the first available train."

Solar Pons blew a little eddying plume of blue smoke up toward the ceiling of our sitting-room.

"It began with noises in the night, did it not?"

"That is so, Mr Pons. Neither Mr McRae or his wife are what you might call sensitive or over-imaginative people. They are, on the contrary, stolid, strong-minded and dependable. Mackintosh likewise."

"The house is a lonely one, I understand?"

"You could say that. The nearest habitation is about five or six miles away but that is irrelevant as the property itself, in extensive grounds, is approached by a long private road and well screened by heavy belts of trees."

"There were noises at first, you say."

"Yes, Mr Pons. Odd scratches, as though someone were trying the shutters at dead of night. McRae got up and ran out, but though it was a fine moonlight night, saw nothing. Another time there were footsteps and after odd banging noises a window was found open, as though it had been forced. On yet another occasion Mackintosh found a set of heavy footmarks across a flower-bed after rain. They had obviously been made during the dead hours of the night, for they were not there the evening before."

Solar Pons nodded.

"Which brings us to the fire."

"Yes, Mr Pons. Though not serious it might well have been. Some outhouses, which stand between the main house and the stable-block, caught fire. Fortunately, Mr and Mrs McRae together with Mackintosh, who lives in a nearby cottage, were able to contain the outbreak with a garden hose but two of the sheds were completely destroyed."

I looked at my companion.

"An accident, Pons?"

The girl shook her head.

"They found a three-quarters empty petrol can near the scene of the fire. It was obviously deliberate. The police were called in but found nothing."

Solar Pons blew out a little plume of smoke from the corner of his mouth.

"What do you make of that, Parker?"

"Why, coercion, Pons," I said. "The Land Trust wants Miss Hayling's property badly. Now they are putting on pressure to force her out."

"Splendid, Parker," said Solar Pons, a twinkle in his eye. "You really are improving all the time. Those are my thoughts exactly and though the conclusion is a trite and obvious one it appears to me that my training is beginning to bear fruit. The question is, what does the Land Trust really want? And why should anyone desire such a remote and isolated property, which has no obvious commercial value."

"Exactly, Mr Pons," put in Miss Hayling. "Farming is a depressed industry anyway and despite the Trust's explanations, the one obvious use to which the land could be put is ruled out, because the estate is unsuitable for that purpose.

The timber might be of some value, if it could be cut and marketed, but even that qualification is doubtful."

"There is more to come, Pons?" I asked.

"Oh, a deal, Parker, a deal. I must apologise for these constant interruptions, Miss Hayling, but such sifting and evaluation of points as they arise, together with the comments of my good friend the doctor here, are a valuable factor in refining the ratiocinative processes."

There was a dry and humorous expression on Pons' face as he spoke and I saw little sparks of humour dancing in the girl's own eyes.

"Well, Mr Pons, as I have already informed you by letter, things got rapidly worse. I had no sooner been apprised of the fire when something even more serious occurred. Mackintosh, the gardener surprised someone in the shrubbery one dark evening a few days afterwards, and was attacked in consequence. He struck his head on a stone bordering the driveway as he fell and briefly lost consciousness.

"But he is a strong and vigorous man, fortunately, and came to no permanent harm. As soon as he was himself he roused the household, the police were called and a search made of the neighbourhood. But the terrain is hopeless as there are so many places of concealment and the perpetrator of this outrage was never found. On receipt of that news I immediately made my way from Norwich and took up residence at Glen Affric."

"When even more serious events took place, Miss Hayling."

"Indeed, Mr Pons. But not before being preceded by two letters, both signed by Mr Mungo Ferguson, and both repeating the original offer of the Land Trust."

"You took no notice of them?"

"Of course not, Mr Pons. On these occasions I did not even bother to reply. But one afternoon, a fortnight ago, I had returned from a brisk walk on the hillside when I heard voices from the stable area. I found Mr McRae, my steward, having a fierce argument with a huge, red-bearded man dressed in riding clothes. He had come up in a dog-cart and the pony had been tied to the railings. McRae had found him wandering about the property uninvited, which had led to words. But he raised his hat civilly enough to me and introduced himself, asking for a private interview. I did not wish to invite him into the house and decided to keep McRae within earshot, so we walked a few yards away to talk.

"He introduced himself as Ferguson and again repeated his offer from the Land Trust and when I refused, somewhat vehemently, he became abusive. I think he had been drinking and it was then, in the course of the interview, that he made an improper suggestion."

Miss Hayling paused and her cheeks were pink, her eyes gleaming with the recollection. Solar Pons' own deep-set eyes turned on her sympathetically.

"An improper suggestion, Miss Hayling?"

"Yes, sir. It was one no lady could repeat to a gentleman. I am afraid I lost my temper completely. Ferguson was holding a riding crop loosely in his hand as we talked and I seized it and beat him about the head and shoulders with it. He was so surprised that he retreated rapidly. I threw the whip after him, he got quickly up into his trap and with many curses drove rapidly off and good riddance to him."

"Well done, my dear young lady," I could not resist saying and Solar Pons looked at the pair of us, a slight smile playing around his lips.

"And what did McRae do all this time?"

"He was as astonished as Ferguson, Mr Pons. But there was no doubt he approved."

"Which brings us to three days ago."

"That is correct, Mr Pons. I felt thirsty after retiring to my room and came down to Mrs McRae's kitchen to get a glass of milk. It was late—or what passes for late in the Highlands—just turned half-past eleven, and I was passing a side-door to get to the kitchen when I heard a sound outside. There was only a dim light burning in the far hallway and the rest of the building was in darkness.

"I distinctly heard a foot grate on the stone step outside and then the iron door-latch was lifted once or twice as though someone was testing to see whether it was locked. I can tell you, Mr Pons, it was somewhat unnerving at that hour of night in such a lonely place to hear and see such a thing."

"I can well imagine, Miss Hayling. You called out, I believe?"

"I shouted, 'Who is there?', more to keep my courage up than anything else. The latch was abruptly released and I heard the sound of hurried footsteps on the flagged path outside. I put on the outside porch light and went out to see who it was, but there was nothing."

"That was a brave thing," I said.

"But extremely unwise, Parker," Solar Pons admonished. And to the girl.

"You did nothing further that night?"

"No, Mr Pons. I re-locked the door, got my milk and went to bed. But I was much troubled in my mind though I did not mention the matter to Mr and Mrs McRae. All the staff had been greatly disturbed by these incidents and I had no wish to lose their services. Which brings me to yesterday afternoon."

Pons' client paused as though recollecting her thoughts and went on in a low, even voice.

"I had been out for a walk after lunch and my ramble had taken me to the northern portion of the estate, which abuts Glen Affric, a wild and lonely place, bordered by one of our local mountains of the same name. It was cold, grey and overcast and I had heard shooting earlier."

"Surely it is not the season?" I said.

Miss Hayling shook her head.

"No, but there are many local people who shoot rabbits and other small creatures for the pot during the winter months, so I took no particular notice. I was standing on the path, looking up the glen, taking in the romantic charm of the scene and thinking about nothing in particular when there came another shot, much closer this time. Mr Pons, it was aimed at me and the bullet passed through the bushes only four or five feet from my head!"

3

There was a long silence which I felt incumbent upon myself to break.

"Good heavens! This is serious indeed!"

"Is it not, Parker," said Pons, rubbing his thin fingers together, suppressed energy evident in every line of his frame.

"What did you do next?"

"I am afraid I panicked, Mr Pons. I took to my heels down the path and did not rest until I was safe in the house again."

Solar Pons nodded sombrely.

"You have done wisely, Miss Hayling. This is a black business. That shot was undoubtedly intended for you."

"But what does it all mean, Mr Pons?"

"That is what I intend to find out. I have formed tentative theories but must wait until we are upon the ground before testing them. That was when you sent me the telegram?"

"Yes, Mr Pons. Some weeks earlier I had remembered my father once speaking of you in connection with some case you had solved. It was then I first wrote you and apprised you of the situation and our ensuing correspondence has been the only thing which has strengthened my resolve in this business. I had Mackintosh get the trap and take the telegram into the village post office for transmission."

"Which was undoubtedly known to McDonald within the hour. He would know you had an interview at Praed Street this afternoon. You saw nobody when you took the London train last night?"

His sharp eyes held the girl's transfixed.

She shook her head worriedly.

"No, Mr Pons. Though I had a strange feeling that I was followed all the way from Scotland."

"You undoubtedly have been. We must be on our guard."

Solar Pons puffed furiously at his pipe, the aromatic blue clouds surrounding him in thick whorls.

"You haven't told us about Colonel McDonald, Miss Hayling," I said.

"I am sorry, Parker. It is my fault. I am au fait with the story and had forgotten it was quite new to you."

"I went to the station that evening, Mr Pons, as I told you. I had to pass the Affric Arms to get to the forecourt. There is a small private bar near the pavement and the window was uncurtained. I glanced in as I went by. Mackintosh was carrying my luggage and had noticed nothing but I could see Ferguson inside, in deep conversation with a man in front of a roaring fire. There was no mistaking him, Mr Pons. The flaming red hair drew my attention to him. The man with him glanced up though I am convinced he could not see me at the window as it was dark in the street. It was undoubtedly Colonel McDonald."

"You know him?" I said.

"Of course, Dr Parker. Everyone in Invernessshire knows the Colonel. He is a celebrated, not to say notorious figure. I must say I was alarmed to see him in such intimate circumstances with such an odious person as Ferguson."

"Why was that, Miss Hayling?"

"Somewhat obviously, Mr Pons, I immediately gained the impression, rightly or wrongly, that he and Ferguson were in collaboration. Or, not to put too fine a point on it, that Ferguson was acting as McDonald's agent in putting pressure on my family to get our estate."

"Have you or your family ever had any personal contact with the Colonel, Miss Hayling."

"So far as my parents are concerned, not that I am aware of. In my own case I have never met the man, though I have read a good deal about him, mostly in the financial press."

"And you do not like what you read?"

"No, Mr Pons. He is certainly not a sympathetic figure."

"I see."

Pons was silent for a moment, his head resting on his breast, his eyes half-closed, as though deep in thought.

"And you have no idea why such a man as Colonel McDonald would have an interest in a small estate like Glen Affric?"

Our visitor shook her head.

"No, Mr Pons."

"Very well, Miss Hayling. You have done well to come to me. There is little point in further discussion. However, I should be very careful while you are in London. Dr Parker will accompany you back to your hotel and I want your promise to stay there until we come to fetch you tomorrow. I believe there is a midday train from King's Cross, is there not?"

"That is correct, Mr Pons. But you do not believe I am in any danger here in London?"

"It is as well to be on our guard, my dear young lady. I would like your promise, if you please."

"You have it, Mr Pons."

The girl got up from her chair, her eyes shining. We both rose also.

"Thank you so much, gentlemen. I feel very much better already."

"I can promise nothing except that I will exert my best endeavours in your interests, Miss Hayling."

"One could not ask for more, Mr Pons."

"If you will just wait a moment while I get my coat, we will be off," I said.

The girl was silent as we took a taxi to her hotel, a comfortable, middle-class establishment conveniently situated near King's Cross Station, but she reiterated her promise to remain in her room before we parted. She was to be ready at a quarter past eleven the following morning when we were due to pick her up by taxi. I saw her into the hotel and waited until she had locked herself within her room. She would dine in the hotel restaurant and would have no need to go out again until we caught the express north.

When I returned to 7B an hour later I found Pons sprawled in his armchair in front of the fire in a brown study. Judging by the swathes of dense smoke which filled the room he had been smoking furiously.

"Well, Parker," he observed on my entry. "What is your opinion of Miss Hayling and her problem?"

"A brave young lady, Pons," I answered, laying down my overcoat and thankfully seating myself opposite him in my favourite armchair in front of the fire.

"But a dark and difficult business. Though it seems obvious that the crude and murderous activities of the Scottish Land Trust were directed toward the purpose of obtaining Miss Hayling's estate, I confess I cannot see the point. From what both you and she tell me it has no possible commercial value."

Pons regarded me through the smoke with very bright eyes.

"You have hit it, Parker. I have already been to Companies House and set my own inquiries afoot. The Trust has ostensibly been set up for the innocuous purpose of recreation and leisure, as they have already suggested to Miss Hayling. They have no need to be more specific than that."

"You think McDonald owns the company and has set it up for some other purpose?"

"There is no doubt about it, Parker. The scheme bears all the traces of his ferocious methods, though his normal native cunning seems to have deserted him. These crude and blunt tactics with Miss Hayling are not typical of him."

"Perhaps the man Mungo Ferguson whom he appears to be using as his agent . . ."

"Perhaps, Parker, perhaps. He may overstep himself. A scoundrel like McDonald has to use the tools to hand and following some of his recent experiences his more genteel and respectable associates may well have been frightened off."

He smoked on in silence for a few more minutes, while I went to the telephone to let my locum know of the situation. When I had arranged for my leave of absence, I returned to the warmth of the sitting-room to find him immersed in a gazetteer and large-scale maps of Scotland which he was studying intently with the aid of a powerful magnifying glass. As soon as I reappeared he swept everything briskly off the table.

"I must apologise for monopolising our quarters with my little problems. We will leave it over until the morrow. In the meantime if you would be good enough to ring for supper, I would be greatly obliged."

4

The weather was, if anything, even more inclement when we set off next day. Though there was no rain an acrid fog hung about the capital which gave the streets a deceptively mild air but the biting cold came through, catching one unawares, so that I had to catch my breath and draw the collar of my heavy overcoat about me. We carried only valises so it was only a moment to engage a cab and with the good Mrs Johnson braving the elements to see us off from the top of the steps we had shortly collected Miss Hayling and were en route to King's Cross.

We had engaged a first-class compartment to ourselves and were soon speeding through the suburbs, the sun attempting to break through the iron-grey clouds which hung over the city. Once north of Welwyn the great locomotive got into its stride and the only indication of our immense speed was the rapid passage of the shadows of the telegraph poles across the carriage windows.

"There is something almost mystical about a great machine," Pons observed. "And the Scotsman is such a locomotive even in an age which has grown blasé over steam power. Eh, Miss Hayling?"

"You are certainly right, Mr Pons," said the girl.

She looked very becoming today in a smart tailored suit. She had put her overcoat and luggage on the rack and still wore the bobbled hat, which gave the carriage something of the atmosphere of our destination.

The trip passed uneventfully; we took lunch and high tea in the dining car and long before darkness fell we were well on our way. Pons spent much of the time studying his maps and occasionally scribbling notes, while I wracked my brains over *The Times* crossword, which I finally threw down in disgust.

"It is digit, Parker," Solar Pons observed with a smile.

"Eigh, Pons?"

"The answer to nine across, my dear fellow. I solved it almost immediately but refrained from filling it in as I did not want to spoil the problem for you."

"You have not done that, Pons," I observed grimly, picking up the paper and scanning the clues. It seemed blindingly simple once my companion had pointed it out and I was conscious of the fair girl's quiet amusement as I somewhat savagely inked the answer in.

I had noticed, as the journey progressed, that my companion, though apparently engrossed in his calculations, had cast sharp glances about him from time to time, particularly at people passing the door of the compartment. Now I was astonished to see him suddenly leap to his feet. We had in fact drawn the blinds as dusk fell, in order to ensure privacy, and Pons strode to the door and swiftly slid it open. A small man dressed in a salt and pepper suit with a bow-tie slid into the compartment with a muffled exclamation.

"Dear me," said Solar Pons gently, as he closed his hand over the elbow of the little man, ostensibly to steady him.

"I beg your pardon, sir," the latter stammered, blinking about him.

"It is rather a squeeze in the corridor here."

"It is rather a squeeze in here also," said Solar Pons, clamping his fingers on the other's arm and propelling him back into the passageway. The fellow howled with pain and tears ran down from beneath his horn-rimmed spectacles.

"You may tell your master that we are *en route* to Scotland," said Pons crisply. "That will save you a good deal of time and trouble. You may also add—though that is expecting rather too much of human nature—that you are doing your job extremely incompetently. There is an art to observing people without being noticed and you have not yet mastered it."

He slammed the door in the other's face and resumed his seat with a dry chuckle, oblivious of my astonishment and that of Miss Hayling.

"What on earth was that about, Pons?" I asked.

"That little man was obviously one of Colonel McDonald's agents," he observed soberly. "But, as I indicated, he is not very good at his job. I have noticed him no less than a dozen times during the day, giving our compartment an extremely close degree of attention. I happened to observe that the door had been slid back an inch or so, though I secured it firmly after tea. He was obviously listening in the corridor."

"Good heavens, Pons," I said. "This is serious. So we are expected at Glen Affric?"

"Of course, Parker," my companion said calmly. "We would have been in any case. I would have expected little less of the Colonel. He is leaving nothing to chance. You forget he has already made several attempts to remove me from his sphere of influence."

He pulled thoughtfully at the lobe of his left ear.

"The question is whether he will try anything before we reach our destination."

He turned to the girl.

"I take it we shall be breaking our journey in Edinburgh this evening?"

"Oh, certainly, Mr Pons. I took the precaution of booking rooms at one of the best hotels as soon as I left Dr Parker last night."

"Hmm."

Pons continued to look grave.

"We must be on our guard this evening, that is all. I think we must stay indoors tonight, Parker. An accident before we reached Glen Affric would suit McDonald's purposes nicely. But I do not think even he would be fool-hardy enough to try anything on a crowded train in broad daylight tomorrow."

And he immersed himself in his documents until we had arrived at our destination. I noticed his eyes were extremely watchful and alert as we alighted in the great, steam-filled vault of Waverley Station. He chuckled as the little man of the dramatic interview scuttled away.

"I fancy we have seen the last of him at least, Parker."

The evening was well advanced by this time and the air raw and damp and he hurried us out to the taxi-rank. In a few moments we were bowling swiftly down Princes Street to the elegant, not to say luxurious hotel Miss Hayling had engaged for us.

Pons glanced back through the rear window several times but as far as I could make out we were not being followed by any other vehicle. As though he could read my thoughts, Pons nodded grimly and put his empty pipe between his teeth.

"Unless I miss my guess, Parker, McDonald would know our destination in advance. He has a big organisation."

"Then why would he set someone to watch us on the train, Pons?"

"He wants to make sure we three have arrived at Waverley. Once we are in the city he can pick us up again without much trouble."

The girl shivered suddenly, though it was warm in the interior of the cab. We were screened from the driver by a heavy sheet of glass and I had already noted that Pons had given the man a very careful scrutiny, being at some pains not to choose the first vehicle in the station-rank.

"I am afraid I have involved you in a very black business, Mr Pons. I would never forgive myself for leading others into danger if something dreadful were to happen."

Solar Pons' eyes rested reflectively on the girl's face, now lit, now dark as the lights from shops in the great thoroughfare glanced across her expressive features.

"Do not disturb yourself, Miss Hayling," he said, solicitude in his tone. "You are forgetting I am operating within my own milieu. The danger and excitement of the chase are like meat and drink to me and the Colonel is an opponent worthy of my steel. My only concern was for your welfare."

The girl smiled winningly.

"Oh, I am safe enough in your company, Mr Pons," she said confidently. "I feel so much better already."

By this time the cab was crunching into the hotel forecourt and the discreet lights of the vestibule were beginning to compose themselves from the thin mist which lay about the city. Gas-lamps bloomed in the square and marched in stately rows along Princes Street until they were lost in the hazy shimmer. At any other time such a noble prospect would have gladdened my heart but our errand and the mortal danger in which Pons' young client stood filled my mind with foreboding.

We lost no time in paying off the cab and while the luggage was being carried in, we hurried the girl through into the warm luxuriance of the hotel lobby.

The evening passed without incident. After we had registered and taken possession of our respective rooms, we dined *à trois* at a side-table in the great elegant Edwardian restaurant with its crystal chandeliers and afterward took coffee in a cavernous smoking-room which had an enormous fire of logs blazing in its huge stone fireplace. Pons sat slightly apart from us, his eyes apparently directed toward the dimly-glimpsed façade of the square through the fog which seemed to have thickened at the long windows hung with filmy gauze. For some reason the hotel servants had not pulled to the thick velvet curtains in here but even as I noted the fact an elderly man in dark blue livery appeared to make a solemn, stately ritual of the drawing.

Pons swilled the whisky round moodily in his glass and turned toward me as the servant withdrew. The girl was facing away from us as the coffee-room waiter poured her another cup from the silver-plated pot and Pons lowered his voice as he spoke.

"I am worried about the young lady's safety, Parker. I am convinced the Colonel will make some attempt against her before we reach our destination. With her removal goes the last obstacle to him obtaining her property. You brought your revolver, as I requested?"

"Certainly, Pons," I replied. "It is securely packed in my luggage. Do you wish me to stand guard tonight outside the young lady's room?"

Pons glanced at me sharply and then gave me an affectionate smile.

"Hardly that, Parker, though it is good of you to discount your comfort in such a manner. I do not think the danger will manifest itself directly and Miss Hayling is safe enough among such surroundings. But there are a number of ways in which she may be approached."

I looked round quickly at the coffee-room waiter, who was exchanging a few commonplaces with Pons' client.

"Good heavens, Pons. Not through her food and drink, surely?"

Solar Pons shook his head, his eyes fixed thoughtfully on the old waiter.

"I hardly think so, Parker. It would be far too difficult for a stranger to penetrate the kitchen of such a hotel as this. And then there would be the difficulty of ascertaining which dish was intended for which guest. I fancy such an approach as I envisage would come from one of two sources. A fellow guest, perhaps . . . ?"

He broke off as if something had occurred to him, and then listened intently to the girl's explanations of our intended travel arrangements for the morrow. We would travel by train to Inverness, catching the ten o'clock fast and the gardener from the estate would meet us at Inverness with a pony and trap.

"That seems perfectly satisfactory, Pons," I said.

"As far as it goes, Parker," he said slowly. "Frankly, I do not like this weather and the thicker it is likely to get the farther north we go, particularly among the mountains."

"There is little we can do about it," I returned.

He shook his head.

"You are quite right, Parker. But a wise general makes his dispositions accordingly, taking account of both the weather and the movements of the enemy."

The girl turned very bright eyes on my companion.

"The danger is not past then, Mr Pons?"

"Not yet, Miss Hayling. I have no wish to alarm you, but we must still remain on our guard. I would like your promise that you will lock your room door tonight and not stir from it, except for any personal request from myself or Dr Parker."

Miss Hayling looked puzzled.

"I am not even to open to the hotel servants?"

Pons shook his head.

"Not even for the servants. In such an event please telephone to my room and I will come along. We will attend your room at eight o'clock tomorrow morning to escort you to breakfast."

The girl rose.

"Very well, Mr Pons. Goodnight."

When I had returned from seeing Miss Hayling to her room I found Pons sprawled in the smoking-room chair, a hazy cloud of smoke about him, a re-filled whisky glass at his elbow.

"Well, I think that about takes care of everything, Pons," I said with satisfaction.

My companion turned sombre eyes to me.

"We shall see, Parker, we shall see," he said slowly.

And he picked up his whisky glass again.

5

I was up betimes in the morning but early as I was, passing through the hotel lobby to fetch a newspaper, I was astonished to see Pons coming in from the open air. It was a bitterly cold day and mist had quite closed in the square outside and beads of gleaming moisture were stippling my friend's overcoat as he strode in through the main entrance.

"What on earth, Pons . . ." I began, when he rudely interrupted me.

"I have just been outside reconnoitring, Parker. A brief conversation with the Scottish taxi-driver, for example, is extremely rewarding. They do not often miss much of importance which takes place outside a large hotel."

"And what did you learn, Pons?"

"Very little, Parker. There has been nothing out of the ordinary. Which has me worried."

"Worried, Pons?"

Solar Pons' lean face was furrowed with concentration. He shook his head toward the misty street outside the vast glass doors.

"I shall not breathe easily until Miss Hayling is once again safe within her own four walls."

"Why do you think, if danger does threaten, that she was not molested on her way down to see us?"

"Because, Parker, it was not in the Colonel's interests to do anything precipitate. And the girl's telegram may have caught him off balance. Now that we are in the field he has nothing to lose."

He glanced up at the clock.

"Ah, it is five to eight. We have just time to collect Miss Hayling for breakfast."

We were ascending the great ornamental staircase that led to the upper floors when the hotel porter came down and met us at a turn in the stair. His face brightened.

"Ah, Mr Pons, I could not find you. I have just delivered the parcel to Miss Hayling's room. She would not open at first until she had identified my voice."

I had never seen such a change as that which came over Pons' face.

"Parcel? What parcel?"

"Why, sir, the parcel for Miss Hayling which came by special messenger a few minutes ago."

"And you have just delivered it to her?"

My friend did not wait for the porter's answer. He was electrified into action.

"Come, Parker! We have not a moment to lose!"

He took the stairs two at a time so that I was hard put to keep up with him. A few seconds later he was beating a tattoo at the girl's door.

"Miss Hayling! It is imperative that you do not open the packet which has just been delivered."

"Oh, Mr Pons. What is the matter?"

To our relief there came the grating of the key in the lock and the surprised face of the girl appeared in the opening of the door. Pons unceremoniously brushed by her and strode into the room, every line of his body denoting energy and purpose.

"Ah, there we are!"

I crossed quickly to Pons' side and looked at the small sandalwood box which the girl had set down on a side table. It bore a plain white label with Miss Hayling's name and hotel inked on it. It was about six inches square and had small holes drilled in the sides. I bent down close to it and it may have been my imagination but I sensed I could hear a faint rustling noise from inside.

Pons turned back to his client.

"You have made no attempt to open it?"

The fair girl shook her head.

"No, Mr Pons. I would not even let the porter in at first, as I remembered what you had told me."

"Excellent!"

Solar Pons rubbed his thin fingers together. The girl's eyes opened in surprise and she turned white.

"You do not think there is any danger in that packet?"

"We shall see, Miss Hayling. In the meantime I suggest you descend to the dining room and order breakfast. We will join you in a few minutes."

I could see by the spirited look in the girl's eyes that she was inclined to argue but the tense expression on Pons' face silenced her. She left us quickly and I stood in the open door of the room until she had descended the stairs.

When I turned back I could not see Pons for a moment and then I heard him call out from the adjoining bathroom.

"Just come in here for a moment will you, my dear fellow."

I found Pons with his sleeves rolled up, a grim look on his face. He started running hot water into the bath.

"What on earth are you up to, Pons?"

"I do not like cruelty to living creatures, Parker, but I fancy there is something abominable in this box. As I have no wish to risk our lives to indulge Colonel McDonald's sadistic instincts I intend to scald and drown whatever is within. There is no doubt it is a living creature for why otherwise would the air-holes be there."

"We do not even know it came from McDonald, Pons."

Solar Pons shook his head with a grim smile, reaching out one lean arm to turn off the tap.

"No-one knew we were at this hotel, Parker. I have Miss Hayling's word for that. It bears all the stamp of McDonald's work. We know we are under surveillance by his emissaries. Why the special box and the special messenger. Just pass me that long-handled scrubbing brush, if you please."

I did as he suggested and watched in silence as he dropped the box swiftly into the boiling water, holding it under with the brush. There were some noises coming from it now but Pons swiftly blotted them out by turning on the taps. He held the box under the surging water for perhaps a minute his face grim and tense.

"Now, my dear Parker," he said eventually, pulling out the drain-plug with the head of the brush. "We have need of your specialised knowledge, if you please."

He was searching around the bathroom as he spoke and grunted as he came across a thin metal spanner at the head of the bath. He held it in his hand, waiting as the last of the water swirled down the drain.

"Let me do it, Parker. We do not want any accidents."

I held the box, while he levered up the lid. There was paper inside, which had been made soggy with water, and we waited a moment to allow it to drain away. Cautiously, Pons parted it with the end of the spanner, his face concentrated and absorbed.

"There is no danger any more, Parker, I fancy."

I stood looking sickly down at the monstrous, bloated thing which was curled in death at the bottom of the box. It resembled nothing so much as a huddled mass of brownish-black fur, though I knew it was the biggest spider I had ever seen in my life.

"What on earth is it, Pons?"

"You may well ask, Parker. A tarantula. One of the most deadly creatures known to man. One bite could have been fatal, had Miss Hayling been unwise enough to open the box."

"Good heavens, Pons! I thought they inhabited only tropical climates."

Pons shook his head, his face set like stone.

"They are found mainly in Southern Europe, Parker. But you are right. This could not have existed long in a place like Edinburgh in January. Hence the warm packing. McDonald is a specialist in such things. I hear on good authority that he has an esoteric private zoo at his Scottish estate."

"Then this came from there, Pons?"

"Undoubtedly, Parker."

My companion became brisk in his manner. He got up, unrolled his sleeves and resumed his jacket. Carefully, he eased the sodden mass out of the box and swirled it down the drain-hole of the bath. He had to force it through the grille with the end of the spanner. He let the water run for a minute or two, his eyes expressing his anger. When he had cleaned the bath to his satisfaction he replaced the spanner and the long-handled brush and rinsed his hands thoughtfully. Then he turned to me.

"Miss Hayling must know nothing of this, Parker. She is worried enough already."

"But what are you going to tell her?"

There were little glints of amusement in my companion's eyes now.

"I shall think of something, Parker. Have I your word?"

"You may rely upon it, Pons."

"Good. And now, I think we have already done a good morning's work. It is more than time to join Miss Hayling for breakfast."

6

The train shuddered and came to a halt. Thin mist swirled about the platform. I huddled more deeply into my overcoat and handed out the cases to Pons after he had assisted Miss Hayling from the carriage.

"So this is Inverness, Pons?"

"It would appear so, Parker, if one can rely upon the station signboards. I believe you said you had a trap waiting, Miss Hayling?"

"There should be one, Mr Pons. I specifically ordered Mackintosh to be here. Ah, there he is!"

A tall, bearded man with a ruddy, good-humoured face was materialising through the groups of passengers who hurried toward the station exits. Carriage doors were slamming, there was the hiss of steam and all the bustle that I invariably associate with travel. Mackintosh, who wore a heavy caped tartan overcoat gave Miss Hayling a respectful salute and took our cases, looking curiously at Pons and myself.

"This is Mr Solar Pons and Dr Lyndon Parker," she explained. "They have come to help us in our problems."

"You are welcome indeed, gentlemen," said the gardener in a rich, smooth burr.

He extended a strong hand to Pons and myself.

"I have the trap just outside here, Miss."

We handed the young lady through the gate of the smart equipage drawn by a sturdy cob and Pons and I settled ourselves down opposite her while Mackintosh stowed the baggage. Then the gardener took his seat at the reins as we busied ourselves enveloping ourselves in the thick travelling rugs provided.

As soon as we had left the town the mist seemed to encroach more strongly and the cold bit to the bone. Pons had been extremely alert all the time we were at the station and in the inhabited streets of Inverness and I noticed that the girl always walked between the two of us, so that we shielded her on either side. But now that we were on the country road that wound up between frowning shoulders of hill, Pons relaxed somewhat and sat leaning forward, a thin plume of smoke from his pipe billowing over his shoulder to mingle with the mist, his lean, aquiline features brooding and heavy with thought.

The atmosphere into which we were going obtruded itself more and more and was not conducive to conversation, so we travelled in silence, the gardener Mackintosh skilfully handling the reins, the sure-footed cob sturdily breasting the rises with its heavy load. We were still going in a northerly direction, despite the twisting and turning of the undulating road and it was soon obvious that we were straying into strange and lonely country.

Not that we could see much of it for the mist clung clammily to tree and hedgerow; but beyond the white blanket, which occasionally drew aside momentarily in currents of air, I could see bleak pine forests and the shaggy shoulders of mountain. The road itself dipped and fell so that Mackintosh eased the cob back to a walk and we jolted on through the damp, bitterly cold winter morning, each of us lost in his or her own thoughts.

Only once was there a change in the landscape and that was when another momentary break in the mist showed us the dark, sullen surface of a large black lake or loch which lay in a vast hollow beyond a fringe of trees to the right of the road. In response to my interrogatory look, Miss Hayling broke the long silence.

"Loch Affric," she said. "We shall not be much longer before we arrive at our destination."

"It is indeed a remote spot," I ventured.

The girl gave a wry smile, her eyes fixed beyond our little group in the trap, as though she could penetrate the mist which had again descended, blotting out the dark and brooding aspect of the loch.

"Just wait until you have seen the estate, Dr Parker. Then will you and Mr Pons fully appreciate the situation in which I found myself."

Pons nodded sombrely, his pipe glowing cheerfully as he shovelled smoke out over his shoulder at a furious rate. But I noticed that his eyes were stabbing glances all around and his whole attitude reminded me of a terrier or game dog whose every sense was attuned to this strange and bizarre atmosphere into which every beat of the horse's hooves was leading us.

The land by now was excessively hilly and the lonely road wound crazily this way and that, bordered by dark plantations of firs and pines so that it was inexpressibly gloomy. I felt my own heart becoming oppressed by the surroundings and marvelled at the girl and her family choosing to make their dwelling in this outlandish place.

As though he could read my thoughts Pons observed to the girl, "Tell me, Miss Hayling, this country, as you have already told us, is almost impossible for farming. It looks equally forbidding for leisure pursuits."

"That is correct, Mr Pons," said our hostess earnestly. "Now that you see it for yourself I am sure you will agree the notion is quite preposterous. There is some fishing, certainly a little shooting but hereabouts forestry with some grazing is about the only possibility."

Pons nodded, puffing thoughtfully at his pipe.

"This Colonel McDonald, Miss Hayling. Do his estates adjoin yours in any way?"

Mackintosh turned round in his seat at mention of McDonald and I saw him and the young lady exchange a long look. The latter nodded vigorously.

"Oh, yes indeed, Mr Pons. You might almost say we are encircled by his property."

Pons' eyes flashed beneath the brim of his hat as he glanced across at me.

"That is extremely interesting, Miss Hayling, and could explain many things."

"I fail to see, Pons . . ." I began when we were interrupted by a lurching movement of the trap and Mackintosh applied the brake. I saw that we were travelling down a steep hill into a valley so deep that it appeared to be nothing more than a vast bowl half-filled with mist.

"This is the river hereabouts, Mr Pons," said the girl. "It is a gloomy place, I am afraid."

I hung on to the rail at the side of the cart and prayed that nothing would happen to the brakes as the cob was having some difficulty in keeping its feet. A few moments later Pons and I, by tacit consent and without speaking descended, and Pons went to take the horse's head. I walked with him and we proceeded like this for some way. It was indeed an awe-inspiring place and we seemed to be descending an interminable distance down the narrow, twisting road.

Presently the slope eased out and Mackintosh brought the cob to a halt to give him a rest. He slipped down to give the beast a knob of sugar.

"Thank you, gentlemen," he said. "The hill is a very difficult place and yon slope the other side is little different."

As a breath of wind slightly cleared the mist I saw that we were almost on to a right-angle turn leading over a large rustic bridge, which had white-painted railings protecting the edges. Pons and I walked across and after a short while the trap followed. Pons paused at the far edge and rested his two hands on the edge of the palings. Far away and below us, apparently at a vast distance, came the rushing of water. The trap was now level with us and Mackintosh drew it up obediently. Pons turned to Miss Hayling.

"I am sorry to revive sad memories, Miss Hayling, but is this the spot where your parents met their fatal accident?"

The girl shivered, though not with cold, and a dark shadow passed across her face.

The Adventure of the Callous Colonel

"That is so, Mr Pons. Just a little farther along. The carriage is still down there."

Pons' languid air was transformed.

"What do you mean?"

"Why, Mr Pons, the place is so steep and the slopes either side so precipitous that it still rests on the bed of the stream."

"Indeed."

Solar Pons' eyes were glittering with excitement and he puffed smoke furiously from his pipe.

"So there was no evidence about the carriage produced at the inquest?"

"I do not quite follow you, Mr Pons."

"No matter, my dear young lady. If you will excuse me for a few minutes I will just satisfy my curiosity."

To my astonishment he walked a little farther over the bridge, skirted the railing where it re-joined the road at another steep turn and disappeared into the dark, misty woodlands which led down to the invisible stream below. For some while I could hear the swishing of his shoes among the leaves and then they died out in the noise of the river. Mackintosh sat politely, his eyes in front of him, though I could sense he was as astonished as the rest of us. In the event more than a quarter of an hour had passed before Pons reappeared, dusting himself down absently.

"You will forgive me, I am sure, Miss Hayling, but I always like to see things for myself."

"And what did you see, Pons?" I asked as we re-seated ourselves in the trap.

"Oh, the vehicle is there all right, Parker. The stream is quite shallow and I could see it clearly through the dark water. We can have it up, if necessary."

"Have it up, Pons?"

Solar Pons nodded but further conversation was again interrupted by the necessity of descending once more as the way again became extremely steep and dangerous, leading upward eventually from the other side of the bridge toward the estate of Glen Affric. We passed two lichen-encrusted gate-posts surmounted by stone heraldic griffins and were then on a sort of plateau which contained the park. Miss Hayling pointed off to the right, where the blank white wall of mist skirted the driveway.

"In good weather one has an excellent view of our local mountain, Ben Affric, in that direction, gentlemen."

"Indeed."

Pons looked musingly about him but it was obvious that even had the air been clear his thoughts were far away and absorbed with calculations that were obscure to me. The road led steeply up the drive which wound between a gloomy avenue of trees, now dank and dripping moisture in the bitingly cold air. Twice Pons glanced back behind him and I thought at first he feared we were followed but then realised he was reconstructing in his mind the tragic scene as the late Mr and Mrs Hayling's trap bowled down that steep hill and through the main gates for the last time.

At length we came up through a dark, almost threatening mass of rhododendron and evergreen shrubbery into a gravelled concourse beyond which lay the long, low granite mass of the house. With its yellowed walls and lichen; the heraldic devices repeated on stone shields below the turret-like roofs; and the Gothic stable-block beyond, it was a forbidding sight and my heart sank at the lonely and oppressive atmosphere of the place, lost in these dank and dripping pine woods.

But Pons sprang alertly down to assist the lady, merely observing, "You will note, Parker, that Miss Hayling has spoken correctly. The estate is the only flat land for miles around. I commend that factor to you."

"I cannot see its significance, Pons," I confessed.

But my companion had already turned to the massive figure of Mackintosh as his client hurried toward the front steps of the house.

"I should like to have that trap up from the stream-bed by tomorrow, Mackintosh, if it is at all possible."

The gardener scratched his head, looking thoughtfully at the horse which was staring wistfully toward the stable-block.

"Well, sir, it would be possible if you are really determined on it."

"I am so determined," said Solar Pons.

The grave eyes were appraising my companion now.

"Well, sir, if it is to help Miss Hayling, I would do anything for the leddy. We have a tenant who farms a few acres just below here. In fact there are two farmers who manage to scrape some sort of a living from the skirts of our land. If he and his boy are not too busy we might try to get it up."

"I would be obliged. It will not be necessary to recover the equipage, merely to raise it from the water in order that I may make a brief examination."

The Adventure of the Callous Colonel

"It shall be done, sir."

Mackintosh raised his whip in salute and rattled off to the stables at a brisk pace.

"What do you hope to find, Pons?"

"Evidence of crime, Parker," said my companion grimly as we hurried across the concourse with our hand baggage to where the slim figure of Miss Hayling waited at the head of the steps.

The house was indeed sombre and lonely though Miss Hayling's hospitality was lavish and Mr and Mrs McRae were kind and attentive. It was obvious that the atmosphere had lightened with Pons' arrival and as we were served a late lunch in an old oak-panelled dining-room Miss Hayling's manner was bright, almost gay at times.

She answered all Pons' questions in great detail and the events at the house and in the grounds were gone through again, this time with the benefit of Pons being on the spot. So dark did it get in these northerly latitudes in winter-time that it was almost dusk by the time we had finished at table but despite this Pons insisted on seeing round outside and listened to our hostess's explanations of the estate with keen attention.

If anything, Glen Affric, the girl's property being named after the nearby glen, was more bleak and remote than before in the fading light. The chill mist persisted but despite this Pons tramped about the stable-yard and the adjoining paths through the fir-plantations with energy and gusto, occasionally asking questions of Mackintosh, who accompanied us, and at other times darting aside silently on small expeditions of his own.

It was during one such that we temporarily found ourselves alone, Miss Hayling having gone in search of her black Labrador which was engaged in chasing an imaginary rabbit.

"I have already spoken to the tenant farmer about that matter, Mr Pons," the gardener said diffidently. "There should be no difficulty. We will try and get the cart up by midday tomorrow."

"Excellent," said Pons crisply, turning his head as the girl came up with the dog at her heels.

"This must be the spot hereabouts, where you were attacked, is it not?"

The good Mackintosh' face turned brick-red and he knotted his thick fist.

"Aye, Mr Pons, a little farther down here. As you can see the shrubbery comes quite near the edge of the path. The black villain sprang on me as my back was turned or I'd have given him a hard fight of it, sir."

"I have no doubt of that," I said encouragingly.

The girl smiled at the gardener's expression, calling to the dog, which was sniffing about in the bushes. But she stopped when Pons held up his hand, an alert expression on his face.

"I believe he has found something."

The dog was in fact snarling at this point, as though he had discovered something particularly unpleasant. I followed Pons as he strode into the clump of bushes. It was still light enough to see clearly and I could make out an area of muddy ground which looked as though someone had trampled over it.

"Have you been through here lately, Mr Mackintosh?"

"Not I, sir," said the gardener in his sturdy manner. "When that villain hit me I lost consciousness and came to myself in the driveway. I must have staggered some yards and I had no idea from what direction my attacker had come. There was no point in searching the shrubbery at any particular point. Of course, the police were called and went all over the place, but the rain would have blotted out their tracks weeks ago."

Solar Pons shook his head, his deep-set eyes searching the ground. "I do not think the police would be involved. Someone has been standing here for a long time, as though watching the house."

He looked thoughtfully at the blanket of mist which pressed upon us.

"Can one see the house from here in normal conditions?"

"Most certainly, Mr Pons," the girl said. "It is only a few hundred yards."

Pons had stopped now and was going over the ground carefully, his thin, sensitive fingers raking in the icy mud. He gave a muffled exclamation and came up with two yellowed slivers of something that looked like wood or cardboard. He held them up to Mackintosh.

"You know what these are?"

"Of course, Mr Pons. Swan Vestas."

Solar Pons nodded.

"Exactly. Someone stood here smoking and watching the house, dropping his matches from time to time and stamping them out on the ground. Perhaps you surprised him when you came along the path in the dusk. He may have dropped something else in his hurry. Hullo!"

I looked round, startled by the urgency in his voice.

"I fancy the dog has something there in his mouth, Miss Hayling."

The Labrador had, in fact, a black bedraggled object which it was shaking and worrying with a dreadful intensity. The animal rolled its eyes and I thought it was going to bite the gardener as he bent to take it from him. When he had wrested it away from the Labrador he handed it to Pons.

"Nothing but an old oilskin tobacco pouch, Mr Pons."

"Mmm."

Pons studied it in silence.

"Half-full of Coronation Mixture, I see. And the initials M.F. in gold lettering on the side. What does that suggest to you, Parker?"

"Mungo Ferguson, Pons!"

"You have not quite lost your ratiocinative touch, Parker. The name fits rather too pat it would appear."

"I do not follow you, Pons."

"Do you not, Parker. We have every reason to believe that Ferguson is the tool of McDonald."

"You mean the Colonel left the pouch here, Pons!"

"Possibly, Parker. Or he has his own reasons for employing a hot-headed and unreliable tool."

The girl's eyes blazed and she looked at Solar Pons in amazement.

"The dog hates Ferguson, Mr Pons. No wonder he was growling."

She paused, controlling her emotions.

"Are you suggesting Colonel McDonald is using the man Ferguson as a scapegoat, Mr Pons?"

My companion looked at her mildly, putting the oilskin pouch into his pocket.

"Nothing is impossible in these romantic surroundings, Miss Hayling. But it is a cold and inclement night, with darkness fast approaching. We can do little more here. I propose we adjourn to the house where we may plan our strategy for the morrow."

7

I was late abed the next morning, possibly because I slept soundly after our journey and the strange change of scene, and it was past nine o'clock when I joined Pons at the breakfast table. Miss Hayling was in the study discussing some matter with McRae and Pons was alone, his head wreathed in tobacco smoke, frowningly studying large-scale maps of the area. He seemed oblivious of my presence but as Mrs McRae smilingly appeared with silver breakfast dishes on a tray he abruptly waved his hand to disperse the tobacco smoke and moved his charts to one side.

"Forgive me, my dear fellow. My manners are abominable when I become absorbed in these problems."

"Think nothing of it, Pons," I said, falling to with a will on the great platter of bacon, eggs and sausages Mrs McRae had prepared.

"I have such an appetite your pipe does not bother me at all."

"It is indeed good of you, Parker," said my companion with a sly smile at Mrs McRae. "Yes, thank you, Mrs McRae, I will have another cup of that excellent coffee if there is enough to spare."

"There is plenty here, Mr Pons," said that good lady, pouring for us both. "And if there were not I would be glad to make a third pot."

I studied Pons between mouthfuls.

"You have made some progress?"

"A little, Parker. Tell me, Mrs McRae, how is your knowledge of these parts?"

"Extensive but not exhaustive, Mr Pons."

"Excellent. Pray sit here for a moment or two, if you please."

Mrs McRae sat down opposite, looking with puzzled eyes at my companion.

"Can you read a map at all with any accuracy, Mrs McRae?"

"Tolerably well, Mr Pons. My husband and I did a great deal of walking in the old days, when we were young."

"I see."

Solar Pons tented his thin fingers before him, his deep-set eyes fixed on the housekeeper.

"The large-scale map of this area in front of you, for instance. Would you be able to indicate to me roughly, using this thick black crayon, the boundaries of Colonel McDonald's estates."

"I think so, Mr Pons."

Mrs McRae sat with pursed lips, studying the map intently while Pons sat quietly smoking, his eyes studying her face. I had finished my bacon and eggs and had started on the toast and marmalade before she stirred. Then she seized the crayon and started etching boundaries over a large section of the map.

"That, to the best of my knowledge, is the extent of the Colonel's lands, Mr Pons. I have no doubt Miss Hayling would corroborate, though I could not vouch for fine detail. The land by the stream there and the more mountainous parts may be inaccurate by a quarter of a mile or so."

"A quarter of a mile or so, Mrs McRae!" said Pons, surprise on his face. "You are a paragon among female cartographers!"

"You make fun of me, Mr Pons."

"By no means, Mrs McRae. I have never been more serious. Those lines you have drawn are invaluable. My grateful thanks."

"You are welcome, I'm sure."

Mrs McRae rose, the surprise still evident on her face and with a reiterated statement that if we required anything further we were to ring, withdrew.

Pons sat for some minutes, studying the map, his eyes glittering with suppressed excitement. I sat back in my chair and finished my second cup of coffee. It was still almost dark outside, but the strengthening light showed only dim outlines of soaked coppices through the thin mist.

"You have found something, Pons?"

"It has confirmed my suspicions, Parker. Except for the main roads, Colonel McDonald's lands completely surround the estate of Glen Affric. More significantly, Miss Hayling's property is the only flat land of any size in these parts, the remainder consisting of bleak hillside, rough glen and undulating forest-land, most of it extremely inhospitable indeed."

"Is that of significance, Pons?"

"Absolutely vital, Parker. It is an essential clue to this bizarre business. Look here."

I drew my chair over, following the tip of the crayon, and carefully examined the map. By using the figures given for contours I was able to see it was indeed as Pons had said. Much of the land owned by the Colonel was precipitous and most of it lay at an altitude of over 2,000 feet.

"Let me have your thoughts on the matter, Parker."

I frowned at him through the pipe-smoke.

"I have not many, truth to tell, Pons. Perhaps it is as the girl says. The Land Trust want Miss Hayling's property for holiday development."

Solar Pons narrowed his eyes thoughtfully through the smoke.

"I fancy there is a good deal more to it than that, Parker. However, McDonald is an expert at floating bogus companies. We will see what the Land Trust office has to say. They are located at Inverness, are they not?"

"I believe Miss Hayling said so, Pons."

I studied the map again but the more I looked at it the more puzzling the problem became. We were interrupted at our occupation by the entrance of Pons' client. She was dressed in a thick sweater, a long skirt and stout boots so it was evident that she was prepared for some heavy walking about the estate.

"I am just off to the Five-Acre Wood with Mr McRae, gentlemen. If there is anything further you require, Mackintosh or Mrs McRae will be glad to look after your wants."

"We are quite well provided for, Miss Hayling," said Pons equably. "And I have my day planned out, thank you."

The girl smiled.

"Very good, gentlemen. Lunch is at one. I will see you then."

We both stood as the girl left the room, her slim, lithe body the picture of health and energy.

"A very brave young lady, Pons," I observed.

"I believe you have already said so, Parker. But it is a truism worth repeating, nevertheless."

A few moments later we saw our hostess walk past the window with McRae.

"You do not think she is in any danger, Pons?"

My companion shook his head.

"Not for the moment. I fancy McRae can look after himself. She is in good hands."

As soon as the couple had disappeared along the misty drive Solar Pons was galvanised into action.

"Now that the young lady is away, Parker, we can set to work. We must first find Mackintosh and I must then descend to the stream at the bottom of the ravine. It is imperative that we get that dog-cart up."

"Just give me a minute or two, Pons," I said. "I need my thick walking boots and an overcoat."

"Very well, my dear fellow, but do hurry."

When I bustled downstairs five minutes later Pons was already standing impatiently on the drive before the house, obviously eager to be off. We could not find Mackintosh at his cottage or the stable-block. It was now full daylight and Pons looked at his watch anxiously.

"I think we will make our own way there, Parker."

I followed him down the drive. The mist had lifted a little but it was still a bleak and inhospitable day.

"Perhaps Mackintosh is already down there, supervising the lifting operations," I suggested, as I fell into step with him.

"Perhaps, Parker. We shall see."

And he said nothing further until we had arrived at the bridge. The way down was indeed steep and precipitous and I must confess my heart sank when I thought of our errand and the terrible end of the girl's parents in their headlong dash to destruction over this very road.

Our footsteps echoed hollowly in the mist and only the harsh cry of some bird broke the eerie stillness. Moisture pattered faintly from the dripping foliage and the bitter air rasped in one's throat while our breath smoked out of our mouths. Pons had thrust his pipe into his pocket and walked along grimly, his brows frowning over his deep-set eyes. I had rarely seen him look so serious. For some reason he had seized a thick hawthorn stick from the hall-stand as he left the house and he slashed moodily at various pieces of foliage at the roadside as we descended.

We had reached the bridge and the sombre gorge now and I could hear the faint fret of the river in the far depths below. It struck with a chilling note to the heart. Pons glanced keenly about him.

"You have your revolver, Parker?"

I tapped the breast-pocket of my overcoat.

"You insisted on me bringing it north, Pons. You told me we were on a dangerous business. I have it here."

A faint smile curled the corners of his lips.

"Excellent, Parker. You are running true to form."

He had turned aside as he spoke and plunged downward between the dark boles of the trees as though he had known the place all his life. I followed rather more hesitantly, as it was slippery underfoot, and I was more than once thankful for the thick cleats on the soles of my heavy boots.

8

It was a dark and gloomy place and the incessant fret of the water, which grew ever louder, only emphasised its sombreness. Pons led at a fast pace, winding downward through the shadowy boles of the trees, the water roaring in our ears now. I saw as we came level with the stream that it tumbled over boulders below the bridge and then flowed level, though swiftly, in a calmer manner.

Pons plunged forward along the bank, following the curve of the stream, until he arrived at a point just below the falls where there was deep, fairly agitated water. He looked up toward the bridge, which was hidden from us by the thick matting of undergrowth and tree-boles.

"A bad place, Parker. They would have hit the head of the waterfall and then come down the fall into the deeper water here."

"You mean Miss Hayling's parents, Pons. An awful business."

I stared at the white, broken water but was roused from my reverie by a sharp exclamation from my companion.

"Extraordinary though it may seem, it has gone, Parker. Mackintosh has been true to his word."

I followed his gaze. Though dark, the stream was clear here and I could see to the bottom. There was certainly no sign of the wreckage of the dog-cart. Pons was already moving again and I followed him across large boulders which made a series of stepping-stones. They were wet and slippery and the water ran surging and deep between them so that I was glad to reach the far bank without a ducking. There were dark runnels torn in the soil here, where the cart had been dragged up the bank. Pons looked sharply about him.

"I shall be surprised if this is Mackintosh' work, Parker," he said drily.

He slashed moodily at the undergrowth with his stick.

"I do not follow you, Pons."

"Do you not, Parker. It is crystal-clear. But it merely confirms what I wished to know."

He turned as there came a crashing noise in the bushes. The angry figure of Mackintosh appeared, with a puzzled-looking farm-worker in corduroy behind him.

"It is disgraceful, Mr Pons! I have never heard the like!"

"I take it you did not remove the cart, Mackintosh."

"Not I, sir," replied the other grimly. "It has been taken out by the people from the neighbouring smallholding and burned in their yard! Despite the fact that this is private property!"

"By whose orders?"

"Mr Mungo Ferguson's sir!"

Solar Pons smiled grimly. He turned to me.

"This promises to be rather interesting, Parker. Let us just find out the situation. Is Mr Ferguson there?"

Mackintosh nodded gloomily, falling in at Pons' side as we walked uphill, away from the babbling stream.

"Aye, Mr Pons. Supervising the burning. I gave him my tongue and he is in no better temper for it. I thought it best to come away for he is a formidable man when the anger is on him. I know not what you wanted to prove, Mr Pons, but there was little left of the cart when I last saw it."

Pons nodded, his deep-set eyes gleaming.

"It was of oak, I should have said."

"That's right, Mr Pons. It had lasted well, despite the action of the water."

"How on earth did he burn it?" I put in.

Mackintosh turned a puzzled face to me over his shoulder.

"He poured petrol over it, Dr Parker. If ever a man seemed determined to destroy another's property, it was Mungo Ferguson."

"Destroy evidence, rather," said Pons, a hard expression in his eyes. "Well, he has played right into our hands."

He increased his pace and as we came up from that gloomy valley I cold see thick black smoke billowing across the trees, where low, poor-looking farm buildings jutted from the landscape. Mackintosh turned to speak to the man in corduroy and he went back across the fields, presumably to his own farm.

Within a very few minutes we had come upon an extraordinary scene. In the midden within the three sides formed by the stout stone walls of the farmhouse, byre and stable, were a group of wild-looking men, standing round a great fire of bracken and wood. They were labouring types obviously and the dominant figure among them, who stood a little apart and directed them, was a gigantic figure in hairy tweeds with flaming red hair and a thick beard. Pons chuckled quietly to himself.

"Mr Mungo Ferguson," he said with satisfaction. "Well, Parker, the best means of defence is attack, is it not?"

And without more ado he strode across to the group round the fire, who watched with a sort of sullen fascination as we came up. The huge man, who had a coarse, inflamed face, had been shouting at the men about the fire and I now saw that it contained the remains of a carriage, obviously the one with which we were concerned. It was almost all consumed and the shafts had evidently been the first to go, for there was no sign of them. Two petrol cans stood at a distance from the bonfire and it was obvious that they had been used to ignite the sodden wood.

"Who is responsible for this?" said Solar Pons, coming to a halt near the group of men, but glancing sidelong at the figure of the bearded man who toyed with a shooting-stick in one gigantic hand. The men stirred uneasily but before they could reply the big man came to life. He stamped forward menacingly, holding the metal stick in his hand, and glared at my companion.

"You are on private property. You are trespassing."

"I am well aware of that," said Solar Pons evenly. "You are burning private property, are you not?"

Ferguson had a loud, coarse voice and his eyes flamed with anger, but there was something about Pons' quiet, resolute manner, that made him pause and choose his words with relative care.

"The carriage has been blocking yon stream for a long time. We thought it was time to have it out."

Solar Pons smiled thinly.

"An odd coincidence, was it not, that you chose the very day we had decided to remove it ourselves?"

"Maybe," Ferguson snapped.

He came closer, his manner bristling and prickly.

"You have a name do you?"

"Solar Pons. And you, judging by your coarseness and lack of manners must be Mungo Ferguson."

There was a hoarse burst of laughter from the men round the fire and Ferguson drew himself up, his red-rimmed eyes filled with hatred.

"Solar Pons!"

He bit the words off savagely.

"The London detective! The meddler and pryer into other people's affairs!"

Solar Pons stood quietly, perfectly at ease, a smile on his lips. His assured attitude seemed to enrage the red-haired man.

"Well, we have a way with meddlers in these parts, Mr Solar Pons! We pitch them down the mountainside, head first!"

Solar Pons drew himself up, his right hand firm and steady on the stick.

"You are welcome to try, my vulgar fellow, but I would not advise it."

With a bellow of rage Mungo Ferguson lurched forward, raising the shooting-stick. Mackintosh had started forward in alarm and I was before him but our assistance was not needed. The stout hawthorn stick moved round so quickly it was just a blur in the air. There was a dull crack as it connected with the giant's shin and he gave a low howl of pain.

Pons turned swiftly as the red-haired man staggered, falling forward; he brought the shooting-stick round in a vain effort to support himself but he had not even reached the ground before my companion caught him two resounding blows across the thick of the body. He fell with a tremendous crash and there was blood on his chin as he scrambled to his feet, a burning madness in his eyes.

"I have some little experience of bar-room brawls," said Solar Pons coolly, "and am able to meet you on your own terms. I would advise you to cut your losses."

There was an enraged bellow from the giant and he came forward, his huge fists flailing. Light as a ballet dancer, Pons moved to one side so that the man's mad rush took him past. The stick came round again, tripping him this time. When he regained his feet, his face plastered with mud and green from the grass, he had lost much of his confidence, but he still came forward with a low growl.

"This has gone far enough, sir," said Mackintosh in a concerned voice, though he could not erase the delight from his features.

The huge man thrust him aside and leapt at Pons for the third time. His blows met only empty air. Then Pons had thrown the heavy stick down; Ferguson staggered as Pons' left caught him on the point of the chin. My companion's second blow, from his right, clipped him exactly in the classic textbook spot and his eyes glazed. He went down, his body square in the heart of the fire, red-hot ashes, cinders and sparks erupting into the air like fireworks.

I rushed forward with Pons to drag him clear and soon saw that though he was unconscious, there was little damage done, except for a scorch-mark on the breast of his overcoat and a smouldering coat-tail. The awed group of men tending the bonfire moved to let us pass. Pons retrieved his stick from the ground, his eyes sparkling, his breathing even and normal, his voice good-tempered.

"You may tell Mr Ferguson when he comes to himself that the Colonel now has me to deal with. He will understand."

He looked down thoughtfully at the unconscious giant.

"If I were you I should lose no time in getting him to his home. He will catch a chill lying on the ground at this time of the year."

And with a dry chuckle he turned on his heel and made his way back across the fields, re-tracing the route we had already followed. Mackintosh caught up with us before we had gone ten yards.

"That was champion, sir. Just champion. I have never seen the like. Allow me to shake you by the hand, Mr Pons."

The old fellow was so sincere in his admiration and delight that Pons smilingly extended his hand.

"It was nothing," he said carelessly. "I was quite a good amateur boxer at one time. But the affair was a single-stick bout for the most part and I must confess I rather pride myself on my prowess in that direction."

I fell into step alongside him.

"At any rate it has demoralised friend Ferguson and thrown the enemy into disorder," said Pons reflectively. "I have no time for such bullies and there is no doubt in my mind that it was Ferguson who downed you in the coppice that dark evening, Mackintosh."

The old man's face was clouded with anger.

"Then you have made ample restitution, Mr Pons, and I am doubly grateful to you."

"You have made a bad enemy, Pons," said I.

"Tut, Parker, he is a tool, merely, and as such of no importance. But unless I miss my guess the incident will bring some reaction from the Colonel. The thing is as plain as daylight to both of us. Each reads the other like a book."

"I do not quite follow you, Pons."

"Ah, here we are at the stream again," said my companion, as though he had not heard my comment, and he was silent and preoccupied with his thoughts until we had again regained the comfortable quarters assigned to us at our hostess' estate.

9

Smoke and steam obscured the platform as we descended from the carriage in the biting air.

"But why are we returning to Inverness, Pons? And by such a roundabout route? That long journey in the dog-cart and then the change of train and boring wait?"

"Tut, Parker," said Solar Pons impatiently, as we gave up our tickets at the barrier.

"It is elementary, surely. The Land Trust offices are at Carnock House, Inverness. Therefore, to Inverness we must go."

"But Mackintosh could have driven us here direct, just as he did when we came," I protested.

Solar Pons shook his head, impatience showing in his deep-set eyes.

"You are not using your brain, Parker," he said crisply. "And give away our destination? The thrashing I gave Mungo Ferguson would have reached the Colonel's ears very quickly. Before he has time to react, we have made our move. I wanted to reach Inverness secretly, before he has an inkling of what we are about."

"I see, Pons," I said, as we hurried down a side-street opposite the station. "But where is Carnock House?"

"I have already looked it up," said Solar Pons, shifting his valise from one hand to the other. "It is a pity that we have to leave Miss Hayling for one night like this but there was no alternative if I was to find out what I wanted. But with Mackintosh sleeping in the house tonight and the McRaes on the alert, she is safe enough for the moment."

"But what do you expect to find here today, Pons?"

"The Land Trust is the key to the whole thing, Parker. I must find out what sort of statements they are issuing. The girl's property is the crux of the matter. This is where you come in, Parker."

"Me, Pons?"

I looked at him in some alarm, as we turned into a broad, impressive-looking thoroughfare, crowded with shoppers and traffic.

"Your grammar is going to pieces in your agitation, Parker, but I follow your drift. I want you to play out a little comedy in the main office and keep the clerk they employ busy."

"What will you be doing in the meantime?"

Solar Pons chuckled.

"Breaking into their private quarters, Parker."

I gazed at him in horror.

"You cannot be serious, Pons!"

My friend stared at me sombrely.

"I was never more serious, Parker. The young lady's life is in danger. McDonald will step up his campaign against her now that I am on his home territory. You surely have not forgotten that creature at the hotel?"

I shivered and drew my overcoat collar closer round me.

"You are right, as ever, Pons. But what are we to do if we are caught? There may be others on the staff."

Solar Pons shook his head as we turned into a large, imposing-looking court, crowded with offices and commercial buildings.

"I have already deduced from what our client says, Parker, that the office is a sham, merely designed to give respectability and credence to the Colonel's operations. It is imposing enough, I give you, but if we are to believe Miss Hayling it is not even on the telephone. The young fellow McDonald employs as a clerk is respectable enough, and no doubt believes in the reality of the brochures and literature he sends out. But he is the only person on the premises so my scheme should not be too difficult to put into operation."

I looked at him with pursed lips.

"Let us hope you are right, Pons. Otherwise we shall not need our hotel reservations while spending the night in police cells."

Pons was still chuckling when we came in sight of the discreet gilt lettering of the Scottish Land Trust offices. They were respectable-looking premises in a narrow-chested building of clean-cut granite, whose bow windows were filled with impressive cabinet photographs and printed literature drawing-pinned to green baize boards. I paused and pretended to examine the windows while Pons turned aside under a small archway which immediately adjoined the building and led to a cobbled courtyard at the side.

He was back again in a few moments, his face bright and alert. He handed me the valise.

"It is just as I thought, Parker. There is a small private office with a glass door which a child could unlock. There are filing cabinets and desks and I should be able to find what I want there. Now listen carefully, because I want you to follow my instructions implicitly."

A few minutes later, as I entered the office, there was no sign of Pons in the street outside. I had begun my task in doubt and uncertainty knowing that we were engaged in illegal, perhaps even criminal proceedings, but the young man with dark hair who rose eagerly from his desk at the back of the office to come to the counter on my entry, was so naive and unversed in the profession for which he was so obviously unfitted that I rapidly regained my confidence.

The elaborate and searching questions about the Scottish Land Trust with which Pons had primed me, soon had young Wilson in a tangle and he had shortly retreated to his desk, pencil in hand, while he searched for a slip of paper on which to note his mumbled calculations. When he rejoined me at the counter, there were little patches of pink on his cheeks and his manner was agitated and nervous in the extreme. But I think I carried out my task with commendable thoroughness. With the brochures and other literature spread out on the counter-top between us, I plied the young clerk with searching questions so that the quarter of an hour Pons had stipulated had seemingly passed in a flash.

Twenty-five minutes had ensued before Wilson had extricated himself from the morass of questions and another five before I had gathered up all the material he had placed before me. I finished up by giving the young man an entirely fictitious name and address and he was so pleased to get rid of me that he actually ran round the counter-flap to open the street door.

I walked on briskly down the road, in the thickening mist, in case he was still looking after me and at the next corner came across Pons indolently studying the contents of a tobacconist's window. He turned to me with a welcoming smile.

"Excellent, Parker. You played your part to perfection. That question about investments overseas was shrewdly phrased."

I looked at him in puzzlement.

"How would you know that, Pons?"

"Because I was the other side of the door to the inner office watching you both," he said quietly, falling into step as we wended our way back through the narrow streets.

"You had some luck, then?"

He nodded, putting the stem of his empty pipe between his teeth.

"It has been a most fruitful expedition, Parker. We have only to visit Mr Angus Dermot at Culzean Lodge and we are free to return to Miss Hayling's estate."

"Mr Angus Dermot, Pons?"

My companion nodded. He drew two heavy sheaves of documents from his pocket.

"He is a geologist and mineralogist who fortunately lives quite close by in Inverness. If he is at home we will have saved a good deal of time and trouble."

And he quickened his pace as though trying to outstrip his racing thoughts. When I caught up with him at the next corner, he had turned into a quiet street of broad-fronted, respectable-looking houses whose trim front gardens led to carved mahogany doors whose brassware winked welcomingly through the mist.

His ring at the bell was answered by a trim, short man of about thirty with dark, tousled hair and a good-natured face. His eyes expressed surprise behind his steel-framed spectacles.

"Mr Angus Dermot?"

"Yes. What can I do for you, gentlemen?"

"My business is private, Mr Dermot, and cannot be discussed in the street. My name is Solar Pons and this is my friend and colleague, Dr Lyndon Parker."

The young man's cheeks flushed slightly and he shifted nervously on the door-step.

"Mr Pons! The famous detective. Forgive my manners, gentlemen. Come in by all means though what you can want with me I cannot fathom."

"We will get to that in a moment, Mr Dermot," said Pons smoothly, standing aside for me to precede him into the hall. Dermot shut the door behind us decisively and led the way into a cheerful study in which a coal fire blazed in a brick surround. With his thick brown tweed suit he looked out of place in the room, as though farming were his natural vocation. He waved us into two leather armchairs set in front of a raised construction which was part desk, part drawing-board. A green-shaded electric lamp was suspended above it and its surface was littered with papers and map-tracings. Pons wasted no time in coming to the point.

"Mr Dermot, you are a geologist and mineralogist, are you not?"

The young man stared at us in frank puzzlement.

"Among other things, yes, Mr Pons. There is no secret about that."

Solar Pons tented his thin fingers before him.

"Just so. I would like you to cast your mind back some time. You made a report, did you not, for the Scottish Land Trust, regarding a property known as Glen Affric."

Dermot was leaning against his drawing-board but now he drew himself up as though he had been stung, indignation on his features.

"That was a highly confidential report, Mr Pons. How you came to know of this is beyond me."

"We will leave that aside for the moment," said Pons calmly. "You confirmed the presence of certain minerals, I believe. I would hazard the guess that there was something strange about the commission. You were employed by Mr Mungo Ferguson, were you not?"

Dermot stared defiantly at Pons for a moment, then lowered his eyes sheepishly. He broke into a chuckle.

"Your reputation has not been exaggerated, Mr Pons. This was a highly confidential report. My sample drillings were carried out by night, in areas of woodland. The whole thing was most unusual but the arrangements were made, I was told, because of the secrecy necessary for a profitable commercial enterprise."

Pons' lean, aquiline features were alive with interest.

"Hmm. This is something you have met before in your experience?"

"Sometimes, Mr Pons. Though it is comparatively rare it is not unknown."

"You have a high reputation in your profession, I understand. One you would not wish to hazard."

Dermot's frank, open features showed his thoughts clearly.

"I have never yet broken my word, Mr Pons. And my reputation is as dear to me as your own."

"Well said, Mr Dermot," I could not forbear adding and Pons glanced at me with amusement, giving a dry chuckle.

"I was not imputing any slur on your reputation, Mr Dermot. But your report—your highly confidential report—revealed the presence of shale oil in great commercial quantity."

Dermot's face bore a puzzled expression again.

"I cannot see how that can be, Mr Pons. My test drillings confirmed the presence of low-grade shale oil, but hardly in commercial quantity. It would not be worth anyone's while to attempt to extract it and I made the matter clear in various letters which accompanied my reports."

My companion was smiling now.

"Excellent, Mr Dermot. Everything is quite clear. You have told me all I wish to know."

"That is all very well, Mr Pons, but I am in some confusion. We cannot let the matter rest here. You have somehow come into possession of a secret document intended only for the eyes of my clients."

Pons nodded.

"You are perfectly correct, sir. You have been open with me. I will be equally frank in return."

He drummed with restless fingers on the arm of his chair.

"I must in turn impose a pledge of secrecy upon you."

"You have my word, Mr Pons," the young man replied quickly.

"I have reason to suspect your work is being used as the basis of a gigantic swindle. A young lady's estate is the key to the whole business, and murder and attempted murder are only some of the ingredients."

There was nothing but shock and suspended disbelief in Dermot's eyes.

"You cannot be serious, Mr Pons?"

"I was never more serious, Mr Dermot. I hope to bring this business to a successful conclusion within the next few days but in the meantime nothing of what we have discussed here tonight must go beyond these four walls."

"I have already given my word, Mr Pons."

My companion looked at our host approvingly.

"Excellent. It goes without saying, Mr Dermot, that your part in this affair is nothing more than that of an innocent person whose work has been made the basis of fraudulent misrepresentation. You may rely upon me to bring the true facts before the police authorities."

"Thank you, Mr Pons."

Young Dermot came forward impulsively and shook my companion's hand.

"You may rely upon me for every assistance."

Solar Pons nodded.

"We will be in touch, Mr Dermot. Come, Parker."

And he strode from the room so briskly that I was hard put to it to keep up with him.

10

"All is well, Parker."

Solar Pons opened the door of the telephone booth outside the station and emerged, rubbing his hands. It was a bright, cold morning with just a hint of mist, and our journey back from Inverness had been uneventful.

"Mackintosh is already on his way and should be here shortly. But let us go into the waiting room. There is a fire and we will be more comfortable than in the street."

I followed him into the small chamber with its leather and horsehair benches, where a glowing coal fire gave off a cheerful radiance that gleamed on the brass fire-irons and coal-scuttle in the fender. I glanced at a coloured poster advertising the attractions of the Isle of Skye as I warmed my hands at the fire. Pons put his valise down on a corner of the bench and busied himself lighting his pipe.

We were alone in the room which shook and vibrated as a fast train went through on the down-line outside. Pons sat frowning for a moment and then fixed me with a steady eye.

"Well, Parker, I take it you have easily seen through Colonel McDonald's little scheme."

I shifted uncomfortably before the fire.

"I get the general drift, Pons, but I am not so sure I see the specific purpose of this blackguard's operations."

Pons stabbed the air with the stem of his pipe, a little furrow of concentration on his brow.

"Tut, Parker, it is simplicity itself. I had a good idea of what lay behind the sinister events enmeshing Miss Hayling before ever we left London. Her letters had apprised me of most of the details and I lacked only the motive. That McDonald was behind it was obvious. Not only did it bear all the hallmarks of his shifty schemes but Miss Hayling's glimpse of him with that scoundrel Ferguson clinched the matter."

He looked reflectively at the black-bearded porter who was vigorously sweeping the platform with a twiglet broom in the hard winter sunshine on the other side of the line.

"Unfortunately, there was little deductive prowess called for, though it was an exercise not without its points."

"You talk as though the whole thing were over, Pons."

"So it is, Parker, so it is," my friend remarked dreamily. "Though I must confess that I am at some pains as to how to bring him out into the open. And I am still going to find it difficult to prove anything against him."

He rubbed his thin fingers together and turned his eyes on the fire as though he could read the answer in the small blue and green flames which leapt and danced and sang as the coals shifted as they burned deeper into the grate.

"Ferguson is a danger to McDonald, Parker," he said almost absently. "Something will happen or my name is not Pons."

I came to stand in front of him.

"What do you mean?"

"We wanted to get that dog-cart up from the stream. Ferguson bungled it by having the thing burned."

"But how did he know?"

"Tut, Parker, the simplest thing in the world. There are two small tenant farmers with properties adjoining. Mackintosh gives his farmer instructions about raising the cart yesterday morning. The other farmer, who is McDonald's tenant, lives in a house only a few hundred yards away. It is my guess that we have been under observation through field-glasses in daylight hours during every journey we have taken in these parts since our arrival. They would have seen me at the stream and McDonald would have known soon after."

"You cannot mean it, Pons."

"I do mean it, Parker. It was only by going far off in our journey to Inverness that we have come close to the truth."

"I am apparently excluded from it," I said somewhat bitterly.

Pons glanced at me with sympathetic eyes.

"Surely not, Parker. We have both had the same set of circumstances before us. McDonald wanted the Haylings' land. He failed by legal means to obtain it so he achieved his object, or so he thought, by the crude methods of Ferguson. That precious rascal or one of his minions half-sawed through the shafts of that unfortunate couple's dog-cart. It had been carefully done and gave at the moment of greatest stress, the right-angle turn across the bridge. But McDonald had not bargained for Miss Hayling and her stubbornness. He found he still could not get hold of the land."

"But why did he want it, Pons?"

My friend looked at me quizzically.

"You have already told me the reason, my dear Parker," he said patiently. "It was surrounded by the Colonel's property and was the only flat piece of land of any size for miles around. The Colonel had to have it for the latest gigantic swindle he was floating."

"This is all supposition, Pons."

My companion shook his head.

"Not at all, Parker. It is as plain as day. It was all there in the brochures and prospectuses I stole from the Scottish Land Trust offices. That gives a glowing and entirely erroneous picture of things, based on young Dermot's report."

My puzzlement must have shown for Pons' face creased in a smile.

"Oil, Parker, oil! An oil boom which, to mix a metaphor, the Colonel wishes to convert into a gold-mine."

I looked at him blankly.

"But there is only low-grade shale-oil there, Pons!"

"Exactly, Parker. McDonald is relying on this to give credence to his fantastic scheme. He is floating hundreds of thousands of shares in a specially set-up company, based on misleading statements from Dermot's confidential report. It is all here. He wants the girl's land for his drilling operations and plant to give the whole thing a plausible basis."

He tapped the breast-pocket of his overcoat.

"There are thousands of gullible fools in this world who will invest in anything providing it promises them a reasonable return. This, if we are to believe the literature, promises them a hundredfold for each share. If McDonald owns Miss Hayling's property and floats his company, I estimate at a rough guess that he will make something in excess of three million pounds before the bubble bursts."

"Good heavens, Pons!"

I stared at my companion for a long moment.

"Exactly, Parker," said Pons succinctly. "The problem is, how are we to stop it, with nothing concrete to lay before the authorities. This was the reason the Colonel was so anxious to get rid of me when he learned I was coming northward at Miss Hayling's behest. And he is equally obviously behind the attempts on Miss Hayling's life, using an odious tool like Ferguson, whom he employs as a figurehead and smokescreen."

"But supposing Ferguson exceeds his authority, Pons?"

My friend smiled thinly.

"McDonald is relying on that, Parker. Ferguson, crude, violent and bad-tempered is ideal for his purposes. If anything goes wrong he would be the scapegoat. McDonald would have covered his tracks perfectly. No-one at the office of the Director of Public Prosecutions would be able to link him with the Land Trust in any way."

"He must be a devil, Pons."

"He is, Parker."

"Then he left Ferguson's tobacco pouch in Miss Hayling's grounds?"

"Not in person, Parker. But he would have given the instructions from far off."

His brooding eyes looked into the heart of the fire.

"I would not like to be in Ferguson's shoes when the Colonel reacts to our latest moves."

He broke off as there came a grating noise from the forecourt outside the little station.

"Ah, here is the good Mackintosh now."

The sturdy form of the gardener was indeed striding toward the station entrance and we hurried out to him for there was something grim and stern in his usually good-natured features. He came to the point straight away.

"A bad business, Mr Pons, though a relief for Miss Hayling. Mungo Ferguson has been found dead in a ravine near Glen Affric."

Pons' face became sharp and alert.

"Ah! I am not surprised. The development we have been waiting for, Parker."

I nodded.

"You believe the Colonel to be responsible?"

Solar Pons' face was as grim as Mackintosh' own.

"I know he is, Parker. When and how did this happen?"

"Early this morning, Mr Pons. The body has been taken to the mortuary in Inverness. I met a local constable on my way to fetch you and he gave me the news. Apparently Ferguson slipped at a steep part of the ravine, fell and broke his neck. Foul play is not suspected."

The Adventure of the Callous Colonel

A bitter smile twisted Pons' lips.

"It bears all the ear-marks of the Colonel. He is a worthy opponent, however evil and warped. Ferguson had served his purpose and had become too dangerous, Parker."

"Even so, Mr Pons," said Mackintosh steadily. "It is a bad business."

"You are quite right, Mr Mackintosh," my companion observed evenly. "I accept your implicit moral judgment. Now, we must put final matters in train."

"What are you going to do, Pons?"

"Send a telegram to the Colonel at Ardrossan Lodge, Parker. I have a mind to bring him into the open. My challenge is one he will find it difficult to avoid."

I felt somewhat alarmed at his words and looked at him anxiously as we took our seats in the trap.

"I would like you to find the local post-office and send this telegram for me," Pons told Mackintosh, who had now clambered into the driving seat.

"Certainly, Mr Pons. It is only a few hundred yards."

Pons pulled an old envelope from his pocket and sat smoking furiously as we rattled down the narrow street, his brows furrowed and concentrated as he wrote with a stub of pencil on the back of the envelope. He looked at it with satisfaction as we drew up in front of a large granite building. Mackintosh' eyes opened wide as he glanced at the envelope when Pons handed it to him. My companion rummaged in his pocket and gave him a guinea.

"Please keep the change."

"Thank you, Mr Pons. Would you like me to go to the village for a reply when we arrive back?"

Pons shook his head.

"I think not. It is my belief that the Colonel will come in person."

My astonishment re-echoed Mackintosh' own as the gardener hurried into the post-office.

"What on earth did you put in the telegram, Pons?"

"Something he could not resist, Parker. I appealed to his vanity."

And with that I had to be content as Mackintosh soon returned and in a few moments we were rattling on our way back to Glen Affric. Pons was silent for most of the journey, only breaking into conversation once.

"Tell me," he said to Mackintosh when we were within a mile or two of our destination. "Does Miss Hayling have a radio at the house?"

The driver glanced at him in surprise.

"Oh, yes, sir. There are two at the main house and I myself have one at my cottage."

"Excellent. You did not listen to the weather forecast this morning, by any chance?"

"Indeed I did, Mr Pons. Such things are vital to country folk in areas like this."

Pons smiled faintly, taking the pipe from his mouth.

"Do you happen to remember what was predicted for Scotland?"

The gardener hunched his shoulders, his eyes fixed forward over the pony's back.

"Fine in the morning with local mist in mid-afternoon, thickening at nightfall."

"Good," said Pons with satisfaction.

He rubbed his hands.

"It is certainly fine this morning. They might be right for once, eh, Parker?"

"Of course, Pons," I agreed. "But I fail to take the point."

"It would not be the first time," said he, with a twinkle in his eye. "It was just a notion which had occurred to me when sending the telegram, but it could be a vital one. I would stake my life that the Colonel would go for rifles. He is a crack-shot and a master of the stalk."

"Really, Pons . . ." I began when we started our steep descent of the hill near the stream, and we had to alight to assist the pony. Our arrival at the house had been noted and Miss Hayling herself stood on the front steps to greet us. She looked pale but her manner was collected.

"A friend has just telephoned from the village to say that Mungo Ferguson is dead."

She put her hand impulsively on my companion's arm.

"Oh, Mr Pons, what does it mean? Goodness knows I have no reason to mourn his death but it is a dreadful thing nevertheless."

"Your sentiments do you credit, Miss Hayling," said Pons, a kindly look in his eyes. "But unless I miss my guess this business will soon be over. I must just ask you to be patient a little longer."

"But what does it all mean, Mr Pons?"

"It means that Colonel McDonald will be here shortly," said Pons sombrely. "I have sent him a telegram this morning which should resolve the business."

There was a look of shock in the girl's eyes but she forbore to question my companion further.

"No doubt you know best, Mr Pons. In the meantime lunch is waiting."

And she led the way into the house.

11

All through lunch Pons had been silent and abstracted and he sat watching the windows which commanded the driveway as though he expected something to materialise at any minute. The sun shone brightly despite the cold and threw the shadows of the mullioned windows across the cheerful, panelled room in which we ate.

The girl had been restrained though her curiosity was obvious and we had chatted desultorily on a number of mundane topics. Afterwards, we took coffee in a small room which overlooked the front porch. We had eaten early and it was still only a quarter to one when I became aware of Mackintosh' sturdy form hovering on the front steps. I glanced at Pons and realised instantly that the gardener had taken up his position on my friend's instructions. He took the pipe from his mouth and addressed himself to our hostess.

"Miss Hayling, you have been extraordinarily patient and trusting in the extreme. In all my long experience I have known few persons of your sex who have exhibited such courage and character."

The short speech was an unusual one for Pons and I saw the girl flush with pleasure while Mrs McRae shot a glance of approval at Pons.

"I know you have my welfare at heart, Mr Pons," the girl said in a low voice. "I am content to leave the explanations for later."

"You shall have them in full, Miss Hayling," said Pons. "In the meantime I shall have to ask you to trust me a little longer. I would like you and Mr and Mrs McRae to withdraw to the upper floors of the house and leave this matter to Dr Parker and myself."

"By all means, Mr Pons."

The girl got up obediently and followed the housekeeper out of the room.

"What on earth, Pons . . ." I was beginning when my friend rose to his feet with astonishingly alacrity and put his hand on my arm.

"Ah, he has risen to the bait, Parker."

I followed his glance through the window to find the shimmering image of a white Rolls-Royce Silver Ghost purring to a stop in front of the main entrance. By the time Pons and I had joined Mackintosh a tall, military figure was descending.

"Just stay within earshot, if you please," said Pons to Mackintosh sotto voce and the burly gardener withdrew a dozen paces or so to the bottom of the steps.

There was no sound in all the great park except for the cawing of rooks in some ancient elms in the distance and the measured tread of feet in the gravel as the tall figure came toward us. I don't know what I had expected but the actuality was a shock. A smartly-dressed but almost emaciated old man with a gaunt face, hook-nose and iron-grey moustache. The only things alive in the dead white face were the burning yellow eyes which were fixed unwinkingly upon Pons. Colonel McDonald came to a halt at the foot of the steps, without a glance at myself or the gardener.

"Well, Mr Pons," he said in a low, soft voice. "We meet at last."

"We do indeed, Colonel," said my companion, descending the steps so that they were on the level, almost face to face.

"You have not wasted much time on receipt of my telegram."

"The opportunity was too good to miss," said the other in the same low, unemotional voice. "You have not lost your dexterity in dealing with my little toys."

"Neither you your ingenuity, Colonel. Spring catches operating surprises were always your specialty, were they not."

A muscle started fretting in the Colonel's cheek but otherwise he and Pons might have been calmly discussing stock-market prices.

"You have been interfering with my operations, Mr Pons. And when you come upon my own home ground I find it intolerable."

Solar Pons shrugged.

"It was a clumsy business, having the wreckage of the dog-cart burned. Though I have no doubt I should have discovered that the shafts had been sawn through."

The Colonel nodded absently.

"That was a tactical error on Ferguson's part."

"But one you have soon put right," Pons observed.

McDonald gave a harsh, mirthless laugh.

"I heard about the accident just before I left to come here. A tragic business."

"Murder is always tragic," said Solar Pons evenly.

McDonald was still standing stock-still but now the muscle in his cheek was twitching almost uncontrollably. That and his blazing eyes were the only indications of the anger within.

"Strong words, Mr Pons," he said in that uncannily soft voice. "Strong words. And ones you are going to find difficult to prove."

"I am not trying to prove them," said Pons with a faint smile. "I am merely speaking my thoughts aloud."

The Colonel nodded again, his yellow eyes now glancing from me to Mackintosh.

"Your telegram implied a settlement between us, Mr Pons. I am in agreement."

"I knew I could rely upon you," said Solar Pons slowly. "Your courage has never been in question."

Colonel McDonald drew himself up stiffly and bowed slightly at the compliment.

"Perhaps we could walk to the car."

"You have no objection to my friend and colleague, Dr Parker, accompanying us?"

"By no means, Mr Pons. I am quite alone."

I hurried down the steps and followed as the two men strolled toward the white Rolls-Royce. The Colonel opened the spring-loaded boot which came up gently with a scarcely audible click. Within I could see two long leather cases.

"Matched sporting rifles, Mr Pons. Neither of us will be at a disadvantage. You accept the challenge?"

"Certainly. After all, it was I who issued it."

As the import of their words sank into my brain I found my tongue. "This is madness, Pons! Are you suggesting something as barbaric as a duel? The Colonel is a crack-shot and an experienced stalker."

"I am well aware of that, Parker. I am not entirely a novice myself with the sporting rifle."

The Colonel bowed again, reluctant admiration on his face. "Then you accept, sir?"

"Most certainly. But on certain conditions."

"And those are?"

"That Dr Parker be allowed to accompany me to act as my second—and see fair play. You to have a companion also. Unarmed I might add."

The Colonel chuckled.

"By all means. I shall not need a companion for I would find him a hindrance. The only conditions of mine are time, place and the question of ammunition."

Solar Pons looked steadily at the other.

"Ammunition?"

"Five rounds each. No more, no less. That should be ample to settle the matter."

"Agreed. And the time and place?"

McDonald looked up at the sun.

"It is now one-thirty P.M. Darkness comes down swiftly in these latitudes. Both parties to be in position on the field by not later than two-thirty."

Pons nodded.

"Agreed. And the venue?"

McDonald slid out one of the leather cases and handed it to Pons before closing the boot. He glanced across at Mackintosh.

"There is a rock called The Sentinel in the glen near the edge of Miss Hayling's property just before the land rises to the skirts of Ben Affric."

"Ah, the mountain beyond the glen. I will find it."

"The gardener will tell you how to get to it. It is only a mile or so from here. I will meet you there. Until two-thirty, then."

"Until two-thirty."

We waited in silence as the Colonel got behind the wheel. The Rolls-Royce glided sedately round the concourse and disappeared down the drive, a thin plume of exhaust smoke hanging behind it in the frosty air. Pons was already opening the case, looking at the sleek, polished rifle within. He broke open the breech.

"Fortunately, I am familiar with this model. It is a beauty. One of a matched pair, as McDonald said. The Colonel goes in for nothing but the best. There are five cartridges, as agreed."

"This is madness, Pons," I repeated, looking at the stolid form of Mackintosh as if for support. "I will not be a party to murder."

"Tut, Parker," said Pons chidingly. "You exaggerate, as usual. I do not think it will be as bad as that."

He glanced up at the sun.

"Come, we must hurry. I have a few preparations to make before we reach the killing-ground."

12

We walked uphill in silence, the sun throwing long shadows on the heather, a faint mist rising, the beauty of the blue-green mass of Ben Affric in the distance making our sombre errand seem like some wild figment of imagination. I still could not quite believe the whole incredible circumstance and walked in silence across the rough ground behind Pons, sick at heart and afraid for my friend.

Pons must have sensed my mood for he looked back at me with a smile, the harshness of the sunlight strongly accentuating the clear-minted lines of his face.

"My dear Parker. You look as though you are on your way to a funeral. Did I not tell you that things were not so serious?"

"That is all very well, Pons," I said. "But there is likely to be a bloody outcome to this business. How do you know that Colonel McDonald will keep his word. He is sure to be up to some treachery."

"I am relying on it, Parker," said Pons gravely, taking his pipe-stem from his mouth. "I have not come unprepared."

He patted the large canvas bag he carried as he spoke. I myself had the loaded rifle McDonald had left with us, slung over my shoulder by the strap and I was finding our progress over the rough terrain rather heavy going. It had now turned two o'clock and we had cleared Miss Hayling's estate and the humped mass of the mountain Ben Affric threw a vast shadow over the glen before us, so that it seemed as though we were advancing into the valley of the shadow. I looked at my companion in surprise.

"I do not follow you, Pons."

He chuckled.

"All will be made clear to you shortly, Parker. Ah, that must be The Sentinel."

I followed his gaze and saw the great hump of rock rising from the plain before us. Already, its base was lost amid the haze.

"What do you intend to do, Pons?"

"Indulge in a little deception, Parker. Normally, I would abide by the rules but I have myself no compunction in being devious when dealing with such a person as McDonald."

We both saved our breath for the next ten minutes, as the going was difficult underfoot. Slowly the huge splinter of granite set in the middle of the lonely glen grew before us. By twenty-past two we were only a few hundred yards off.

"There is no sign of McDonald, Pons," I observed as we stumbled the last few yards across the boulder-littered ground.

"I would not expect there to be, Parker. Unless I miss my guess he is up on the skirt of the mountain there, where the ravine runs, watching us through glasses. That would be a perfect vantage-point."

"Good heavens, Pons!"

"There is no danger for the moment, Parker. The Colonel will not make his move until he is absolutely certain."

We were within the shadow of the rock now and scrambled, by means of broad ledges to a position just below the top. As Pons had hinted the place was empty and there was no sign of the Colonel. It was bitterly cold here in the shadow and the surface of the granite was damp and slippery. I put down the case and busied myself in unstrapping it and removing the rifle. Pons had his back to me as he knelt and rummaged in the canvas bag he had brought.

When I turned I was amazed to see what appeared to be a dummy, dressed in old tweeds. Pons produced a crumpled deer-stalker and jammed it on the figure's head. He surveyed it critically.

"I think that will do nicely, Parker."

"But what are you doing, Pons?"

"With the aid of a few bolsters borrowed from Mrs McRae and an old suit of her husband's I am making a passable facsimile of myself. I think it will pass muster, even through the Colonel's glasses, if I pull the hat well down."

Pons put the finishing touches to his creation and then carried it to a position a few feet below the ridge of the rock. Then he cautiously hoisted it there, with its back to the mountain, and pinned it with a dead branch he had broken from a stunted tree which projected from the rocks just below the sky-line. It stood up well and the silhouette so presented must have been visible for miles around. Pons dusted his hands in satisfaction and then came back to me.

"It is almost half-past two, Parker. I do not think we shall have long to wait."

He took the rifle from me and went cautiously back. In a niche in the rock below the summit, where I joined him a few moments later, I found I could see right up the glen to where the purple-brown mass of Ben Affric was becoming slowly rinsed with haze. Nothing moved in all the vast expanse of the glen before us.

"You see, Parker," said Pons calmly. "Colonel McDonald never had the slightest intention of keeping this appointment. At least in the way we intended."

No sooner had he spoken than there came a bright flash from the sombre darkness of the mountain before us and a moment later the echoing crash of a high-powered rifle which thundered about the glen. At almost the same instant the tweed-clad figure which sat on the summit of the rock above us somersaulted in the air and landed some yards from us. Feathers floated down after it. I ran across and was stupefied to see the large hole torn in the material of McRae's jacket.

"It would have been right through the heart, Pons!"

"Would it not, Parker."

Solar Pons was lying in the niche of the rock, his keen right eye sighting along the rifle, his cheek close in to the stock.

"The flash came from the head of the ravine. Ah, there he is!"

He squeezed the trigger gently and the rifle cracked, the stock jerking against his cheek while blue smoke curled from the breech and barrel.

"You have not killed him, Pons!"

My friend looked at me with a grim smile.

"Hardly, Parker. I have no wish to appear as the principal figure in a murder trial. I fired to frighten him. As near as I can judge the bullet struck the rocks a dozen feet away from him."

No sooner had he finished speaking than the most dreadful cry sounded from the head of the glen and went echoing round the heights. Pons started to his feet but I put my hand on his arm.

"Careful, Pons! It may be a trap to lure us out. He cannot be wounded and we shall be at his mercy in the open."

Solar Pons smiled.

"His rifle is useless now, Parker. The weather is closing in. I relied on it in my calculations of the risk involved."

I soon saw what he meant. Already, as we had moved off The Sentinel heavy banks of mist were gathering around the skirts of the mountain.

"So that was why you asked Mackintosh about the weather, Pons?"

"Naturally, Parker. I do not believe in taking unnecessary chances in face of such an enemy. It is no bad thing to enlist the help of nature when possible."

Pons was scrambling down the base of the rock now and I followed, carrying the rifle, which he had cast aside. As I gained the ground I could see Pons striding away at a great pace among the scree and boulders. By dint of great effort I caught up with him and we went forward side by side through the rapidly thickening mist.

As we mounted up the flank of Ben Affric the air grew ever more raw and dank. The mist was breast-high now and Pons guided us over toward the right of the mountain.

"Be careful, Pons. We are coming near the area of the ravine."

"I am well aware of that, Parker. I am endeavouring to memorise the salient features of the terrain before the weather closes down completely."

Even as he spoke we seemed to walk into an impenetrable white wall. A few yards behind us the sun had been shining; now, it was almost as though we were in the middle of the night, as the great fog-bank rolled on, borne inexorably forward from the heights above by the wind at its tail. Instinctively I had faltered, but Pons' hand was on my elbow, guiding me on as though all were daylight and absolutely clear to him.

"It is only a few yards now, Parker. Please be extremely careful. Ah, here we are!"

A few seconds later I saw what his keen eyes had already noted; the matching rifle to the one I carried was lying on the damp rock floor of the gully we had been mounting. On top of a flat boulder from which McDonald had obviously fired, were four spare cartridges.

"At least the Colonel kept his word in one respect," said Pons grudgingly. "Keep behind me and mind your footing."

He went forward slowly and I followed, anxious not to lose him for the mist had grown remarkably thick. Our journey did not take long. After only a few yards the terrain shelved steeply on to slippery rock. Pons stopped and held up his hand.

"We can go no farther, Parker. This is the edge of the ravine."

As he spoke there came a terrible groan from the chasm before us; the sound was so unexpected that I felt an indescribable thrill of horror run through me. Pons' reaction filled me with alarm. He went forward on the steep slope and lay down, supporting himself by a small nodule of rock which rose from the precipitous surface.

"For heaven's sake be careful, Pons!"

"If you would come here and hold my legs, Parker, I would be obliged," he said in a low, almost gentle voice. "And pass me the rifle if you would be so good."

I did as he bade and came forward, lying down in a flat place by a boulder and leaning forward to grasp his ankles. Pons was slowly extending the rifle and its sling before him.

"My shot startled him and he obviously slipped into the ravine," he said musingly.

At that moment there was a sudden breeze and the mist parted briefly. I think I shall never forget the sight it revealed. The Colonel's gaunt face with the burning yellow eyes glaring savagely over the iron-grey moustache was suspended in the blackness. He did not see me, for his intense, malevolent gaze was fixed entirely on Pons. I could see only his head and the upper part of his shoulders; his body must have been hanging almost vertically in space.

His fingers were frenziedly locked in a clump of heather which was growing from a crevice in the rocks in front of him. I could see now where his heels had scored a distinct passage in the damp, mossy surface of the gorge. Inch by inch Pons advanced the rifle toward him. Pons' arms were extended to the limit in front of him and I felt his ankles vibrate beneath my hands.

The end of the rifle sling was still a foot short. The Colonel opened his mouth as if to say something, then shut it with a snap. Little flecks of saliva dribbled down his chin. There was a mixture of anger, pain and regret in his eyes. Then the stems of the heather tore out with a convulsive movement and the head and arms whipped backward out of sight into the mist.

The dreadful cry which echoed and swelled from that terrible abyss I hear still in my dreams to this day.

Then it was cut off abruptly and we heard the sickening impact of broken flesh on rock as the body bounced from boulder to boulder until the sound died away in the distance. For a long time there was nothing but the patter of scree and small rocks rattling down the sombre depths.

Pons slowly dragged himself back to safety. He was white and trembling. Despite his efforts the rifle slid over to join its owner in the chasm below. I got up and we two sat on the edge of a boulder for several minutes to collect ourselves. Pons lit his pipe and soon had it drawing comfortably, his head wreathed in tobacco smoke.

"Well, Parker," he said eventually. "Poetic justice, though I would not have had it happen like that."

"You could not have helped it, Pons," I said. "That dreadful creature would have murdered you in cold blood."

He nodded without speaking, his eyes hooded and brooding as he stared into the misty deep before us.

"Fate is unpredictable, Parker," he observed presently. "Unless I miss my guess it is somewhere hereabouts that McDonald's tool Mungo Ferguson met his end."

I stared at him, still too shocked to say anything. He looked at me sympathetically and roused himself.

"We must get back and inform the police, my dear fellow."

I nodded, my thoughts still elsewhere.

"What did you put in that telegram, Pons?"

"THIS MATTER MUST BE SETTLED BETWEEN US. YOUR TERMS OR MINE. PONS. I knew he could not resist the challenge. I accepted his terms, with the result we have seen."

Pons sighed and I looked at him sharply.

"Unfortunately there was little in the case which appealed to my ratiocinative instincts, but it was not without interest. And it has disposed of one of the most dangerous opponents I have ever come up against."

I nodded.

"The Colonel's was an ingenious scheme, Pons. The shale-oil report was a stroke of genius."

"Was it not, Parker."

Solar Pons stared at me with a far-away look on his clear-minted features.

"Who knows, Parker, there may well be oil beneath Scottish soil and Scottish seas. Whether it will come in our time is another matter. We shall have to wait and see."

He turned abruptly on his heel.

"Now we have a tidy step before us and it will soon be dark. And I really owe a most gallant young lady some detailed explanation."

The Exploits of Solar Pons

First Edition

1993

The Exploits of Solar Pons by Basil Copper was published by Fedogan & Bremer, 700 Washington Avenue, S.E., Suite 50, Minneapolis, Minnesota 55414. Nineteen Hundred copies of the trade edition and one hundred copies of the limited edition have been printed from ITC New Baskerville by the Maple Press Company.